BREATHING
UNDER WATER

Also by Sophie Hardcastle

Running Like China

BREATHING
UNDER WATER

SOPHIE HARDCASTLE

For my sisters — Georgia and Gemma

 hachette
AUSTRALIA

Published in Australia and New Zealand in 2016
by Hachette Australia
(an imprint of Hachette Australia Pty Limited)
Level 17, 207 Kent Street, Sydney NSW 2000
www.hachette.com.au

10 9 8 7 6 5

National Library of Australia
Cataloguing-in-Publication data:

Hardcastle, Sophie.
Breathing under water/Sophie Hardcastle.

ISBN: 978 0 7336 3485 7 (pbk)

Twins – Australia – Fiction.
Life change events – Australia – Fiction.
Young adult fiction, Australian.

A823.4

Cover design by Christabella Designs
Cover illustration by Sha'an d'Anthes/furrylittlepeach.com
Author photograph by Craig Peihopa
Typeset in 12/17.25 pt Adobe Garamond Pro by Bookhouse, Sydney

Printed and bound in Great Britain by Clays Ltd, Elcograf S.p.A.

'People dived into this teeming world and saw how the ocean could be itself.'

– TIM WINTON, *Blueback*

PROLOGUE

Chilled bones. Red skin. White clouds exhaled as teeth chatter, and the ocean, just waiting for them . . .

Beneath a silk veil of silence, feet sprint across wet grass, wet sand, and then lift. Hands grip the rail edges of surfboards and for a brief moment in time bodies fly over a roll of vanilla foam. As torsos land on wax, they stretch arms forward, dig down and draw back, pulling themselves through the cold morning milk.

White wash approaches and in unison they each lunge forward on their boards, pushing themselves deep beneath the turbulence. They ride up through the dark belly of the wave and emerge through its shoulderblade. With their lungs expanding, a new day is born. New life.

As they reach the line-up, the cold is pinching every place their wetsuits cannot conceal: their wrists, Achilles tendons, the napes of their necks. They sit up on their boards and, without passing a word between them, float effortlessly. Both have red-glass eyes and cheeks that sting, licked by the tongues of winter tides.

Across the sea, the sun catches fire on the horizon; he looks across at her and smiles.

For hours they dance on waves of molten gold, blissfully unaware that today the sun will set at noon.

I WEAR THE OCEAN

I feel Ben's patience wither.

Rattling the metal bar, unable to release it from its rusty hinges, his cheeks flush pink. Finally, my twin brother kicks the wiry old gate. It flies open and slams into the side of the chicken coop. The sudden bang wakes BBQ and Honey Soy from their sleep, sending them into a frenzy. Laughing, Ben lifts the roof with his spare hand and I bend over to fetch the eggs. Honey Soy kicks up a cloud of dust as I'm sifting through straw. Grit makes my eyes dry, and there's the foul taste of chickenfeed where the back of my nostrils connect to my throat. I cough, splutter and hear his laugh deepen.

'Shut up, Ben!'

Moments later, I touch my fingertips to shell and draw three eggs to the surface. Carrying them to the house, they warm my palms.

Ben takes my board and places it with his in the shed and we dart around the house to the outdoor shower, leaving emerald footprints in the morning dew. Like the first heavy droplets to fall from storm clouds, water rains from a large round showerhead, freckled with orange and turquoise spots of corrosion. Ben pulls a flaking strip of white paint off the house's outer wall. I slap his hand. 'Don't, Dad will get pissed off.'

Nailed to one of the slats is a shelf made of driftwood with a bar of coconut soap, a bottle of home brand shampoo, a conch shell, a sea sponge and a succulent in a silver teapot. I lay the eggs on the shelf beside the teapot and wriggle my way under the hot downpour.

We peel off our black skins and my body quakes as the cold air bites my thighs. 'I'm telling you,' he says, lathering himself in coconut suds, 'You're skin and bone, Grace – you're making me cold just looking at you.'

'It *is* cold.' Shuddering, I wrap my gangly arms around the bones where my womanly hips should be.

For a few years now, I've watched time carve beautiful figures out of prepubescent marble blocks. Polished femininity. I crave the way the other girls' busts fill bras and bikinis, the way boys second-glance. I crave the curves between their hips and their thighs when they wear their high-waisted shorts. 'Something to grab,' the boys say. But most of all, I crave the way heads turn when the other girls enter a room and how conversation seems to slow.

Dad walks from the shed across the yard with two surfboards beneath each arm. I admire the retro that he has reconditioned. The others are new – two white and one with a psychedelic paintjob on foam – only needing to be sanded back before he can sell them. Walker Surfboards. A family legacy, something to pride myself on. He loads the boards into the back of the old Rodeo, which he has parked oh so neatly, half on our dirt driveway, half on the grass, almost squashing a hedge of agapanthus. 'Get out of the shower!' Dad calls over his shoulder. 'You're going to be late for school!'

'We don't have school!' Ben calls back. 'It's a strike today!'

Dad laughs but then loses the grin. 'Very funny boy. Turn it off!'

Ben holds his hands around the shower taps so tight his knuckles turn white, counting, 'One, two . . . two and a quarter . . . two and a half . . . two and three-quarters . . .' pausing before he yells, 'THREE!' and twists the taps off. I grab the eggs and we sprint up the steps of the old wraparound verandah. Mum has left towels out, I put the eggs down and we madly rub our limbs as if to rub away the chill of autumn.

In my bedroom I put on underwear, a singlet and my school dress, washed and ironed for the start of the week. Shivering, I pull my school jumper over my head and wrap a scarf around my neck, but even that is not enough to turn my purple nails pink again or to soften the ache in my lower back.

When I emerge, Mum is in the kitchen. I slouch over the wooden bench, worn and smoothed by this family like a piece of driftwood worn and smoothed by the sea.

'Oh love, your lips are blue,' she tells me. 'Have a bowl of this.' She hands me a glazed terracotta bowl and fills it almost to the rim with black rice pudding. 'Your dad was snoring,' she tells me, 'so I made a whole pot last night.'

Noticing her frying pan starting to smoke, she puts one hand up like a lollipop lady. 'Wait, wait! I forgot the banana.' With a loving smile, Mum removes her pan from the stove and pours warm coconut milk into the bowl, lifting out the fried banana with a spatula and laying it on top of the pudding. 'Bon appétit!' she says in her finest French accent, handing me a Thai brass spoon that is probably as old as the house. Ben strolls up to the bench and pulls up a stool beside me. Mum turns to him, 'Do you want some too, honey?'

He nods and she pours him two bowls of the pudding, serving them with four slices of the spelt sourdough she made the other day, each piece spread with homemade nut butter.

As I eat, I listen to the two of them chat. It's as if Mum and Ben speak in another tongue. It's a language I can almost understand but know I will never speak. Words come naturally to them. No conversation is ever awkward; their sentences don't just break the ice, they melt it into pools of water, warm enough to bathe in.

Mum's in her one-piece swimsuit, the one with the turquoise and purple paisley pattern, a towel wrapped around her waist. Her toes are sandy and she leaves wet footprints on the spotted gum floorboards. I love to watch the way my mum moves, her effortless beauty. Her blonde hair with its few silver strands is still dripping, matted between her shoulderblades. Since she was my age, she's graced the tides every day at dawn, swimming laps with us inside her, right up until the day we were born. In nothing but her paisley swimsuit, she bears the pain of winter and celebrates the pleasure of summer.

Sometimes when I was younger I would wander with her down the grassy hill, when the sky was that cool ash shade between purple and blue, and sit on green rocks with my toes dipped in the sea. Waiting for the sun, I'd count her laps as she moved through the water so smoothly it was as if she were a fish born underwater and was living on land by mistake.

Ben finishes eating, grabs his things and wanders out to stand on the verandah with his skateboard under his arm and schoolbag hanging off one shoulder. He calls out for me to hurry up.

'Yeah, just a minute!'

I can't find my sneakers and it's not until I walk back through the lounge room in odd socks that I realise Monty has taken them. He's old and doesn't chew things; he just collects them. I lift his tired legs to retrieve my shoes from his doggy bed. Mum says he collects our things because they smell like us, his family. Our sense of smell is our most powerful sense, she tells me. We commit scents to memory before any sight or sound. We can even smell inside the womb.

~~

I love the way water slides down my neck in the hours after I've towel-dried my hair. I love the way it soaks into my cotton collar. I love the damp.

I love the way I wear the ocean walking through the hallways at school, standing at my locker, sitting in class. I love the way I carry the morning's surf on the nape of my neck, the way lovers carry each other's scent long after they have parted.

We're dissecting the first known telling of Sleeping Beauty, *The Sun, the Moon and Talia*, written long before fairytales were sanitised for children by the Grimm Brothers. I pick at my nails as we read the tale of Talia, alone and paralysed in the forest.

Suddenly Mia comes rushing in with her head down. She takes the seat I've saved for her. Mr Woodlow turns from the blackboard, scowling, and she mouths *sorry!*

He turns back to the blackboard without acknowledging her and I slide my exercise book across the desk so she can jot down my notes.

'You'll never believe what just happened!' she whispers, although not quite quiet enough. Mr Woodlow whips his head around with sharp eyes.

'Mia Ellis!' He spits her name across the room like it's sour food. 'Don't make me turn around again.'

As I write, she shifts in the seat beside me, tapping her hands on the table. Mia is a wild bushfire that consumes, a desert storm that rips. In my peripheral vision, she gathers her strawberry blonde hair, pulling it up into a high ponytail. 'Hold this.' Mia passes me a crimson ribbon, before looping her hair tie around thick locks. 'Thanks.' She takes it back, fastens a bow, winks at me, and then races her pen across the page to catch up.

No more than five minutes pass before I'm squirming as her elbow drives into my side. What? I swing my head to see her wearing a pair of paper glasses she's cut out from a page in her exercise book. A laugh cracks my lips open.

This time when he jerks to face us, Mr Woodlow's nostrils flare. 'Get out!'

'But Sir,' she begins.

'No buts. Take your books, Mia. You'll be continuing your analysis of the text in the hallway. Sit where I can see you. I'll be checking your work at the end of the class.' Mr Woodlow wipes his forehead with a handkerchief and settles his ruffled comb-over. As he presses on with the class, his chalk handwriting betrays the slight trembling of his hands.

Everyone knows he would love to drop her to second stream or, better yet, force her to leave extension English altogether, but when Mia spends the occasional lesson in the hallway, and still manages to top every exam, he is a lone firefighter, unable to control the blaze.

Waiting for Mia at my locker, I exchange my English textbook for one on ancient history. She bounds up the corridor from Mr Woodlow's room, bumping, smashing, pinning me against my locker.

'Calm down!'

'Have you seen him?' she cries.

'Seen who?'

'Harley.'

'Harley who?'

She flaps her hands in the air theatrically, the gold glitter on her fingernails catching the light. 'I don't know! I don't remember. He went to our school, ages ago, like ages ago, as in primary school. He moved away with his family, up north maybe. He was in our class in year one . . . the one who wet his pants on the oval!'

Out loud, I ponder, 'Harley Mathews?'

'YES! Harley Mathews!'

'Shh!' I giggle, glancing around for onlookers, or worse, *Harley Mathews*.

As young girls, Mia gave me one of her old Barbie dolls, one with brown hair. She kept her blonde-haired doll for herself and coloured the hair strawberry pink. She then cut their hair to look like ours and altered their clothing and even cut a surfboard for my doll and a beach towel for hers out of cardboard.

When Mia went shopping for her first bra, she dragged me along with her, and not because she was nervous. Mia insisted that the shop assistant fit us both, despite the woman's awkward hesitation when she looked at me.

'We don't stock cropped tops.'

'We don't want cropped tops,' Mia replied, feet planted. 'We want bras.'

The two of us walked out of the shop with a gorgeous red lace bra and a modest lavender bralette that we both knew I wouldn't be wearing anytime soon. When we arrived back at her place, Mia pulled her new lingerie from the bag. The shop assistant had wrapped our purchases in pink tissue paper. Mia tore hers open and held her bra up to the light, explaining that even if she didn't have a boy *yet*, it was important to be prepared. She told me her new lingerie was going to make a boy as hard as a diamond one day, and although I wasn't quite sure what that meant, I agreed. Later, when older boys with P-plates whistled out of their cars, she always assured me they were whistling at both of us.

Moving faster than everyone else, I love the way she allows me to run with her. Some mornings she comes over before school and shows me YouTube videos she's found of parrots saying funny things, cats sticking their faces in vacuum cleaner hoses and teacup piglets sitting in pot plants, telling me how they're so cute that even though she's a vegetarian, she *just wants to eat them!* Other nights she reads essays on Plato, or manifestos by early modernists, or her science textbooks cover to cover. She's read the dictionary, the bible, and completed four Where's Wally books. Before going to sleep she sometimes embroiders or draws or does Sudoku. In the morning Mia tells me about everything she did the night before. I'm in awe of what she's accomplished and I'm always left feeling dumbfounded when she pulls out her finished homework and the school captain speech she's written for the weekly assembly.

Most of the time she talks so fast her words blur into one and even I have trouble understanding. Her bag is freckled with badges from music gigs or political rallies that she's gone to with her brother in the city. And whether or not the other kids at school can appreciate the stars she has hand-stitched into the sides of her bottle green Docs, Mia is the wind – the hot, dry western wind. And I am gravity.

⌒

'Oh my god.' She nudges me as we walk out into the schoolyard. 'That's him!' Mia points and I smack the top of her hand.

'Don't make it so obvious!'

'He's sitting with *our* friends!'

Sudden sunlight washes over us as we step out of the dim corridor. I squint to make out Harley among the group.

They're sitting under the same tall pine tree we always sit under. Sometimes I think that the boys' territorial approach is a little pathetic, but I am grateful to be part of the pack. They look out for us, regardless of how often Mia reminds them she is more than capable of looking after herself.

As Mia and I approach, Jake picks up a handful of cheesy corn chips and throws them at Mia. 'I hear *someone* has a crush on Blake,' he taunts. 'Could he be the *one*?'

Mia's cheeks flush as she kicks a pine cone at him.

'Calm your farm,' he says, reclining on the grass, bearing his weight on his elbows as he stretches his legs out in front of him.

'Well I heard about Michaela . . .' Mia retaliates. 'Fifteen? That's got to be an all-time low.'

'That blondie from Saturday night?' he says, flicking his Whitsunday white hair to one side as he glances across the yard at a group of girls, teasing them with fleeting eye contact.

Mia rolls her eyes, arms crossed. '*Yes* . . .'

Jake's laugh bursts from his chest, 'I swear her name was Amy.'

'You're disgusting,' Mia scoffs.

Across the circle, Ben calls out my name. I turn to see him point at me as he explains to Harley, 'You remember my twin sister don't you? Grace, Harley. Harley, Grace.'

'Hey.' Harley's voice is steady, his lean shoulders relaxed, and when I smile, I'm suddenly unsure if I actually said hi, or if I just said it in my head.

'Toby was meant to be showing him around,' Ben says, 'but he was doing a shit job, so I took over.'

'Rack off,' Toby mutters, his freckly cheeks pale pink.

'Just kidding, man.' Ben slaps Toby's shoulder. 'You know I love you!'

Mia pulls on my skirt and I realise I'm still standing. 'Do you have those almond biscuits your mum made on the weekend?'

I sit cross-legged beside her.

'Well do you?' she asks.

'Do I what?'

'Have any of the biscuits?'

'Oh, yeah.' I peel the cling wrap off the two biscuits and pass one to her.

'Thanks.' She shoves the whole thing in her mouth. 'You're such a weirdo sometimes.'

I think of Harley Mathews, the boy from primary school who wore goggles and a wetsuit band around his ears in the water – the only kid we knew with grommets in his ears. Scrawny with coffee-ground skin, he was the boy who refused to venture into the deep end of the rock pool. The one with the runny nose who wet his pants on the oval. And then I look at *this* Harley Mathews . . .

Munching on her biscuit, Mia talks with a full mouth, spitting crumbs onto her lap *and* mine. 'Honestly, what does your mum put in these? I don't think I'll ever understand how a biscuit with no sugar can taste this good. And with no milk and none of that other stuff everyone's saying they're intolerant to . . . Gluten! That's it – every hipster is getting on that bandwagon, aren't they? Then again I did read this article about how it's better for your gut – your mum would know. Regardless, yum! They're delish – who even needs a gluten?'

I'm looking at his hair – dark, probably shoulder length, pulled back into a low bun. I'm looking at his jagged middle part, his jet-black eyebrows.

Mia snaps her fingers in front of my face. 'Grace!' She laughs. 'You're hopeless.'

I'm looking at his crossed legs, his grey Converse, slender calves, his brown socks, the tan leather string around his wrist.

'Okay, fine,' Mia says, reaching over me. 'I'm eating your one too.'

Mia sinks her teeth into my apple, chewing loudly in my ear. I can feel the spray, tiny droplets of apple juice landing on my cheek, yet somehow all is quiet, all is still.

Harley catches my gaze and with a slight curl of his lips, smiles as if he's known me his whole life – as if he never left.

Two

FAT FRIDAYS AND VEGO PIES

'It's official, I am failing,' Jake says, dumping his schoolbag on the ground beside me under the pine tree. With a melodramatic huff, he collapses in the Friday sun.

'Well, what do you expect?' Mia smirks. 'You've spent the term sleeping with half the girls in the class.'

I love watching the way Mia's mouth bends around her words.

Jake grins. 'Certain sacrifices must be made for the betterment of humanity.'

'That there,' she waves her hand in the direction of his crotch, 'will be humanity's downfall.'

'Maybe I need some tutoring.' He leans across the grassy circle to Ben. 'Mel wouldn't mind a couple of hours after school with Jakey, yeah?'

Ben takes a long, drawn-out breath.

'Okay, okay!' Jake retreats. 'Settle, bro.'

I overhear Harley whisper to Mia, 'Who's Mel?'

'Ben and Grace's mum. She teaches biology at that all-girls Catholic school in Port Lawnam.'

'South, isn't it?'

'Yeah, about twenty minutes or so.'

'I remember Port Lawnam – Dad took me and my brother there a few times, fish and chips by the harbour.'

Sitting beside Mia, in the shadow of the pine tree, I open my mouth to tell Harley the fish and chip shop is still there, but before I have time to join their conversation, Ben butts in.

'Come over to ours tonight, Harley,' he suggests. 'For some beers and a feed.'

'For sure. You still living in that big white house on the headland?'

'That's the one! End of Walker Street.' Ben winks, basking in the supposed fame of living in a street named after your family.

Our school bell sounds for the end of lunch. Standing, I haul my backpack off the ground, slinging it over my shoulder. Mia and I part from the group, dawdling around to the B block for our final class for the week, extension English. She complains about Mr Woodlow as we stroll, annoyed that he still hasn't let go of Monday morning's incident. I wipe my palms on my school shorts, wondering what Harley will think of our home, whether Mum will be there bombarding him with questions.

'Grace.' Mia pokes me in my side, a teasing wide grin on her face. 'Why are you blushing?'

⌣

With Oatley nipping at our ankles, we hurl our schoolbags over Mia's picket fence. Late for work as usual, we sprint from Mia's place down the Avenue to the string of shops that line High Street, the main drag in Marlow. Our leather lace-ups are heavy on the pavement. Beads of sweat collect under our arms, behind our knees. Weaselling our way through a crowd of little grey-haired ladies, we make it into the bakery, my hair falling out of its elastic loop.

As we scuttle around the counter, Margie crouches behind the display cabinet, words sharp, voice hushed. 'If I didn't have customers lined up out the door, I'd give you two a right serving. Now hurry out the back and get changed.'

Between the benches, cooling racks and ovens, we unbutton our blouses and wriggle into staff shirts. Neither of us really likes the way flour lines our nostrils out the back here, but the bakery and the butcher's were the only places that would hire the two of us . . . and with Mia being a vegetarian, we settled for kneading dough and working an ancient till that all too often refuses to open and share its wealth. Plus Margie isn't all bad. She loves every pie she makes, in particular the avocado, brie and chicken, the sour cream, pumpkin and potato, and of course the classic chunky steak. It's a love that is evident in the wide curve of her hips. She wears gold bangles that turn white when she handles the dough and clatter when she kneads. We help out a few afternoons a week, and early on Saturday mornings, when the people of Marlow and farmers from the hills queue down the street, all the way to the bank, to buy warm loaves straight from the oven. Hers have a golden crust with a slight crunch and a heavenly soft centre. When we aren't in trouble, I quite like working here. The skylight out the back is tinted, so I spend most of my time in blue shadows, while Mia stands at the counter dealing with customers. She is a kaleidoscope, and as she works, I watch the way she refracts light, the glorious way in which colours bend and twist around her.

Mostly, I find myself slicing bread or icing cupcakes, dotting each with lollies or chocolate droplets. When Margie's brother, a slow giant with a warm smile, is in making pastry, I help him fold it and put it in boxes to freeze. Other than that, I clean. Mia, on the other hand, chats, captivates, listens, learning the latest gossip from Marlow's circle of pearl-necklace pensioners. Her world is loud with conversation, the bell tinkling above the door every time someone enters or leaves, the crunch of the till drawer when she forces it shut and the clink of coins emptying from purses onto the glass counter.

Although mere metres away, my world is quiet. I slide between shadows with a wet rag in hand, wiping flour from cool surfaces. Sometimes I close my eyes and let my hand find its way across metal, letting the cloth glide along bench edges, curl around handles and stretch over fridge doors.

When I glance at Mia packing sourdough into a paper bag and passing it over the counter with words on her lips, I think, maybe boring *is* easier. Back here, blind in silence.

<hr>

I check the mirror twice before changing my top. Navy seems to look better than emerald on olive skin.

'You like him.'

'What?' My skin warms.

'Harley.' Mia grins. 'You like him.'

'I don't even know him.'

'You want to know him.' She pinches my cheeks.

I squirm, laugh forced.

'Grace, you look fine.'

The boys are in the fibro shed, playing Nintendo on couches that were once yellow but have been worn grey. Nestled in between surfboard racks, a lawnmower and wetsuit hangers, the old TV set lights up their faces as Mario and Peach race around pixelated tracks. Crossing the finish line, Jake yells, 'HA!' waving his controller. He jumps up for a celebratory dance and knocks over his beer.

'You idiot!' Ben pushes past him to grab a towel and mop up the mess while the others scramble to save the Nintendo box from the frothy tide.

When the commotion settles, Mia pauses the game and steps in front of the TV, holding up a paper bag of bakery treats.

'Presents!'

Together, we hand out the leftovers Margie gives us every week to take home for Fat Friday. We dish out everyone's favourites.

'Ben,' Mia says, throwing him two banana muffins and some white choc chip berry scones. I pass an olive roll and two ham and cheese rolls to Toby. Mia passes Jake a custard tart and a jam doughnut before lobbing a plastic bag of pink icing cupcakes at his head.

Turning to Harley she says, 'We didn't know what you would like, so I brought you two finger buns.' She hands him one with pink icing and coconut flakes and another with white icing and hundreds and thousands.

'Thanks.' He takes them. 'You can never go wrong with finger buns.'

'You're going to fit right in.' Mia laughs. 'Is that your van in the driveway?'

Mouth full, Harley nods, swallows. 'It was my dad's, but he can't drive anymore.'

Jake butts in, holding up two game cases. 'Which one?' Everyone votes for the game in his left hand. Jake, disagreeing, puts on the one in his right.

Mia pops a bottle of sparkling wine that she's bought for $3.99. She pours me some in a kid's plastic mug and I take tiny sips, pretending I'm enjoying it. We're barely into the first scene when Jake, already halfway through his bag of cupcakes, lights up a cigarette.

'Do you have to?' Mia rolls her eyes. 'You're going to die of cancer.'

'Or will cancer die of me?'

'That doesn't even make sense.'

'Think about it.' He taps his finger to her temple and the boys laugh. I scrunch my face, smoke ruining the sweetness of the apple chunks in the Danish Mia and I are sharing.

Above us, the tin roof is rusted from years beside the sea. Last week's rain leaked through cracks and we're sitting now on carpet that smells like wet Monty. On the walls are surfing magazine cut-outs and pictures from the mid eighties of Mum and Dad and their Holden parked on red earth in West Oz with boards stacked on the roof. On the shelves beneath the fishing rod rack are some surfing trophies, mostly Ben's, and if a surface isn't covered in dust, it's covered in sand.

Relaxing against a pillow that smells of vanilla incense, the one the boys light to mask the smell when they smoke, I look around the room. As they race, Ben's tongue sticks out the corner of his mouth. Jake's foot jackhammers the floor and he holds the controller in one hand, his cigarette in the other. Toby's torso twists and turns with his character on the screen. And then there is Harley . . . wedged between them in the middle of the couch as if he's been here with us since we were kids. His hands own the remote, thumbs and fingers sliding over the buttons as he edges forward on the lounge. On screen, characters emerge from a dark tunnel into an icy cave. The blue light bends around his jawline. He's in the lead. He beams and says something I don't quite catch, taunting Jake, who is chasing after in second place.

Mia elbows me. 'Are you even listening to me?'

'What?'

'There's a bonfire tonight, on Tarobar Beach, just got a message. Heaps of people are going.' Mia's mouth races faster than the characters on screen. 'It's for some older guy's birthday – don't know who . . .'

Harley. His eyes, as blue as the sky on the sea, catch mine. The TV becomes deafening.

Suddenly, Jake takes the lead, crossing the finish line again in first place.

'Grace!' Mia elbows me again, I flinch and Harley looks away, leaving me in dead water. 'It's only eight o'clock,' she says. 'We should go. What do you think?'

'Sure, see what the boys say.'

Standing up, she turns the TV off to make the announcement. With a unanimous *yes* vote from all members, we go into the kitchen to fill our esky with ice from the freezer. Mum tells Mia she's all class for purchasing the absurdly cheap bottle of bubbles.

Giggling, Mia responds, 'It's a wise investment.'

Embracing the two of us, Mum whispers, 'Just be safe, girls.'

Ben straps the esky onto a little wooden wagon we've had since we were kids, towing it as he rides on his skateboard down the street with the other boys. Mia mounts her bike, and I climb onto the back, arms wrapped around her stomach as she pedals behind the boys, down High Street and over the hill to Tarobar, the next beach south of Marlow Point.

⌒

I'm curled up on the sand with tails of smoke and dancing flames. Grains stick to my skin, and shift as I move my legs, my bottom. Harley Mathews sits down next to me and the sand shifts again. The fire is blazing, radiating heat. It makes my skin raw and red, but I can't pull myself away. Someone throws an empty wine cask into the flames and I watch orange and blue dance together.

Mia is sitting across the circle from me next to a brawny guy with shoulder-length hair and a half-buttoned shirt. He's at least a few years older than us with curls of brown chest hair. His arm is wrapped around her fine frame, his thumb stroking the side of her breast. Harley's cotton sleeve brushes my forearm and my hand tightens around my plastic bottle.

'How's your night?'

I take a slow sip from the bottle Mia had drained of water and filled with vodka and cranberry juice, waiting a moment to be sure he is talking to me.

'Good,' a girl says and I turn to see him facing a girl wearing a low-cut singlet on his other side.

My next sip is a gulp. Vodka burns a hole in my stomach and when I burp, my eyes water. As he chats to her, I spy his hand from the corner of my eye. His beer snug in the stubby holder Ben forced him to use, which reads *I remember my first beer.*

Her name is Lilly, she lives in Port Lawnam and it is her brother's birthday bonfire. She asks why she hasn't seen him round, saying his face was one she would definitely remember. Harley tells her his family has just moved from the far north coast. She makes some sly comment about him being hot up there. His laugh is awkward and strained.

'Of all the places, why'd your family move to this shithole? Other than sunbaking, there's nothing to do around here except fish, talk smack and step on cow poo.'

Harley clears his throat, sips his beer. 'I used to live here,' he said. 'I was born in Marlow. Moved up north for my dad's job. Shit happened . . . He got paid out and we came back.'

I wonder whether Lilly is listening, whether she cares, whether she can feel her heart beating in her throat.

'Oh . . . Heavy.'

She tells him she likes sunbaking and photography and has a blog. When Harley asks what she writes about on her blog, she admits she just finds pictures on the internet and reposts them, which makes me feel better because it seems less impressive. He says he has an old Pentax.

'What's that?'

'A camera . . . You said you liked photography.'

'Oh!' She flicks her hair over her shoulder. 'I knew that,' she laughs. 'I just forgot.'

Harley tells her he loves working in the darkroom but his old school had shut theirs down because most of the kids in his class were using digital cameras and a darkroom was expensive to maintain. He says he likes reading, surfing, and used to play a lot of chess.

I imagine for a moment that I am Lilly, soft-speaking, eloquent and effortless. I bet she knows how to kiss.

Harley explains that when he was eight, he'd received a glass chess set for Christmas, and all of a sudden I can't tell if she is laughing at him or with him.

Harley leans back onto his elbows, distancing himself, and the sand moves again.

'Grace,' he says as he turns to face me and notices my hands choking the neck of the plastic bottle. 'You all right?'

'Yeah, just a bit flustered.' I shake the bottle. 'Too much maybe.'

With Harley's attention no longer on her, Lilly gets up and leaves.

'You don't drink much, do you?'

'Not really.'

'Me either.' He smiles. 'I've got these, though,' he says, holding up a packet of marshmallows. 'Jake and I bought them from that petrol station on the way here.'

'I love marshmallows,' I admit with a shy grin. 'We need sticks.'

Harley stands, brushes sand off his jeans, and then offers his hand to pull me to my feet.

Slipping into the night, no one notices our silent departure. Drenched in moonlight, we wander over the sand dunes. Creatures of the darkness rustle in bushes and insects hum in the grass while silver waves lap against the shore. Somewhat intoxicated from Mia's concoction, I follow him through shadows scented by burnt gumleaves, trying not to step on sand dune succulents as we draw closer to the forest. After several minutes of searching, a branch snaps beneath Harley's shoe. 'Here!' Leaning down, Harley breaks two sticks off the fallen branch, handing me one before leading me back to the orange haze.

Finding our place in the circle, Harley tears open the packet and we each skewer marshmallows onto the ends of our sticks.

Hot embers fly. Bark flakes from blackened wood on a bed of white ash. We peel back charcoal skin, placing hot gooey marshmallow on our tongues. It sticks to the roofs of our mouths, and as we lick the pink leftovers off our fingertips, I can't help but notice the way light flickers on his skin.

⌒

I use my sleeve to get the vomit out of her hair.

'I swear you didn't even drink that much.' Jake exhales a grey cloud and throws his cigarette in the gutter. Lying back, his shadow is stark. Haze from streetlights drown out stars.

'It was that guy at the end's fault. He gave me a swig of green something, green fairy.'

'That's absinthe!' Ben laughs as she leans over to spew again at the road's edge.

Around us, the car park is dead, trees are still, and for a moment it is only us in the world, six kids lost, as if nothing exists beyond that jagged line of gums. There's a rustle in the bushes as possums growl in argument and the air smells of damp grass. I brush loose strawberry blonde strands behind Mia's ear. Spreading her jacket on the ground, I help lower her down to rest and she closes her eyes.

In spite of Ben's and Jake's banter, all I hear is the crunch of peanuts as the boy beside me munches on a nutty choc bar. From the corner of my eye, I see a grey Converse edge closer toward me. I hear the slosh and slurp of chocolate milk from a carton and feel his shoulder brush against mine.

Mia moans, rubbing her stomach. 'Vego pies from servos are a bad idea.'

'Don't you know not to take candy from strangers?' Ben teases as she sits back up, dry-retching. 'Honestly, he just wanted to get into your *fairy* knickers.'

Her body crumples. 'Did not . . .' she mutters.

Ben sighs, shuffles across to her and rubs her back as she empties the rest of her insides onto the bitumen.

When Mia catches her breath, she wipes her mouth and tells him, 'I'm a catch, a perfect ten.'

A fleeting smile crosses Ben's lips as he wraps one arm around her shoulder.

Three

WALK ON WATER

'Oh, Dad, you shouldn't have . . . this place is *way* out of our budget!'

My dad grunts, pushing Ben through the door. I scurry in behind them and slide the coffee table, topped with dated celebrity mags, to the side of the living space, making room for our boards and bags on the floor. Timmy, the young boy Walker Surfboards has just sponsored, hauls bulging paper bags, packed with groceries for the week, onto the kitchenette's tabletop. He's half Ben's size yet carries twice as much from the car into the motel, looking over his shoulder repeatedly to check whether my dad is watching. Mia does little to help unload the car, instead spending her time skipping around the kitchen on the small square cut of lino floor, putting away the food.

'Really, Mia?' Dad says, and I turn to notice the way she has arranged our refrigerated items from tallest to smallest, and bundled the items in the pantry into groups according to colour. There are a few pieces of fresh fruit, spelt sourdough, fig jam, Vegemite and homemade muesli bars, but Mum would keel over if she saw the packets of instant noodles, chips, sugary cereals, lollies and cheap 'do it yourself' Mexican family pack Dad permitted.

Mia giggles. 'What?' She bats her blonde eyelashes and I catch Ben's sheepish grin.

When we've settled in, Dad's mobile rings. 'Garry, mate, how are you! Yeah, we just got here . . . Ben, Grace, Timmy and the unit . . . Nah, Mel stayed at home . . . I'd love to . . . The Brownlow Pub? See you soon.' Dad throws on a coat and ducks out while the four of us kick back on the couch. I turn on the local news to see a young reporter, red hair flying beneath charcoal clouds, standing on the sand dunes at MacAndrews beach, relaying the weather forecast for the week. We lean forward as if she's a fortune teller, reading the ocean swell like the lines on our palms.

'Great news for the directors of the annual Black Wave titles, the largest junior surfing competition on the east coast, boasting the best up-and-coming surfers in both the amateur and professional divisions. Be sure to come and watch the action unfold, starting just two days from now on Tuesday, and finishing with what is expected to be an epic day of finals on Sunday.'

'I told you,' Ben says, breaking open a pack of potato chips. The scent of lime and cracked pepper fills the air. 'That storm way down in the Southern Ocean . . . the waves will be pumping this week!' His fingers shake with excitement as he shovels chips into his mouth. We each take a handful, except for Timmy, who draws two chips from the packet.

'It's okay,' I whisper. 'The food is for all of us.'

Smiling, he nods, reaching in for more.

Ben pushes his broad shoulders back into the somewhat itchy cushions and spreads his legs wide, taking up half the couch, crowding Mia against the fat armrest.

'You're squishing me!' She squirms, stands and then plants herself on his lap. 'That's better!'

'Piss off! Your arse is so bony!'

'Deal with it,' she sneers, wriggling her bum on his lap, driving her sit bones into his thighs.

Ben grins and shoves her off his knees. Landing on a bag of wetsuits, she is still for a moment before rising to her feet and kicking him in the shins. I recline against a cushion, settling in to watch a game that has entertained me since childhood. Timmy however, never before exposed to the pair's antics, is shocked, his eyes widening as Ben flies off the couch and tackles her to the floor. The twelve-year-old watches them play fighting, unsure as to whether anyone is actually getting hurt.

⌒

It's a new address, but we've been here a thousand times before. Budget accommodation — close to the competition is preferable. This place has cream walls with green architraves and skirting boards, a couch still with the impression of its former tenant's bum, a Monet print hung on the wall above the box TV in a tacky frame spray-painted gold and linen that smells of lemon wash powder, wrapped tight around plastic-covered mattresses. Mia takes the top bunk, and I slide into the shadows beneath. I fluff my pillow and roll onto my back, staring up at wooden slats. Her every movement on the bed above me makes the wire frame clank against the wall.

'Are you nervous?' she says.

Ben rolls onto his side on the bunk bed he and Timmy are sharing on the opposite wall. He props himself up on one elbow, his silhouette that of an Athenian royal. 'Nope.'

'I wasn't talking to you, Ben. Timmy, are you nervous?'

There's a moment of grey silence. 'A little,' he admits.

Timmy tells us it's his first time out of state – he's been to Port Lawnam, and up the coast to the city a few times, but this is the furthest he's ever travelled from Marlow, and although he doesn't say it, I know this is the furthest he's ever travelled without his mum. 'But I'm excited.'

What kid wouldn't be? Picked from the thousands of keen grommets who attempt the Australian waves, chosen to surf for the famous Walker Surfboards. Better yet, taken away to a major surf competition with the man behind the sanding mask . . . Ray Walker himself. He's the hard-faced surfing legend, the man whose attention and affection are highly sought after but not easily won. And it doesn't matter who you are in the fight for his respect. Sharing blood has made no difference.

'What about you, Grace?' Mia rattles the bed frame.

Outside, in the middle of the holiday park, fibreglass fish statues in the pool spit water out of their mouths into shells. Cold splashes in the dark.

'Grace?'

After a while, she gives up, deciding that I am already asleep.

⌒

'Good luck, Grace,' she says, handing me my competitor's rash vest, still wet from its use in the previous heat. Wearing the volunteers' T-shirt, this girl smells of the frangipani spray they're handing out in the girls' complimentary competition bags. We've been introduced before, but her tousled blonde hair and beaded leather bracelets are nothing out of the ordinary in this crowd. Dad has introduced me to plenty of these volunteer girls, plenty of directors, plenty of sponsors, plenty of judges . . .

'Thanks,' I say, not taking the risk of getting her name wrong, instead smiling with closed lips.

Wandering down the path, through the dunes, to the beach, I hear the shuffle of sand as someone sprints after me. Ben, panting and red faced, stops beside me. 'You don't need luck, Gracie, you're going to kill it.' He hugs me tight before jogging back up to the competition tents.

Reaching the shoreline, I plant my feet in the wet sand and listen to the deep cry of the ocean. Down the beach my fellow competitors do cartwheels, stretch to touch their toes, twist their spines, flap their arms, jump on the spot, jiggle their legs. One is wearing headphones that cover half the sides of her head. I see another kissing a block of wax before she rubs a final coat over her deck.

I scratch the sand, digging down until I sink my hands into an icy pool of water. Out the back, waves break well over the heads of young surfers, churning on the sandbank in the impact zone. Salty waves crunch, the power reverberating through the seabed, up the shore, through the sand. I feel the ocean's energy charge my limbs. Electric currents shoot up my arms and set my collarbones on fire.

Blaring over the loudspeaker, the commentator calls five minutes remaining for the heat in the water. Myself and the three other girls in coloured rash vests charge down to the shore dump. We leap over the first roll of foam and duck-dive the second. Grey icy water washes my hair back.

We reach the line-up, and after a few minutes the horn blows. I watch the two progressing through and the two knocked out of the former heat turn and ride on their stomachs to shore. Thirty seconds later, a second horn blows, and with fingers that shake, I set my watch to count down twenty minutes. Moments later, a set approaches and I grasp that the others are a good ten metres away. I'm in position. I spin my board beneath me and drive forward as the wave builds behind me.

On the beach, the commentator traces my actions with words, describing my movements to the crowd of onlookers.

'Only seconds into this heat, we see Grace Walker in yellow, dropping down the face of this left . . . That's got to be at least twice overhead for this young girl, don't you think, Mark?'

I crouch, touch my hand to the water, pivot and then drive up toward the lip.

'Sure is, Adam, and WHOA! Grace absolutely annihilates the top of that section!'

Bouncing off the foam, I descend and lay into another heavy bottom turn.

'Such style from this girl. The pocket rocket proving yet again, big things come in small packages!'

I fly through three more sections, whacking the lip on each, before kicking off the back and paddling out through the rip to make the line-up again.

'Just like her brother and dad, the celebrated Ray Walker, this girl undeniably, walks on water.'

A smile squeezes my cheeks as I race back to the other girls in coloured rashies, bobbing out the back. 'And here comes her score, a whopping 9.12 out of a possible perfect 10. It's a solid score to kickstart Grace's campaign for the week.'

In the moment before I duck-dive my next wave, I imagine my dad, chuffed, and wonder how wide his grin is.

When I reach the line-up again, I make eye contact with one of the other girls. I've surfed against her a hundred times before. Erin, scorning with a puffed chest. There is a lull, and no decent waves come through for a good five minutes. When a set finally approaches, I lie down on my board and paddle into position but soon hear the splashing of arms and feet, thrashing the water. She pushes past, almost knocking me off my board. Erin makes the inside and steals the ride. A second wave approaches, but before I can straighten my torso on my board, another competitor, Jamie, shoves me to the side and takes off. By the time the third wave arrives, I barely manage two strokes before Ash drives forward and jumps to her feet in front of me. Alone, and with no waves on the horizon, I sink into the grey.

⌒

I trudge over dank dead seaweed back to the competitors' tent. Handing back the sandy rash vest, I can hear the contest director talking to Dad in the next tent.

'Ray, she surfs better than almost every girl in the competition — everyone can see it . . . She just doesn't have the confidence. Grace doesn't have the fight like the others do. I mean, she was ripping on that first wave, the highest score in the heat — it's just a shame she couldn't back it up.'

The girl at the desk takes my rash vest and gives me my show bag. 'Better luck next time.'

Mia finds me at the outdoor shower, with a towel in one hand and a hot chocolate in the other. 'Ah, well,' she sighs. 'We've got the rest of the week now to enjoy the eye candy.' She glances at three boys strolling past with boards and unzipped wetsuits. '*Oh my god!*' she mouths. 'I just don't know where to look!'

I shed my black skin and feel the sting of the icy shower. When I step out she wraps my towel around my shuddering body and my hands around the hot chocolate. Carrying my board and dripping wetsuit, Mia leads me to the marquee we're sitting beneath. I put on dry undies beneath the privacy of a towel around my waist and rug up with trackies, uggs and a jumper. Together we plant ourselves down in our camping chairs on damp grass, gazing out at the next heat in the water, with hot cocoa running down our throats.

'What do we have here?' Mia reaches down and grabs my show bag from my feet. Sifting through it she pulls out a small bottle of frangipani spray, a necklace with a pink pendant shaped like a hibiscus flower, a *Black Wave Surf Titles* magnet for the fridge, a 10 per cent off voucher for the local surf shop, a ticket to win a new surfboard, a surf mag and some sunscreen and moisturiser samples courtesy of the competition sponsors. While she inspects the freebies, I swirl my hot chocolate around my mouth with my tongue, letting a tiny bit seep out, warming my purple lips.

'Ew, stop it,' she demands. 'You look like you're drooling brown saliva.'

Her smartphone buzzes. Immediately, she types her password to unlock the screen, holding it close to her face. 'EEE!' Mia bounces in her chair.

'What?'

'He messaged me!'

'Who?'

'That boy!'

I wait until she's stopped bouncing.

'Who?'

'Eric, the one from Friday night!'

'The one who gave you absinthe?'

'Yes!'

'That made you vomit . . .'

Ignoring me, she punches the mobile keys. In celebration, she puts on the necklace. It matches her pink freckles.

'It looks pretty,' I say.

'It would look pretty on you too if you would wear jewellery.'

I shrug as someone's arms wrap around me from behind.

'Aww, Gracie,' Ben says, squeezing the air out of me. 'Who cares if you're in the comp or not? That first wave was epic!'

Dad walks under the marquee, giving me a nod and a weak smile.

'Hey!' Ben shakes my shoulders, whispering in my ear. 'That wave *was* epic, Gracie, okay? Nothing else matters.'

⌒

In the hours between Timmy's final and the prize giving, I cannot count the number of times he checks his watch.

'The prize giving is at two, yeah?'

'*Yes, kid!*' Dad says, quick to turn his attention back to Ben, surfing his final.

The loudspeaker blares, 'And taking to his feet here is Ben Walker in the red, and oh! He kicks off the back of that one.'

Dad is nodding, claps his hands together, speaking softly under his breath, 'That's it, son. Come on, Ben.'

'Wise decision there from the young seventeen-year-old. With two solid scores beneath his belt, he could see that wave didn't have the potential to better his position in first place.'

'You're right, Adam – it just goes to show his maturity as a competitive surfer, and haven't we seen him evolve?'

'We certainly have. Right from his early start in the grom comps, this boy has been a force to be reckoned with.'

'Ray Walker would be very proud right now, but of course this heat is not over yet as we see Connor in the blue pick a cracking right-hander . . .'

'Answering back on the very next wave we see Ben laying deep into his bottom turn, he comes up, stalls, and OHH!'

Ben disappears behind a curtain of water.

'Will he make it out? Wait for it . . .'

Suddenly the wave spits and Ben comes flying out of the barrel, executing two impressive turns before the horn blows to signal the end of the heat. The commentators go crazy, the crowd along the fence line applauds, and I see Dad shaking hands with one of Ben's sponsors.

⌒

Timmy takes second place in the grom division and doesn't let go of his trophy – or his grin.

When Ben is announced as having taken out the under-18s division with unanimous first-place scores from every judge, he takes the microphone. He thanks Mum and Dad for their ongoing support before rattling off a list of sponsors. Afterward, he thanks

Mia for letting him eat the last packet of instant noodles and for spitting on his board for good luck. 'Disgusting but it seems to have worked.'

Chuckles ripple through the crowd.

Finally, his eyes find me through the sea of people and honeycomb softens. 'Most of all, thank you to my twin sister . . . my best friend, Gracie.'

Handing back the microphone, Ben takes his $1500 bank cheque, raising it high above his head as someone shakes a bottle and sprays him with fizzy drink. Onlookers applaud and whistle, yet Ben holds his gaze on me.

On the podium, Ben thanks me in silence, in a way only I can understand. A lump grows in my throat and soon I am clapping louder than anyone else.

⌒

The four of us kids are all woken up when Dad pulls off the highway just outside of Spring Valley, gravel and orange earth crunching beneath our tyres. A bushman with white stubble, an Akubra, hard leather boots and an oilskin jacket sits on a weathered chair by the gate to his property. Piled on the rusty wagon beside him are trays of peaches, apples and nectarines.

But Mia is looking in the other direction. 'Whoa,' she says, pointing across the highway. 'Look at that.'

Turning around, I see trees stripped naked, blackened limbs, torched bodies on ashen earth. Without foliage, I can see for miles through the forest, all the way to the mountains. A wave of grief washes over me. I wonder how many creatures caught fire.

Dad forks money from his pocket for the fruit, gazing across the highway to the scorched bush. 'Bloody hell, it's amazing it didn't jump the road.'

'Believe me,' the bushman says, 'every fire truck within a fifty-kilometre radius was on this highway.'

'Were you still here?'

'They evacuated everyone in the area, but my wife and I stayed.' He carries a tray of peaches to the Rodeo ute. 'I was born on this property . . . I've spent my whole life breathing through these trees. This place is my home. You don't abandon that.' He shakes Dad's hand as we climb back into the ute. 'Looks bleak now but bush always grows back . . . I'll stand by it until it does.'

Four

BROWNIE POINTS

He doesn't even like eggs that much, yet he can poach and top them with hollandaise better than anyone else I know. I can't compete with him in the kitchen, can't last five minutes without setting off the fire alarm, having incinerated the contents of a pot. Even on the barbecue, I turn the outer layer of a steak to charcoal while the inside remains blood raw.

The culinary skills that both Dad and I so tragically lack are compensated for by Mum's and Ben's fluid movements between stovetop and chopping boards. I sit and watch the speed at which he can slice carrots and capsicum, tossing to me tail-end pieces to munch on. I marvel at the way he creates by taste, not a single recipe in sight. Dipping the end of a pinky finger into a soup, or pulling back the lid on a wok, he judges spice and flavour through a single drop of liquid, a sudden cloud of steam. He nourishes everyone around him, energy from the sun nourishing the earth.

Ben lays my poached eggs down in front of me on a slice of toast, and I get stuck right in. 'I swear if you didn't have me around you'd starve.'

I laugh with egg yolk oozing down across my chin and he passes me a cloth. 'That's not true,' I say. 'I'd still have Mum.'

'My poached eggs leave Mum's for dead.'

Mia bursts through the front door in her usual fashion, rays of sunlight streaming in behind her. In her bathing suit, with a towel over her shoulder, she plants herself down on the wooden stool beside me. 'Morning!' she grins, picking at my breakfast.

I slap the top of her hand.

'What?' She giggles. 'We all know how slow you eat. Work's in half an hour – if I don't help you eat we won't even have time for a swim.'

Ben interjects. 'What time do you start?'

'Ten.'

I glance at the clock: 9.20 a.m.

Mopping up a pool of yolk with my slice of spelt toast, I thank Ben. He winks, says he's going to meet Jake, grabs his wallet and ducks out the back door, his skateboard under his arm. From out in the yard he shouts, 'Have a good day, Gracie, and tell Margie she's a sex bomb!'

Ignoring him, I wash and dry my plate, gazing through our sun-drenched living room across the verandah and through our lush garden to where the wire gate opens to the grassy hill, rolling down to the sand . . . the sea.

'Come on, Grace.' Mia stands at the dining table holding up a pair of my bathers. When I get close she throws them.

Although there is no one around but the two of us, I am slow to remove my top. 'It's okay, you'll grow,' she promises.

'And what if I don't?'

'Well, let's just say your babies will be very thirsty!' she teases.

'Yuck!' I wriggle into my swimsuit as she places her hand on my shoulder.

'Seriously, Grace, it doesn't matter – you shouldn't care so much.'

Our ocean is a sapphire stone liquefying in the sun. Waves are small and gentle, they kiss the shore. There is a boy with board shorts and a black wetsuit top, unzipped at the front, sitting on a smooth, wooden plank. Swell lines ripple on the sea and he lies down. He strokes his arms deep into the water and as the wave picks up his board he takes to his feet in one fluid motion. The old board slides down the blue face and he kneels, leans against the wall of water, rises, placing one foot in front of the other until he has walked the plank and is standing with ten toes hanging over the nose of the board. He glides, effortlessly. It's the most beautiful thing I have ever seen, and it is not until he kicks off the back of the wave that a breath caught in my throat is released into the sky.

It's Harley.

I let slip, 'Wow.'

Mia giggles as we wade out of the sandbank. She prods me in my side, 'You do like him!'

'Do not,' I argue, splashing water at her. 'I just didn't know he could ride a longboard – that's all.'

'He used to live at Ivory Point. Grace, I can hardly surf and even I know that is where any longboarder dreams of surfing . . .'

'Okay . . .' I blush. 'I didn't know he could ride like *that*.'

'Oh my god!' Mia sprays me with water and I freckle with goosebumps. 'Grace has a crush. Grace has a crush!' she sings.

'Shut up!' I protest, legs turning to jelly.

The next wave of white wash knocks my feet out from under me and I plunge beneath. When I surface, coughing, laughing and spluttering, Mia calls out to Harley.

Sitting on his board a hundred metres away, out behind the rocky point, he calls back to us, a smile stretching his lips. I hold my breath and dive under the next wave.

⌒

If it weren't for our dripping ponytails, we might have gotten away with being five minutes late, but Margie is tired, having been up baking since the dark hours of the morning while the rest of us slept. She smiles politely as she hands a man his paper bag of scones and then rounds on us as he turns away. Following us out back, her words are a prod in the arse. 'We don't all have time to swim in the sea. *Some* of us have to work.'

It's a busy morning and we're rushed off our feet and by two o'clock, Margie looks as if she's about to fall down. 'Go down the road and get a coffee,' Mia suggests. 'There's a lull in customers now anyway – it's after lunch.'

Cat-whisker wrinkles around Margie's eyes smooth as she sighs, and her face softens. 'Okay,' she says, picking up her handbag and dusting off her hands. 'See you soon. I'll go to Angelo's on the corner so you know where to find me.'

'No worries, enjoy!'

The little bell rings above the latch as the door shuts. Once we've watched her cross the road Mia turns to me, winking. 'Brownie points.'

I softly tap my hands together, offering a silent round of applause. 'More points if someone's sitting out front with a dog,' I add, picturing the hopeless way Margie turns to butter when she stumbles upon a cute dog, how her voice jumps an octave.

'Even better . . . a puppy.'

'A sausage dog.'

'A puppy sausage dog!' Mia lines the top shelf of the display cabinet with croissants. 'Fingers crossed. With that many brownie points we'd probably get an early mark.'

The bell rings. A familiar voice says, 'Speaking of brownies.'

We look up to see Jake and Ben stumble into the shop. Observing their red-rimmed irises, I know any brownies they've been eating haven't been legal ones.

Behind them, one of our regulars, Janine, makes her way through the door. She's a slender woman with a long grey braid and a colourful shawl who swims some mornings in the ocean pool with Mum. She tells me she placed an order with Margie a few days ago and I ignore the banter tossed over the counter between Mia and Jake, focusing instead on the orders booklet. I find Janine's order, write out her receipt, and then fetch her box from out back. At the counter, I open the box to check the contents with her. 'Perfect,' she says with a warm smile. 'My youngest granddaughter, she's turning five today. She's having a mermaid party in the ocean pool.' Janine holds up one of the cupcakes from the box. Little mermaids made from gummy babies and M&M's swim in blue icing atop each cake. 'These are wonderful, thank you so much.'

'You're welcome.'

As she walks out of the store, I think of how many birthday parties Ben and I hosted in the ocean rock pool.

'I also placed an order . . .' Ben says, leaning against the counter.

'Oh yeah, and what did you order exactly?' Mia grins, her hands on her hips.

'Two firm, round buns.'

Jake cracks up behind him as Mia teases Ben, 'I've got samples, would you like a taste test?'

Ben nods, closes his eyes, letting his tongue slide out of his mouth and reaches blindly over the counter toward her.

'I'd like to finger your bun . . .' Jake slurs in the background. 'Oops, I meant I'd like a finger bun.'

Consumed by their own hilarity, the boys sink to the floor.

Suddenly Mia snaps, 'Get up!' and as I follow her gaze across the road, I see Margie with a coffee in her hand, waiting for a gap in the traffic.

The boys look for a moment as if they're about to stand, but then crumple to the floor again, as if their limbs are failing them.

'Ben! Jake!' I beg, 'Get up, she's coming back!' but our demands only make them laugh harder.

Dashing around the counter to the front of the store, Mia drives her foot into Jake's shinbone.

Still laughing hysterically, they crawl onto their hands and knees. Jake uses the edge of the bread stand to haul himself upright, then, before either of us have time to react, he leans over and plucks a jam doughnut from the cabinet.

'Mmmmm! Oh, baby,' he groans. 'Firm bun. Sweet, gooey inside . . . This here is wife material.' He holds out the jam doughnut in front of his face. 'Kiss me, sugar!'

'That's the closest you will ever get to a wife!' Mia says, throwing her weight against him in an effort to push him out the door but he just stumbles sideways.

'Aw, come on, cupcake!' Jake bats his eyelashes and puckers his lips, glazed red with jam.

'Uh oh.' The words slip off my tongue as I watch Margie make it through a break in the traffic.

'Piss off, Ben!' Mia slaps him and I notice that he has taken a meat pie.

Biting into the pie, he moans. 'That's how I like my girls . . . *chunky.*' Jake and Ben drop to the floor again, rolling around on the tiles, laughing as though their sides are about to split.

All of a sudden, Mia has a loaf of bread that Ben pulled off the stand and is hurling piece after piece at the two of them. Slices fly all around as the bell above the door rings.

I don't know if the boys shutting up would help at this point, but they don't.

I just stand there.

Margie is frozen in the doorway, taking in the mess on the floor – slices of bread, several pastries and two boys, high as kites – and Mia standing there with the bread bag in her hand.

'Get. Out. Of. My. Bakery.'

To my horror, Jake rolls onto his back, spreads his arms and legs wide like a starfish and says with a smile, 'No thank you.'

Bright red blotches appear on Margie's face and neck. She rolls up her sleeves.

Ben, still caught in a fit of laughter, wipes tears from his eyes and rises to his feet.

'Boy, I'm warning you,' she says, nostrils flaring.

'Okay, okay!' Jake stands up with his hands raised. 'Don't get your knickers in a knot,' he snickers as he stumbles out the door.

When both boys are outside on the pavement, Margie looks at us and says, 'I meant . . . all of you.'

⌒

'Pricks!' Mia kicks a rock along the footpath. It tumbles into the pole at the base of someone's letterbox, stone on metal rousing a dog behind a wire fence. The ball of white fluff bounces and yaps.

'Oh my god. *Shut up.*' Mia rolls her eyes. 'What do you think the person in that house says when someone asks them if they have any pets?'

I shrug.

'I don't know either,' she says. 'You'd be lying if you called *that* a dog.'

My chuckle is short lived. 'Do you think we'll get another job?' I ask.

'Yeah,' she loops her arm through mine, 'and I won't get another one until we find another together. Besides, I reckon it sounds kind of bad-arse . . . *We got fired.*'

'I guess so.' I squeeze my arm tight in the loop. 'I would have totally freaked if I was by myself.'

'Probably . . . but you're not by yourself.'

⌒

I lie down on Mia's bed beside her toy kangaroo. Mia slides open the glass doors to her garden, and a line of feathers strung up between her bedposts begins to flutter. Kookaburra, cockatoo and budgerigar all take flight.

'Do you want something to eat?' she asks.

I nod, 'Yes please,' and she leaves for the kitchen.

Rubbing my hairline with my sleeve, I wipe off a fine crust of flour and dried sweat and gaze around the room. Like Mia, her bedroom is a constellation of stars, impossible to recreate, impossible to absorb. By my head, on her bedside table, there's a notebook with a sequined cover, like scales of a rainbow fish, a piece of rose quartz, pawpaw cream, Japanese manga comics and a buttermilk candle in a marmalade jar. I reach over and light it with her Hello Kitty lighter, and as flames warm wax, heavenly smells soften my limbs and I seep into the mattress.

Above her desk, which is stacked with books, are several photos pinned to a corkboard. My favourite is a washed-out picture of the three of us – me, Ben and Mia, with me in the middle – at the steps to the kiddie end of the ocean pool, three years old, sandy and naked with goggles sucking our faces. Even then I was half a size smaller than both of them.

Beside the photo board is a poster of her favourite book, *The Lorax*, and I think about all the environmental protests Mia's attended with her brother Jackson in the city, how she always saw the very real, adult message in the story of the Lorax, while the rest of us were just children, delighted by Dr Seuss.

'Here.' Mia hands me a banana she has rolled in hundreds and thousands and then skewered with a kebab stick. 'A fairy wand.'

I sit up and tap the tip of my wand against hers. 'Here's to happier days.'

She laughs. 'To dolphins and guys that know how to kiss girls!'

I sink my teeth into the magical rainbow creation, drawing it off the wooden stick, and grin like a child. Colourful beads of sugar crunch and pop as creamy banana mashes against the roof of my mouth.

On the shelf, I notice a glass bottle filled with foreign coins and notes. 'Where'd you get that?'

'Jackson, he's down for the weekend. Sleeping now though, I think. He visited twenty-six countries – how insane is that!'

Mia's phone buzzes. The plastic kitten mobile accessory she bought from Chinatown when she was last in the city lights up as the phone vibrates.

Checking her phone, Mia gasps. 'Wow!' she says, and holds the fairy wand out, examining it with one eye shut. 'I knew these were good but I didn't know they were *that* good.'

'You've lost me.' I flop back onto the bed.

'The wand . . .' Mia passes me her phone, 'Look at this. *Here* is a guy that I bet already knows how to kiss . . . from the bonfire, remember?'

I take the phone and glance over the message on the screen.

If you're free tonight, my friend is having his 21st in Port Lawnam.

I pass the sparkly mobile back.

Mia punches the keys and a minute later the handset buzzes again.

'It's a house party!' She beams. 'With DJs and a band. Will you come with me? He told me to bring a friend. Please, Grace!'

When I don't answer, she taps her half-eaten fairy wand against mine. 'Please.'

'Okay, but I want to drive.'

'Fine by me! We'll take Gran's car,' Mia says. Her grandma's old Corolla has been idle in the driveway since she moved into the retirement village behind Marlow's public school.

'Sweet,' I say, and she bounces onto the bed, crushing me with her embrace.

'You never know. Tonight could be your night . . .' She grins. 'He might have a friend for you!'

⌒⌒

Like father, like daughter. I watch the way they peel the lids off their pies, scooping out and devouring the spiced lentils. They finish by lifting the empty pastry shells and eating them like biscuits. William, lean and silver haired, wears glasses with wooden frames, loose white trousers and an open cotton shirt. He works from home building software, does yoga and moves slightly out of time with the rest of the world. In that way, he moves in sync with Mia.

We eat on cushions on their back deck, and when I've finished, William says there are more pies that he can heat up if we're still hungry. He tells us how he had popped into the bakery this afternoon to say hi after a swim and taking Oatley for a walk, only to find us missing in action. Upon learning the reason for our absence, he'd started sweating, toyed with his wallet, rolled back onto his heels, and before he knew what he was doing, he had purchased all eleven vegetarian pies off the shelf.

'Sympathy shopping . . . You're hopeless under pressure,' Mia giggles, then reaches across his lap to collect his plate. 'So you're not mad?'

'Honey, a baker needs to be patient and exact with measurements. Let's just say I knew you were never quite going to cut it.' He lies back on his cushion. 'Plus it sounds to me like those boys are largely to blame.'

'They're completely to blame,' Mia says and I suppress a grin, recalling her flinging slices of bread like frisbees.

'I'm sure Mel will have a word with them.' William picks up his book and takes out the bookmark Mia made for him – a feather with a string of colourful beads dangling from the shaft. With his index finger, he raises his glasses slightly on his nose. 'You will need to get another job.'

Mia leans down to kiss him on the cheek and says, 'I love you.' I cannot help but wonder how different *my* dad's reaction will be.

We rinse the plates and cutlery as Jackson stumbles out of his old room, now converted into a guestroom. 'Something smells good,' he says.

'Lentil pies, just heat one up,' Mia says.

Wearing odd socks, boxers and a loose singlet, he rubs sleep from his eyes. 'Still haven't gotten over this bloody jet lag.' Then he notices me. 'Grace!' Embracing me with long, wraparound arms, he scruffs my hair. 'How you been?' Loosening his grip, he steps back. 'I swear you've gotten taller!'

'Really?' I blush.

He chuckles. 'No, not really, but you're looking good.'

'How was it?'

'Indescribable. The best and worst days of my life.'

'Why the worst?'

'I was travelling by myself . . . meant there was no one to share the great moments with, and no one to cry with when it got hard.'

'Well, you're home now,' I say. 'And everyone is here.'

Five

ANY STORY

Because I have no clothes at her house other than my work clothes, I am forced to obey when Mia decides to dress me for the party. I end up in a high-waisted denim skirt, a cropped black bralette and a vintage denim jacket. Feeling kind of edgy in double denim, I sit on the edge of the bed while she colours my lips dense burgundy. When Mia permits me a glance in the mirror, my eyes, as dark blue as the ocean at midnight, have a certain light, a certain energy, a reflection of the moon.

'You're so lucky,' she complains. 'Your eyebrows and eyelashes are so dark, you don't even need make-up.'

I draw a breath deep into my belly, warm and dark, picturing his jagged hairline, wondering what would happen if he were to see me with tinted lips and eyes that swim.

If he saw me, would he be at my mercy? The sea to the moon?

'You look really pretty,' she says and kisses my forehead, before finishing off her own make-up and outfit.

When we're ready to leave, we say goodbye to William and Jackson.

'Are you coming back here tonight?' William asks.

'Either here or Grace's,' Mia says.

'Okay, well, your mum got called in this afternoon, so she'll be at the hospital all night. If you do come back, try to be mindful of her tomorrow – she'll want quiet . . .'

'All good, love you!'

'Bye, thanks for the pies!' I call, and it's not until we're in the car, me turning the keys in the ignition, that I look across at Mia, see her pull a flask from beneath her jacket and think maybe tonight isn't the *best* idea.

'What's in there?'

'Rum,' she beams.

'But where did you . . .'

'I took some from a bottle in the house and filled it back up with apple juice.'

'Apple juice? Is that even the same colour as rum?'

'A bit lighter, I think, but it doesn't matter – neither of my parents drink rum. No one will notice.' Mia tucks the flask back under her jacket. 'Let's stop somewhere on the way and get something to mix it with.'

'Okay.' I turn on the engine. In the dark, she might not notice the slight tremble of my hands.

⌒⌒

Even at night, we wouldn't have needed the address to find the house.

Music pulses through an otherwise quiet neighbourhood. There are cars and skateboards and bikes parked across the front lawn, and a girl already losing her dinner in the gutter while a friend holds back her hair. A second friend with her arms crossed is just far enough away to look like she *might* not be here with them. The crowd is already thick on the street, people hanging in clusters, holding silver pillows of wine above their heads, guzzling on them.

I follow Mia up onto the front verandah and spy a group of boys at the edge of the yard, trying to find a place to jump the fence into the main party out back. As we go to enter the house, two older guys step up off a ratty couch planted at the front door. The skinnier one's beady eyes scrutinise us. He wears a black beanie and has two sleeves of tattoos. Drawing back on a cigarette, he takes a heavy swig from his longneck and snickers, 'This isn't a kids' party.'

A lump swells in my throat.

Mia steps forward, tossing loose curls over her shoulder, puffs her chest and says, 'I'm with Eric Rockwell.'

The two guys exchange a glance and crack up laughing. 'Babe,' the chubby one in the doorway says, 'no one is *with* Eric.'

'Fine,' she snaps. 'I'll call him.'

Mia fishes her mobile from her purse and starts to dial his number.

'Okay, okay.' The skinny one reaches out and pushes her hand down. 'Come on in.' They move aside, granting access. Mia takes my hand and draws me toward the entrance. It's only in the moment before I step through the doorway that I recognise two faces from the crowd on the street – a boy from our English class, a girl I used to play netball with. All of them . . . *our* age.

Suddenly, it dawns on me that we're leaving ourselves behind and stepping into something else entirely.

Deep house beats throb, so loud it feels as if my heart is being forced out of rhythm. Clouds of smoke loom like late May, and I wonder if anyone plans on actually living here after the party is over. We weave our way through the back living area. Beneath the bursting light of a strobe, someone launches themself off the breakfast bar, taking out a mob dancing on blackened floorboards. I squeeze Mia's hand and quicken my pace, trying to stick close to her.

Outside, worn couches and glass bottles litter the lawn, right down to the bottom of the yard where a makeshift stage has been set up. A local band are playing beneath a dark sky. Mia spots an empty armchair closer to the fence and steers me over to it. Sitting down, she draws me down onto her lap and whips out her phone. 'It's too hard to see anyone,' she explains. 'I'll just message him.'

'Maybe we should just wait here,' I suggest. 'Let him find us?'

'Grace, we're not sleeping beauties lying in the forest. I'm sick of lying still and just waiting for Prince Charming.'

A couple walks by while I wait for her to text Eric. I see the girl nudge her partner and cock her head in our direction. 'What is this? A Wiggles concert?'

I shrink back, wanting to sew myself into the green leather upholstery that stinks of lint and tobacco.

'Hey.' Eric wades out from the murky shadows behind the stage and leans down to kiss each of us on the cheek. 'Sorry,' he pauses in front of me, 'what's your name again?'

I open my mouth to speak as Mia answers, 'Grace.'

'Nice to meet you.'

'You too.' I manage a smile at the feet of this giant.

'Come dance,' he says and takes Mia's hand, pulling her out from underneath me. Eric makes for the patch of mud in front of the stage and I feel my best friend's arm hook around my waist. Like a fish caught on a line behind a boat, I am towed in their wake whether I like it or not.

When we make it to the middle of the dance floor, Mia looks down at my two left feet and shouts in my ear, 'Do you want some? Might help you loosen up, yeah?' I see the flask in her hand.

'I'm *driving*,' I say. Suddenly I notice her eyes. Pink glass, sliding in and out of focus. The flask slips from her grasp, and when I pick it up off beaten earth, I discover it is empty. 'There is nothing in here, Mia!'

'Don't worry.' Eric wedges himself between us. 'I'll fix it.' I watch him reach under the stage and draw out a bottle of vodka, pouring clear liquid into the flask until it starts to overflow. The band hits the chorus and the sea of bodies bob and sway. An elbow pokes my spine, a boot stamps my foot.

'Mia, I don't think you should . . .'

Eric's arms slither around her. He grinds his crotch against her. I watch his hands slide over her buttocks, thighs, back around her hips, up over her breasts.

'She's fine,' he says through clenched teeth and takes her head between his two wide palms to stop it toppling off her shoulders. Then he leans down and kisses her, and I see her eyes roll into the back of her head.

'Grace!'

I spin around and see a guy in ripped cord jeans, his shirt over his shoulder like a rag. How does he know my name? He is tall, his head shaved and his jaw angular. He answers my unspoken question, 'I'm Angus – Eric's mate,' and sneaks a hand beneath my jacket, brushing the skin between my skirt and bralette.

I glance back to Mia and see a boy with a tie-dyed tee and long hair where she and Eric *should* be. Blood begins to pound in my eardrums as I scan the yard in search of Mia. The blood is so loud in my ears I don't even notice the break in the music.

'Where is Mia?'

'She's with Eric.' His fingertips touch my lower ribs, soft at first, and he draws me closer to him.

'I have a boyfriend.'

He maintains his grip and smiles. 'Yeah? Where is he?'

My skin tightens, my shoulderblades squeeze together. 'He didn't want to come.'

Angus laughs, only the sound is hollow and cold. His fingers curl, nails dig into my waist. He leans over me, breathing bourbon and Coke hot against my now naked collarbones as he slides my jacket down my arms. 'What's his name?' he taunts.

'Harley,' I say, quickly biting my tongue.

'Never heard of him.'

A bug in a spider's web, I writhe and wriggle.

Through welling tears I barely see the singer stumble off the front of the stage. The sea of bodies turns wild with waves of cheering and chanting and I am ripped out of Angus's hold. Swimming out of the crowd, I escape up the yard, ducking into a shadow beside the house. I dig for my mobile, calling the number at the top of my favourites. Ben picks up on the second ring.

'Hey, did you get my message? I'm so sorry about today! Trust me, I'll make it up to you, Gracie – I promise, okay?'

I close my eyes and lean against the fence, pressing my face against the rough wood.

'Where are you? What's all that noise?'

Down the hill, the singer is hoisted into the air by three guys. He's showered in beer and screams of praise.

'Are you at a party?'

When I don't answer, his voice goes up. 'Gracie, are you okay?'

It's not until I hear myself speak that I become aware of my sobbing. 'I can't find Mia.'

'Take a deep breath.'

I exhale, taking comfort from his voice.

'Have a wander, and if you can't find her maybe go wait by the car?' he suggests. 'I'm with the boys in the shed – we have pizza, Mum made it with some healthy shit. There's still heaps here for when you get back . . .'

There's a blackout, the winding down of a generator, and as the party is plunged into darkness my grip slackens, the phone bouncing off the ground and into a crack between the stairs and a fence. I drop to my hands and knees and stretch one hand into the gap, trying to reach it. The screen light stays on for a few seconds, but after that I am left groping for it blindly. The mob starts booing, calling for the lights to come back on. I hear someone banging metal together. 'OI!' they shout. 'COPS! Everyone out! The cops are here!'

Finally, I touch my phone, just as a boy on his way out trips over me in the shadows and I graze my head against the coarse timber of the fence. 'Fuck! Watch yourself!' he spits at me, dusting himself off.

I bring the handset to my ear to find Ben still waiting on the other end. 'Are you okay? Gracie, I heard that. You have to stick up for yourself.'

'The cops are here,' I say, cupping my other hand over my mouth so that he can hear me over the racket – empty cans crunching beneath shoes, screams, chatter, and sirens already blaring in the street. 'I'm going to go find Mia.'

'Okay, but call me back.'

⌒

Caught in the current, I flow through the house, pouring down the front driveway and emptying into the street where the lights flash blue and red. I try to stay there, at the river mouth, darting between the schools of fish, scrutinising every face, until there are only a few left stumbling down the drive and I come to understand she must have come out before me. She's already out *here*.

I blink and tiny drops chase down my cheeks. I swallow, draw a deep breath, wiping my eyes on the sleeve of my jacket. Black blotches come away on denim.

Weaving my way out of the crowd, I swim toward the car. Neighbours are out on their front steps in dressing robes and ugg boots, several clutching torches, as if a mere beam of light is enough to stop a teenager vomiting on their flowerbeds.

And then I see her, a girl without her jacket, walking up the centre of the street. Her arms are wrapped around her stomach, and despite the chaos unfolding on the street all around, her every step is calm and measured, strides of equal distance, equal timing. *Nothing* like Mia.

She stops on the bitumen no more than a metre in front of me and in the glow of the streetlight, I see her face, ghost white, deep sunken eyes. She's silent.

I notice his meaty shoulders. Trailing ten or so metres behind, Eric Rockwell comes to stand at her side, adjusting his crotch, doing up his fly.

My heart sinks.

Her stare is vacant, her hair matted and damp at the hairline. The giant stamps her lips with a kiss, but she doesn't blink.

'I'm going back to find my friends. See you, Mia,' he says, and then he is gone.

She doesn't speak. She can't speak.

It's sickening. My heart starts to ache.

'Oh, Mia . . .' I begin, just as whatever strength she had, holding herself upright, burns out and her body folds in two.

⌒

We stop twice on the way home. The first time because she vomits out the door into the gutter. The second time because her cries are so hysterical, I have to turn off the engine, pull her out of the car and lie her on the kerb so that the night air can fill her lungs.

Ben, as he has always been able to, knows something is seriously wrong before we're even home and is waiting in the driveway when I pull up. Lifting her out of the car, he asks me what happened, and I say nothing, because with Ben I sometimes don't need words.

I watch the colour drain from his face. His body shrinks a little, and then his arms tighten around her, as if wishing his embrace could undo someone else's wrongs.

'Who is he?'

'Eric Rockwell,' I whisper, and she sobs harder, soaking his shoulder with her tears. 'What should we do?'

'Go tell the boys to go home—' Ben begins, but then we hear Mia's voice, her breath ragged and uneven.

'I just want to go to sleep,' she manages, and as I watch him carry her into the house, I think about Sleeping Beauty.

⌒

I wake in the night to the sound of feet at my bedroom door.

'Mia,' Ben whispers, 'are you awake?'

'Yeah.' She's barely audible. 'I can't sleep.'

I hear the rustle of cotton sheets as he eases himself onto the single trundle bed I pulled out for her on the floor.

'Come here,' his voice soothes, and there is another rustle as he gathers her bones. Whispers pass over the pillow, my two best friends entangled on a single mattress.

'Can you tell me a story?'

'A story about what?' he asks.

'About anything . . . Any story. A story about something *else.*'

Six

LIKE THE SUN

Nineteen minutes and eleven seconds separated us at birth.

On the official documentation, he is older.

Ben came into this world screaming, his presence bold. I, on the other hand, was still caught in the shadows, lagging. Ben had left me and I was aimless in a world without him. The womb, our first home, was hollow and empty now.

I was the moon beneath a dark horizon. And when I rose, I began my orbit around the sun.

On the birth certificate, I am younger.

Although it really has nothing to do with age.

I recently discovered in a personal development class at school that fraternal twins are the result of hyperovulation – multiple eggs being released from the ovaries, which are then fertilised by different sperm, possibly even at different times. There is no way of knowing which one of us is actually older.

It has nothing to do with age.

What it really means is that I am, and have always been, *second*. Second to breathe. Second to be weaned off breast milk. Second to walk unaided. Second to say the alphabet from start to finish. Second to stand on a surfboard. Always one step behind Ben, always lagging.

Whenever he took a new step, Mum would look at me almost apologetically, until one day, she began pushing me down paths Ben had not already marched. Girl guides, netball, clarinet lessons.

For a year, I even attended ballet. I was a seven-year-old unable to touch my toes, and rarely stood without the teacher poking my stomach. *Tuck in this banana belly, Grace!* One day, she shuffled the class and I was placed at the front of the ensemble. With no one to look to for the next move, I stumbled out of time and put each girl behind me off beat as well. I quickly returned to my place at the back and was comfortable, guided by the girls in the front row.

These days, Mum has to lift Monty into her car, his legs too thin and tired for him to jump up on his own. Without Ben in the car, I happily take the front seat and strap myself in next to Mum. She turns on the ignition and shifts the car into gear, telling Monty to lie down in the back so she can see out the mirror.

'I still don't see why he has to be so mean . . . it's been over a week,' I say, thinking of Dad's cold shoulder in the days since Mia and I were fired from the bakery.

Mum pulls out of the driveway. 'Oh it's okay honey, he'll get over it soon enough.'

'Well he's being nice to Ben and it was Ben's fault, not mine.'

Turning down the radio, Mum says, 'It's different for you two. You're his little girl. I'm afraid he just doesn't know how to react sometimes.' Mum sighs. 'He really does care.'

I turn to look out the window as we turn onto High Street. 'Got a funny way of showing it.'

'You know, when you were born—' Mum begins and even though I have heard her talk about the day a thousand times, I never get tired of listening. We're cruising past the strip of main shops in Marlow as Mum recalls Dad clasping her wet palms in the delivery room. She tells me how Dad, a hard-skinned man, came undone, tearing at the sides like tan leather slit with a knife when Ben was drawn from her body. At the sight of his baby boy, he leant into Mum's shoulder and cried.

'The nurses had whisked Ben away,' she says, reaching across the gear stick, rubbing my knee. 'I could turn my energy to the tiny body still inside me. The little person I was *yet* to meet.' Smiling wide now, Mum tells me that when my dad set eyes on me, his baby girl, frighteningly small for thirty-six weeks, his next breath was laced with a slight anxiety. Mum explains that his fear, in that moment, stemmed from a sudden feeling of inadequacy, the realisation that he could never guarantee my full protection. He would never be able to shield me from every girl who bullied me for being a tomboy, or catch me every time I fell from my bike. 'Although,' Mum laughs, 'he will always try.'

I fold my arms, 'How is being mean *protecting* me?'

Mum comes to a gentle stop at the only set of traffic lights in Marlow. 'Like I said honey, he cares so much. He just doesn't know how to react sometimes.' The light turns green and Mum leans on the accelerator. 'Your dad has never been good with his emotions.'

I shrug. 'I guess so . . . Can you tell me the story of what happened after?'

Mum chuckles and I realise that I probably didn't need to ask.

'*Mrs Walker,* the nurse said to me, *we have a minor problem . . .* Maybe I was being over the top but I thought I was going to have a heart attack when she said that!'

Mum pulls into the parking lot at the edge of the sports fields where the local farmers markets are held each week. She finds a park, puts on the handbrake and turns off the ignition, but I leave myself buckled in, patiently waiting for her to reach my favourite part.

'They told me Ben was crying and that none of the nurses could calm him,' Mum says, 'and so I told them to bring him in. It was motherly instinct,' she boasts. 'I had them put you in the same crib.' I unfold my arms as Mum describes the way Ben's wails silenced as soon as he was brought to my side.

'Just remarkable,' Mum says. 'A little boy yearning for his sister — a tiny wolf, howling for the moon.'

I unbuckle my seatbelt; hop out of the car and with Monty waddling at my feet, think of all the steps Ben has taken before me. But then, I consider that he has stopped, each and every time, looking back over his shoulder with a dimpled grin, patiently waiting for me to catch up.

⌒

At the markets, I drift in Mum's brilliant, colourful shadow as she sails between fruit stalls and clothing racks. She is barefoot, in a cotton dress that loops around her neck, hugs her slim waist and thighs and then falls loose around her ankles. A pashmina scarf with iridescent orange stitching draped around her shoulders makes the blue water in her eyes ripple.

I'm still while she contemplates cherry or grape tomatoes, eventually buying both. I linger while she presses an index finger and thumb to avocados to judge their ripeness. I smile when she introduces me to someone who then asks, 'Where's Ben? How is Ben?' I hold open the hemp bag for her kale and celery stalks, and I blush when two young girls with braces and sparkly lip gloss point and giggle, as if the very idea of seeing a teacher outside of school defies one's imagination.

'Hi, Mrs Walker!' one of the girls says before they both burst into laughter and duck behind a stall of organic marmalades and jams.

Soon we run into neighbours, Nicole and Pete, whose daughter, Jess, two years older than me, has just flown to England to see the sights and nanny for a young family for the summer. Mum rubs Nicole's arm, comforting her, and says, 'I know how you feel. This is my babies' last year in school. I can't believe it! You know Ben is expected to make the circuit next year, if he keeps performing like he is – fingers crossed – but I don't know how I'll go next year, when he's halfway around the world. How do you manage having Jess so far away?'

'We miss her, that's for sure,' the woman says.

Her husband chimes in then. 'But she's on an adventure.'

My mum nods. 'Of course. We can't hold on to them forever, right?'

I wonder if Mum has forgotten I'm at her hip.

Nicole rests her temple on her husband's chest, saying softly, 'It helps to know she has a return flight.'

⌒

By noon, when we meet Mia at the gelato stand, we have filled a mere three bags in three hours. 'Oh!' Mum giggles. 'I didn't even notice the time.' It's her catchphrase, yet I don't think it is so much that time escapes her. Rather, my mum melts time.

I think that's why Dad fell so hard for her, because suddenly he felt there was not *enough* time.

Mum puts her bags on the grass and wraps her lean arms around Mia, blanketing her shoulders with the pashmina scarf. 'How are you, my little sunflower?'

Squished, Mia mumbles a reply into Mum's armpit. Mum holds her a fraction longer than usual, until Mia's limbs, rigid, finally slacken.

Walking into a tent that sells infused olive oils, Mum dips a cube of sourdough into an oil, then into the small dish of macadamia nut dukkah on the sample plate. Popping it in her mouth, she closes her eyes and the muscles in her face soften. She licks her lips, compliments the lady behind the table, and turns to Mia. 'Have you eaten?'

When Mia shakes her head, uncharacteristically quiet, Mum suggests a picnic. 'I'm almost finished up here. Why don't we buy some extra things, whatever you like, and have a picnic lunch, just the three of us. How does that sound?'

She caresses the nape of Mia's neck, her touch gentle.

'Sure.' Mia gives Mum the biggest smile she's managed all week, though even this one looks like it could slide off her face in a heartbeat. 'That sounds good.'

We decide to have our picnic at the base of the grassy hill at home because the clouds have parted a little. Sunlight falls through the small opening, a drop of blue ink in a grey sea.

Mum and I unload the fruit and vegetables from the old Range Rover with Mia in tow, then gather some cups, plates, cutlery and a rug from the house and wander down the hill.

We settle ourselves on a patch of level earth and spread the rug. It's thick, with colourful ribbons and little copper bells sewn around the border. Beneath the fabric, the grass is dark and lush, thriving after the rain we had at Easter. Mum draws from her bag a collection of small plastic containers and arranges the garlic-stuffed olives, marinated button mushrooms and sun-dried tomatoes on a platter with a handful of homemade crackers in the centre. I slice banana and chop the green tufts of hair off the heads of strawberries on a wooden board, offering one to Mia but she shakes her head. Mum empties a bag of honey-roasted macadamias into a cup, then opens a pot of eggplant dip. Taking a loaf of spelt sourdough out of a paper bag, she pulls off chunks and lays them on a platter, as I settle the fruit in a bowl.

'I hadn't bought this dip before,' she says, taking a piece of bread and plunging it in the pot.

After consuming the whole thing in one mouthful, Mum reaches for another. 'Mmm! Delicious! Try some.'

Again, Mia shakes her head, so I reach across and grab some. The eggplant is smoked and seasoned with garlic, paprika and cumin. A hint of chilli hits me after I've swallowed.

'That lady by the bread stand . . . the little round one . . .' Mum looks a bit embarrassed at what she's just said, but she goes on. 'She had a plate with some of the dip, told me what it was, said it's Moroccan inspired and that I simply had to try it. I'm so glad I did, it's divine!'

I reach for another piece of bread and scoop up dip. 'Yeah, I like it.'

'Gorgeous woman. Can't believe I didn't recognise her. Nila . . . you remember her? Nila Mathews.'

I nod, picking up my drink and biting on the end of my straw, jiggling the ice floating in the cup.

'She said this was the best Moroccan dip she'd had in Australia, just like her grandfather's.'

Slurping up the fresh lemonade, I wait for, hope for, Mum to continue.

Did her grandfather smoke the eggplant himself? Was there a secret to his recipe, some slight alteration that made all the difference? A family secret, passed all the way down the line, to her sons, to Harley?

Mum says she's invited the Mathews around for dinner next week.

I shake the ice again, gulp my drink down.

'The way someone nourishes their family, it says a lot about their character,' Mum says.

I suck the cup dry.

'What's her boy's name?' Mum asks. 'She showed me a photo on her mobile . . . He was always a bit odd, wasn't he, but hasn't he grown up! *Very* handsome.'

'Harley,' Mia says, biting on a slice of banana.

Mum nods. 'That's it!' She's silent for a moment, pondering. 'Funny, she remembered Ben, said Harley had mentioned him.'

A weight in my abdomen draws me into the earth. *Everyone* knows Ben.

Mum pours kombucha into a cup, 'Would you like some?'

I turn to Mia, watching her politely decline as she picks another slice of banana from the bowl. Her nail polish is fading, flaking off. I notice water diluting her blue eyes, the slight puff of her eyelids, the wash of pink skin at the base of her throat, the way her limbs seem to hang. Her breasts are flattened, cupped tight in a sports bra, concealed beneath a plain white top and green cardigan. Her spine curls.

It's as if Eric set foot on her red earth and dug a gaping hole.

Mia hadn't let me tell her mum until Sunday night.

At the hospital, the counsellor said that it was up to Mia to decide if she wanted to involve the police. Mia couldn't have legally given Eric her consent while she was intoxicated, the counsellor explained, and if she wanted to report the incident to the police, she would have the full support of both the counsellor and the hospital. She also said, in some cases, even though it's wrong, young girls experienced more trauma when they pressed charges as the rumours were exaggerated, and the slander intensified. The counsellor had taken her hand and assured her that the choice was hers and hers alone to make – that she would be safe and supported either way.

Mia drops a strawberry in her lap. The juice bleeds into her grey leggings. She doesn't bother to pick it up, instead reaching for another.

Mum and I are quiet now, staring into this hole, desperate to know how we can fill her back up.

Ben stops to say hello on his way back from the beach, wetsuit peeled to his hips, revealing a snail trail and pronounced V-lines. He fishes in a shallow pool for something appropriate to say. It's a rare sight, Ben Walker strangled by silence. He manages a smile but I know he is kicking himself for the times he teased Mia for waiting for the one. *Where's Prince Charming tonight? You should invite him to the party . . .*

It was different for him. The girls at school wished they'd been the one to go with him into the sand dunes. With childish notes and cards, texts, wall posts and late-night phone calls, they made themselves available. He had been somewhere no other boy our age knew how to take them.

Guys in grades above nodded at him casually, as if he'd been received by some secret society. In our own year group, boys gravitated toward him, envy in their eyes. Ben was seen as a hero. Like the sun, they bowed down before him, with subtle but regular offerings of beers, attention and respect.

And although my mum didn't silently congratulate him the way Dad did, realising there was a part of her child that didn't belong to her anymore, she didn't mourn what she had lost by spoiling him or tiptoeing around the void. She didn't buy him freshly squeezed organic lemonade, choosing the only coloured straw left in the tin like she did for Mia. She didn't caress the skin between his shoulderblades. She didn't take his hand for the fourth time in an hour and say, 'Is there anything else I can get you?' because unlike Mia, he'd been proud. He'd made a choice – hers was stolen.

I think about Ben and Mia and their cool distance this past week. I think about how he kept an eye on her from across the circle of friends under the pine tree, from down the hall, but did not dare to tread too close. I think about how he snuck out of my bedroom last weekend before Mia woke me up at eight o'clock for pancakes. How maybe they'd thought it would shock or upset me to know they'd lain together, half-naked, beneath a feathered quilt. Maybe they had shocked themselves. I think about how in reality *I* had woken first, around five-thirty, to soft white light that was neither night nor day.

I had seen the way her pale cheek fit in the groove beneath his collarbone. I had seen the way his torso cradled hers. I had seen the way her palm rested on his heart. I had seen the rise and fall, their bodies breathing together.

I think about how in the few minutes before I fell back asleep, I had seen a girl and a boy, perfectly conforming to each other's skin and bone, yin and yang. I think about the way they looked together, the way in which they fit, and wonder if this is something even they have not yet realised, or come to understand.

Seven

THE SHADOW IN BETWEEN

We're picked up from school at midday because the surf is pumping, boards already in the back of the Rodeo. This is what being grounded looks like for Ben. After all, it's hard for Dad to discipline Ben for smoking weed when the boys discovered Dad's stash just last summer.

With no job, I am free on Wednesday after school, so I skip lunch, maths and history as well, and follow Dad and Ben out the side gate. Already this term, blue autumn swells have granted us two visits to the orthodontist and now an appointment with a chiropractor. Although Dad would kill us if we were to leave school early for any other reason, surfing has never fallen into the 'truancy' category. Perhaps he sees it as an investment in Ben's professional career.

I am sure the woman at the front desk knows we aren't on our way to Port Lawnam to align our postures, but Dad's sinking green eyes are enough to persuade her. That is the effect he has on women.

We drive north as sunlight falls and shatters into a million gold pieces on the sea. Waves curl and crack. White wash tumbles against the foot of the cliffs, spitting foam high into the sky as we round headlands in search of the perfect peak. Ben suggests we check Boulders, a rock shelf ten minutes further north.

'Grace, I practically did you a favour.' Ben laughs and kicks his feet up on the dash. 'Look at what you'd be missing out on if you were working this afternoon.'

'That's enough,' Dad warns.

Sinking into my seat in the back, I consider my shallow savings account, how it will no doubt run dry in a few weeks. And while Ben has made the effort to buy both Mia and me treats from the canteen at school and offered to renew my yoga class card, I will soon be in need of another job.

It's easier for Ben. He works at the factory on weekends and sometimes on weeknights, coating boards with resin and routing spaces for fin plugs. He gets along with the older guys who work there full time, playing practical jokes and grooving to deep house turned up so loud the speakers wobble on their hooks. *And* he is overpaid, tremendously. After all, I can't remember a time when Walker surfboards weren't in demand.

I was offered a job there too when we turned fifteen, but the chemicals burnt my nose, and though it was unspoken, I was never really welcome. I was there only because I was Ray Walker's daughter. I knew they were waiting for me to mess up, to coat an epoxy blank with the acrylic paint meant for a polyester board, or to mix in too much catalyst and set off the resin too early, turning it to jelly before the rails – the edges of the surfboard – were completely covered. They didn't want a girl in the factory; it was a male space, with posters of naked women taped to the insides of cupboard doors, beers in the fridge and the toilet seat forever upright.

What few understand is, for Ben, factory work is merely pocket money. Cash in hand, money to play with. His *real* savings are frozen in an account, inaccessible until he's left school. Seven years of prize money, sponsorship endorsements and contracts, amounting to a sum even I am not privy to.

As we pull into the clearing, loose pebbles and dirt crunching beneath tyres, clouds of orange dust rolling over the bonnet, we catch a glimpse of the point through a trough in the sand dunes. A magnificent mountain of water builds, becoming darker until it can't grow any taller and starts to fold. White wash cascades down the face as the lip arches, splinters on the rocky shelf. Boulders is the best we've seen it all year. As soon as the handbrake is on, Ben decides to climb out the open window with his school shirt already off, bouncing on the dry earth. 'Told you so! It's epic!'

Dad calls Ben around to the back of the ute. 'Got a surprise for you,' he says.

'You're kidding!' Ben says.

'Nope, all yours.' Dad's smile splits his face from ear to ear as Ben pulls the board out of the tray, running his hands over the freshly sanded rails. Sunlight bounces off the surfboard, pristine and white, making me squint. Ben flips the board in his hands and Dad points to a cartoon sketch of a 1960s pin-up girl bathing in a martini that the factory artist has drawn just above the fins. 'Mark thought you would like that.'

'Shit, yeah – tell him it's awesome! Love it!'

I turn away, dropping my towel and pulling my wetsuit over my naked chest, the sun hot on my shoulders. I can hear Dad saying that the new board is to congratulate Ben for his big win a few weeks back, but I know, we all know, Dad has never needed a reason to congratulate his son.

⌒

Burnt red and cracked – the backs of my hands, the soles of my feet, my earlobes and face. We spent four hours in the water at Boulders, just the three of us, and now, with thick steam clouding the bathroom, the scorching water from the showerhead almost feels cool against my skin.

My bones had felt the vibrations of the rock shelf, pummelled every few minutes by the monster swell. Maybe I'd been too excited to think about sunblock. Had we even had sunblock with us? My skin is not as tanned as Ben's, and certainly not as dark as Dad's – I should know better than to let myself fry. Maybe the new board glistening beneath Ben's arm had been our greatest distraction.

'Gracie, I'll give you a turn once we're out there!' he'd beamed, waxing the deck.

Mum will kill me. I'll almost certainly peel.

I slide down to sit on the pale green tiles and rest my head between my knees. Water bends over and around the rivets of my spine like pebbles in a stream. I lose myself beneath the downpour, and it's not until I catch myself thinking of him in science class on Monday, first period, just one row in front, with a bun of black hair still damp and sandy from that morning's surf, that I stand and turn the taps off.

I swing open the door and step off wet tiles onto cool floorboards. The sun has set since I've been in the shower. I catch a whiff of cumin seeds, sizzling and popping in a pan of oil. I hear Nila laughing. They're already here. A hot cloud of steam rolls out of the bathroom, a summer storm cloud, engulfing me. I tiptoe down the hall toward my room but in the final few feet before my bedroom door, Mum calls out to the boys and Harley emerges from Ben's room.

I look at Harley, the flare of his blue iris brilliant even in the dim hallway, and wrap my arms around my abdomen, the towel suddenly too small, too thin to possibly conceal me. I shrink back against the wall.

'Oh, sorry! I didn't mean to . . .' Harley's usual cool air is hot, he's flustered, his confidence has evaporated.

My breaths are shallow, incomplete, as if oxygen is no longer enough. Warm droplets drip from my hair at the nape of my neck and run down between my shoulderblades. They tickle and tease, pooling on the floor between us.

A moment later, Ben wanders out of his room, takes one look at me and laughs. 'Wow, Grace, go put clothes on – we have guests!'

Later, lying on the couch with my legs draped over Dad's lap, I catch myself again staring over Dad's shoulder to Harley sitting at the dining room table. Beside me, Dad is describing a new line of longboards he's designing for a Japanese shipment next summer. Steve Mathews rocks forward in his wheelchair, elbows on knees, palms cupping his chin, keen and attentive. A fine patch of silver hair sprouts from the open collar of his shirt.

On the floor, Ben and Ryan, Harley's older brother, talk about Ryan's plans to travel down through Europe to North Africa.

Ryan says he's spent the year working, saving up. Moving down from Ivory Point meant he had to leave his old job. It's taken him the past few weeks to secure one down here but he's working as a labourer now in Port Lawnam and says it's paying enough. He'll be leaving Australia early next year.

Ben rants, telling Ryan he can't wait to travel, that he can't wait until graduation at the end of the year, when he's old enough to qualify for the pro surfing circuit. 'I'll be out of here in a heartbeat!'

Leaning back, chest tight, I think of languages I wouldn't understand. I imagine the rules, recipes, roads – how would I get my bearings?

Ryan edges forward as Ben brags about the places he intends to visit in between competitions.

'Yeah?' Mum laughs, almost teasing, as she crosses the lounge room to place another log on the fire. 'With what money, my love? I doubt your sponsors are going to cover a leisurely trip to Amsterdam.'

'Drug money, Mum. Filthy drug money.'

Mum asks him to stop showing off in front of our guests, and our fathers chuckle.

As Mum takes a seat at the dining room table next to Nila and Harley, pouring Nila and herself a glass of red, I can see the faint smile rounding her lips.

'Well, I've always got my savings,' Ben taunts.

'Oh no you don't – that's for university. You can't stay on tour forever.'

Ben rolls his eyes, murmuring something to the boys. Dad winks and nods in agreement.

Propping myself up on my elbows, I peep over Dad's shoulder. Sitting with our mothers at the dining room table, Harley takes a sip of Nila's wine, his eyes cruising around the room. I follow his gaze as it skips from a Star of David pendant on the bookshelf across to rosary beads hanging from the mantle, down to a framed picture of Ganesh on the wall and back to Mum's buddha in the centre of the table. Nestled between a candle and a bouquet of acacia and bottlebrush flowers, the tiny buddha is frozen in bliss. Harley picks him up, cradling his bone belly, smoothing the buddha's bald head with his thumb.

The fire crackles and spits, and Harley looks at me, bands of orange and purple light dancing on his cheek. There's a foreign warmth between my thighs.

'Mel?' he begins, elbows resting on dark wood. 'What do you believe in?' He knows Mum is a science teacher at a Catholic school, and he's trying to make sense of all these religious artefacts.

Mum loops her arm around the back of her chair and twists to face him. 'Do you want to know why I love science, Harley?'

'Oh, now you've started her!' Ben jokes. 'Get ready to have your ears chewed off!'

Mum ignores him, swirling the wine in her glass.

Eucalyptus logs blacken in the grate. Harley, twiddling the tiny buddha between his fingers, nods and smiles. 'Sure'.

'Well,' Mum beams, 'I love knowing what plants need for photosynthesis, what they need to turn energy into matter. It's so simple – just water, carbon dioxide, sunlight and chlorophyll. That's why I love science. But even more special is knowing we can take those things, put them in a test tube, shake it up and still can't replicate it! I know how we came to be, but I don't know *why*.'

Harley's hand grips the buddha and he edges forward. 'Science can only explain so much . . .' he offers.

Mum nods and takes a sip of her wine before continuing. 'Religion fascinates me, for obvious reasons – the traditions, culture, it's all very beautiful at the core. Religious doctrines, though – they're what I find most interesting. They claim to have the answers, but faith is *not* answers. Faith is the shadow in between.'

Mum sets her glass down on the table, her red wine lips spread into a smile. 'I believe in the sun and the moon,' she says.

The sun, radiant and alive.

The moon, a mere reflection of his light.

Eight

TANDEM

I am at the kitchen bench, half-dressed, stuffing my face with toast and eggs, when Harley walks through the door with Jake and Toby. I smile with closed lips – in case I have something in my teeth – and quickly excuse myself. In my room I put on one of Mia's hand-me-down bras and then pull a spaghetti strap singlet over the top so the white lace bra straps are obvious.

In the weeks since Harley plucked the buddha from the mantle, Mum has taken a particular liking to him, roping him into conversation as soon as he sets foot in the house. When I return, he is sitting at the breakfast bar, chatting to Mum as she pours blueberry banana pancake mix into a skillet. The scent of coconut oil liquefying in the pan drifts through the house.

I sit down next to Toby on the couch and he shifts his lanky limbs, making sure I am comfortable. He is acutely aware of his body, always making room for others – unlike Jake, his cousin, splayed across the Afghan rug on the floor as they watch the Saturday morning cartoons.

I catch snippets of Mum and Harley's discussion during lulls in conversation on the TV.

'So easy,' she explains. 'The mix is egg, banana and blueberries . . . Then I add some flax seeds, almond meal, vanilla – whatever really!'

I hear the splat of a pancake landing back in the pan after a high flip.

Harley admits he's already eaten. 'But it's the most important meal of the day, or so my mum says . . . I'm sure I have room for seconds.'

'She's a wise woman,' my own mum laughs. 'It's the first thing we bless our bodies with each day . . . breaking our fasts, a new sun rising in the sky . . . something to celebrate, no?'

Harley agrees, and Ben calls out to Mum to stop annoying our guest.

On the couch, I arch my neck back, trying to see past Toby's bony shoulder as Mum serves a pancake from the skillet. 'Try it,' she beams, offering Harley a knife and fork.

'Mmm,' he nods, speaking through stuffed cheeks. 'Delicious!'

'My dad,' she says, crossing back to the stove, 'had his days. Called it the dark cloud, said it would descend, black and heavy . . . that the ocean would turn a dense blue. Some days he didn't get out of bed. Then my mum, Sasha – you'd love her – the genius that she is, started making him breakfast every day, and not just any old jam on toast. She'd make scrambled eggs and marinate a side of mushrooms in chilli, garlic, herbs and olive oil. Other days she'd make granola from scratch, even soaking nuts and seeds overnight before baking, then she'd go and buy goats' yoghurt or fresh milk and honey from the growers.'

Mum offers Harley some blueberries. He takes a few and sprinkles them on his pancake.

She shakes the punnet. 'Oh, come on! Take a proper handful.'

Blushing, he reaches back for more as she cracks another egg into the bowl and whisks it into the mix.

Harley swallows a mouthful of pancake and clears his throat. 'When my dad finally came home, after his accident and everything, he didn't talk, barely ate . . . so Mum got up one morning before sunrise and went as far as the fish markets, almost two hours from Ivory Point, bought him a fresh piece of swordfish, seared it on the barbecue in the yard with sesame seeds and served it with dill sauce. Ryan and I carried him outside to sit in the sun. Our yard was really cool, heaps of plants. It wasn't everything, like it didn't just fix Dad, but it was something, you know?'

'That's beautiful.' I hear the splat of another pancake. 'Who else wants one?' Mum calls.

In the living room, hands shoot up, and she laughs. 'Breakfast is an incentive . . .' she says. 'A reason.'

Joining Harley at the worn breakfast bar, Mum serves us each a plate of moist, fluffy pancakes. Her hair is still matted and damp from her early morning swim, her eyelashes crusted with salt. Mum washes her hands and dries them on a tea towel. 'Enjoy, boys!' she says, and I cringe, just a little, as she heads off to take a shower.

Enjoy, boys. She doesn't mean to blot me out, erase my presence. When I was younger, I hated being singled out. I wanted to be one of the boys. I was a part of them, a part of Ben. So why was my body shrinking now when her words looped me into the male pack?

As hot, sour blueberries burst in my mouth, I edge forward on my stool into Harley's peripheral vision, a little closer to the window, and that's when I see them – a collection of retro surfboards, one even from the sixties, decorating the lawn outside.

'Whoa! Look at those,' I say, pointing to them.

'Epic.' Harley says, a smile reaching across his cheeks.

'I say we take them out,' Ben suggests.

Jake agrees instantly, but Toby sounds doubtful. 'Do we know who they belong to? Maybe they're not meant to go in the water.'

'They're surfboards, idiot.' Jake snickers.

'But maybe Ray has refurbished them, for a museum or auction or something?'

No one listens to him, and within minutes it is settled.

When they've scoffed their pancakes, Ben rinses the plates and skillet in the sink while Toby and Harley dry and Jake climbs into the pantry to reach a box of pink icing biscuits, saved for when my younger cousins visit.

In the yard I pull my steamer wetsuit off the Hills Hoist and stretch it over my limbs beneath our towering fig tree. Flecks of sunlight fall through the gaps between leaves, gold dances on the grass. I choose a yellow board with a black lightning bolt on the deck and a fin set in fibreglass with rainbow resin on the bottom. Along the stringer, in pencil, it reads, *For Mark, 1974*. I wonder how long it has been since this board has tasted the ocean. Is it thirsty?

The morning is unusually warm for late May. Waves with sparkling faces spill behind the rock pool, sweep over the sandbank, lap on shore. White wash caresses the sand. I leap from ankle-deep water, landing on my stomach, gliding, stroking, and duck-diving a tumble of foam. The sea combs through my hair. It peels back the layers of my life on land, peels back the hours. For all I know, it could be 1974.

When we reach the line-up, we sit higher out of the water than usual, and it makes us laugh. These old-fashioned boards are more buoyant than the ones we're used to. Riding without a leg-rope, my feet sway freely with the tides. I wonder about Mark, what he knew about this board, what wisdom he'd acquired. Wisdom, of course, that only mutual experience could have granted him. Getting to know a board is like getting to know a person, a deep impenetrable friendship with secrets and shared memories.

Ben finds his feet first. His board drags him back in time, warping his technique, yet his power, fluidity and precision prevail as he slashes the lip with a single fin. When Harley takes off on a wave, I steal my eyes away from the swell to watch. He slides down the face of the wave, his timing so cool his movements blend with that of the water. I watch his silhouette move through the back of the wave, rising up to its shoulder, painting the blue sky with a fine spray of white.

We surf as the sun melts hours into the sea, until my arms ache and my ribs are bruised, but I don't want to stop. I paddle onto a wave, rise to my feet and fly down the face. As I throw my back into a bottom turn, I hear someone whistle, then call my name. 'Grace!'

I glance over my shoulder to see Harley riding down the face on my inside, hand outstretched, gaping smile. I lean on my back foot, stalling the board, allowing him to catch up and ride beside me.

'Jump on!' He beams, and before I really know what I am doing, he's taken my hand. I leap from my board, landing on his wax. His free hand finds my hip and I find my balance.

We ride, rising and falling on the wave's turquoise face until it closes out and we fall together into the frothy soup, still holding hands. It isn't until he pulls me to the surface that I realise I've been holding my breath the entire ride.

Feet on the sandbank, he wipes my hair from my face and I open my eyes. The glare burns. My knees buckle slightly.

'Amazing,' he says, and I burst into laughter, so dizzy I can't find words.

'Sorry about your board,' he adds. It has washed up on the wet sand nearby.

'Sorry about yours!' I point down the beach to where his has been swept into a rip.

'Hey . . .' he says, smile slackening, 'isn't that your dad?'

I turn to shore to see a man yelling, probably swearing, flapping his arms about as he stamps across the sand.

'Yeah.' I gulp. 'Shit.'

It is my dad and he is furious.

On the sand, he gives me a death glare, then peers out at the waves, shielding his eyes with his hand. 'Ben!' he shouts. 'Get your arse back here NOW.'

By the time Ben emerges from the water, Jake and Toby behind him, Dad looks ready to explode.

'How dare you!' Dad shouts.

'Cry me a river,' Ben retorts and I honestly think Dad is going to hit him.

Toby, Harley and I hang back while Jake and Ben, being the smart-arses that they are, fuel the fire with sly comments. They are enjoying watching Dad burn.

'Do you have *any* idea how much these boards are worth?'

'Enough to leave them lying out on the grass,' Jake says under his breath and Ben struggles to suppress a giggle.

Dad's balding scalp shines brilliant crimson. *'Arseholes!'* he stammers, kicking the sand, then turns and marches back along the beach toward the house, calling over his shoulder, 'I want them back on the lawn by three o'clock. Washed!'

'I love you!' Ben shouts, and Dad flips him the bird.

A wave rides up the shore, cold splashing around my ankles, as Jake turns to me and says, 'Grace, maybe you should lend him a tampon.'

The boys cackle, and I feel myself sink a fraction in the wet sand.

Nine

INDIGO

There are only a few big storms a year. The ones you can smell the day before, when the sun is still shining, yellow light draping the coastline. Dusk descends with air that is laden, damp, and the shadows are eerie and still, like the earth has inhaled deep and now holds its breath, preparing for the onslaught. When we were young, a big winter storm was one with waves so fierce they broke the barrier pool on the point, flooding the main rock pool with clumps of seaweed and sand.

This storm, I heard first in my dream. A deep hum turned wail, as the earth tore open. A branch ripped off the fig tree and shattered a window in the sunroom at 4 a.m. Monty whimpered beneath the dining room table as Mum, in her white nightgown and slippers, swept broken glass, while Dad, Ben and Jake taped a sheet of plastic over the gaping hole, a temporary fix until dawn. I went back to bed, letting Monty sleep at my feet.

I am woken no more than two hours later by Ben sneaking into my room with his quilt draped around his shoulders. 'Grace.' He shakes my shoulder. 'Wake up, you gotta come see this.'

I step into my ugg boots and trudge out the door into silent purple shadows, following the boys across wet earth to the gate. The air is still, the rain and wind have passed. 'Look, down there.' Ben points across the grassy hill to the rock pool. Dark waves have breached the barrier pool. The pool chains are submerged under grey foam, and then I see what he's pointing at. I gasp. A small fishing boat has washed onto the rock stairs.

'Holy shit!'

Beyond, the beasts that carried this boat on their shoulders roar. My breath catches as a wave cracks in half on the rock shelf. The ground shakes, deep vibrations.

'Pinch and a punch for the first of the month!' Ben taunts. 'No returns!'

Squealing, I lunge at him with a clenched fist, punching, narrowly missing his chest.

'Hey!' he says, laughing, 'I said no returns!' and puts me in a headlock.

Wriggling free, I catch my breath and gaze out to sea. Grey, wet clouds hang low. On land, the earth's soul lies still in the mud, beaten and breathless. Tree branches sag with fatigue.

Only the ocean still rages, retaining the energy of the storm like charcoal retains heat in the hours after red flames have died. Enough heat to burn you.

Enough strength to drown you.

Jake swears. Teeth chatter.

'Stop complaining, you pussy,' Ben hisses.

'You were the one who left the wetsuits on the line,' Jake retorts. 'It's your damn fault they're wet.'

'You won't even notice once we're in the water,' I say.

'Exactly,' Ben adds. 'So hurry up, I want to beat the crowd.'

I pull my zip right up to the nape of my neck with fingernails already lavender, chilled by the first day of winter. In the shed, Ben pushes a couch against the wall and climbs onto the arm to reach the top shelf. He passes down the 'guns' – longer, narrower boards with hard rail lines, saved for swells that punish the shore. Mine is sprayed silver like the moon, and I walk with it into the yard as Dad hops down the verandah stairs. He stops, and his eyes dart from my board to me, back to my board. I shiver, charged.

'I don't think so,' he says, shaking his head.

Saliva sticks in my throat.

'It's triple overhead.'

'I know it is.'

My dad repeats, 'It's triple overhead.'

'Yeah . . .'

'I think you ought to take that wetsuit off, Grace. Wait till tomorrow, when the waves are smaller.'

'I don't want to wait till tomorrow.'

'You'll get hurt.'

Jake interrupts. 'Where are you going, Ray? I thought you'd be the first one out – it's pumping!'

'Mick just rang, that wind last night took half the roof off the factory.'

'Shit . . . Good luck.'

Dad jumps into the Rodeo, slamming the door, but before he turns on the ignition, he cracks the window. 'Grace, get out of your wetsuit.'

I glance at Ben, glance back to Dad.

'I mean it.'

Slowly, I unzip the wetsuit, my body quaking as the icy air hits my skin.

Gravel crunches and as he pulls out of the driveway, I feel Ben take my wetsuit string and pull the zip tight. He fastens the velcro around my neck. 'He can piss off . . . he worries too much,' Ben assures me. 'You're just as capable as us.'

Jake nods with a smile and though I'm gripped by the cold, I feel a warming in my chest.

Waiting for Harley at the base of the grassy hill I don't know what I'm more nervous about – seeing him again or the size of the surf.

Waves chomp on the reef, the sound deafening.

When Harley arrives, Jake bounces like a child. 'Let's go!' The four of us hop and skip over slimy rocks, wet emerald. With surf as big as this, paddling out from the beach is near impossible. Instead, we make our way to the edge of the rock shelf, where we will jump into the murky tide. As we wade along the perimeter of the pool, up to our thighs in foam, I spy a dead seabird washed into the pool and fathom that I am well beyond the point of return.

Ben is the first to jump. I study his movements, which rock he takes, his stance, his timing. A wash of grey tumbles to his feet, he compresses, he leaps, landing on wax, paddling ferociously as he races away from the suction zone around the rocks.

'You should go next, Grace, so we're behind you . . . just in case,' Jake says. I barely manage a reply.

There's a slight lull between swells. 'Go now!' he says.

I skip across three rocks, landing where Ben took off with my gun under my arm and my heart thrashing in its cage. In the distance, a monster bares its teeth and I prepare myself for battle. The wave breaks, sprays and spits.

'You have to jump!' Jake yells over the thumping swell. White wash thunders toward me, I swallow, save a breath, and with only a moment to spare I spring up and over, the monster nipping at my heels.

It's not until I land that I realise my timing was off, too late, and I don't clear the wave fully. Huge bubbles rise from the underwater shelf, pushing my board sideways as they rupture the surface. Struggling through the frothy mess, I can hear the boys screaming, 'Paddle! Paddle!'

I glance up, and there it is, another mountain of white wash. With only a few metres of water between me and the rocks behind, I flog the sea with panicked strokes, grip the rails and push underneath. Still in shallow water, my knuckles graze the reef before I'm shot to the surface. Adrenalin now fuels my every muscle and I move through the water faster than ever before. I clear the next wave, and the three beyond that, arriving out in the line-up starved of oxygen with a smile splitting my face in two.

Ben paddles up beside me. 'I saw you get pinned! That was heavy! You all good?'

I look down at my fingers, strips of skin flapping from my knuckles, blood dripping onto a blackened sea. 'Looks worse than it is.'

Ben winks. 'I'm glad you're out here.'

Jake howls as he makes it to the line-up with Harley close behind. Together, we rise and fall with the mighty swells, our skin burning in the icy tides. Sitting up, Jake hurls a clump of seaweed at my head, scratching my cheek raw pink.

When he laughs, Ben scowls at him. 'Piss off, Jake, leave her alone.'

Harley props himself up beside me, glances at my hands resting on a glass sea. 'You're a tough little nut, aren't you?'

I shrug and he laughs. 'Don't worry, it's a good thing.'

My gaze touches his, and I don't know if I will ever get used to the wild stroke of blue in his eyes.

'Quit the flirting!' Ben taunts. 'There's a set coming!'

Dark waves rally, marching toward us. I hang back, watching Ben pull into position. He paddles, pushes up and disappears down the face. A glorious throw of grey spray clouds the sky as he whacks the lip and I watch his shadow through the wave as he drops again. Jake takes the one behind and Harley the one after, leaving me floating in their wake.

Ten or so minutes pass before they are all back in the line-up.

'Your turn now, Gracie,' Ben says, but all I hear is my heartbeat.

'This one is yours!' Jake yells as another set approaches. I fill my lungs and begin to paddle. The wave builds beneath me, lifts and carries me. I slide to my feet. The boys' cheers are drowned out by the crack of the lip and white wash tumbles down the face as I descend. At the base, I grab the rail, driving through my bottom turn and flying back up to smack the head of the wave. My fins slash, foam flies. My stomach lifts into my throat as I swoop down like a seabird from the cliffs.

By the time I kick off the back of the wave, I am laughing.

As I paddle, Harley takes off behind the point. He sails, effortless, his hand touching the wave's smooth, dark skin.

I duck-dive the white cloud. Behind, a clean break in the swells allows for a quick return to the line-up, where Ben and Jake sit, now joined by two other locals. Ben high-fives me.

I beam. 'I wish Dad saw that!'

'Oath!' Ben laughs. 'But screw him . . . *I* saw it.'

With a fire now blazing in my eyes, I look to the horizon.

Mere minutes pass before it disappears. Out of the ocean, a wave, deep indigo, grows bigger than any we have seen this morning, and before I really have time to think, I am paddling. On the inside, closest to where the wave is breaking, which gives me priority. The wave picks me up on its shoulder, and in the split second before my feet touch the wax, I hear Jake's voice. 'OH. MY. GOD!'

It jacks up, and I'm too deep. I ride down the jagged face, slide over a step in the wave. My board sticks and I fly, landing face first on a slab of water. The sea shoots up my nostrils, into my ears. That is just the beginning.

Above, the wave breaks, a ton of water, its weight heaving down, squeezing the life out of my lungs. I'm dragged by the hair. Tossed like a rag doll. Blind, I kick until my head grazes the seabed and I choke; I've swum in the wrong direction. I pull on my leg-rope, but it's snapped clean.

I remember the training, all those hours spent in the pool at the high-performance camps. *Don't fight it. Save your energy.* I let my limbs go limp, and I hang there, at the bottom of the ocean, waiting for the remaining air in my body to deliver me to the surface. Then I hear it, a second wave, breaking metres above me.

I'm flung, spun, twisted and yanked, my body annihilated by the turbulence.

Ben begins to panic, I can feel it, hear it, the beating of his heart.

I scream for him, salt water stripping my oesophagus, filling my stomach.

The arms of the ocean hold me on the black seabed until I am neither alive nor dead.

~

A torrent of sea water, acid and bile scalds my throat, turns my teeth to chalk. I cough and splutter, hot vomit dripping off my chin. Two warm hands grip my head. Another set grips my hip and shoulder.

Sand is everywhere, like a thousand shards of glass embedded in my flesh, stuck beneath my eyelids.

'She's going to be okay, right? She vomited – that's good, right?'

I gag. A second wave spews out of me.

A gloved hand takes mine as a man speaks into my ear. 'Grace, squeeze my hand if you can hear me.' It's a foreign voice, older, calmer.

I manage some pressure.

'My name is David. I'm an ambulance officer from Port Lawnam. You've swallowed a lot of water but you're okay. We're going to give you some oxygen.'

Wet hair is swept off my face and a mask is fitted. I feel my next breath in my veins.

'Three, two, one.' I'm rolled onto my back and hear the crinkling of foil. As I open my eyes, a sudden wash of light scorches my retinas and I squeeze them shut again. My head pounds, my bones ache. I try to sit up but I'm stopped, held, lowered back to the ground.

'Easy now . . .' the paramedic says. There's a sharp ringing in my ears and he sounds far away.

Opening my eyes again, I catch a flash of the silver space blanket. The hands roll me onto my side and back down onto hard plastic. My eyelids droop, as I'm lifted, carried. A new hand takes mine, only this one is ungloved and cold. It doesn't lose grip, even as I'm loaded into the ambulance.

As the truck pulls out of the driveway, Ben bends over and rests his head on my shoulder, sobbing. 'Gracie, don't ever do that again, holy shit, never again. Gracie, I thought you were dead. You hear?'

I try to nod, movement sending pain down my spine, as tears stream freely across my cheeks.

'Don't ever leave me, okay?' Ben's warm tears seep into the skin of my wetsuit.

'I promise.' My words are barely audible. Still, he hears me.

⌒

Curtains are drawn when I wake. The tiny monitor on my index finger has a light at the tip that glows pink in the cool shadows.

There is a knock. 'Come in.' My voice is raspy and weak.

Harley walks in, stopping at the foot of my bed. I pull the sheet over my hospital gown. There is sand in my hairline still, sand beneath my nails. The slow, steady beep of my monitor quickens. Harley glances at the machine, smiles, gaze dropping to his feet. He takes a seat beside me.

'I think they're letting Ben have a shower here somewhere. He was still in his wetsuit in the ambulance. Jake and I drove down – he's just gone to the cafeteria to grab some lunch for us – and your parents are on their way. Sorry . . . too much info? How you feeling?'

I try to speak but my voice cracks.

'Have some water,' he says, unscrewing the lid to the bottle on my bedside table and holding it to my lips, as I lift the oxygen mask to take a sip.

'I've been better,' I tell him, 'but I'm here, right?'

Harley's gaze falls into his lap and he twiddles his thumbs.

'Honestly, Grace, when I pulled you out . . .'

'*You* pulled me out?'

'I was paddling back out when I saw you stack it. I was the closest.'

I fix my mask and draw back heavily on the oxygen.

'You were so cold . . . You were blue.'

'I've been told blue suits me.' I try a joke but it is as itchy as the sand in my bed.

He looks up at me now, fixing his eyes on mine. 'Grace, I think you're beautiful, but that blue isn't pretty on anyone.' Harley takes my hand. 'Seeing you like that . . . Honestly, I don't think I've ever been more scared.'

He intertwines his fingers with mine. My eyelids, heavy with fatigue, begin to sag.

'It's okay.' He smiles. 'I'll wake you when your parents get here.'

⌒

'I told her! You heard me tell her and you still took her out with you! And now look where she is, in hospital! She nearly drowned, god damn it!'

A woman interrupts him. 'Excuse me, sir.'

'Oh, bugger off!'

The commotion in the hallway rouses me from my nap. Still in the chair beside me, Harley squeezes my hand. 'I think your parents are here . . .'

'Sounds like it.'

He offers me some water and we listen to the argument.

'You're an idiot, Ben, a bloody idiot!'

I hear Mum pleading, 'Ray, stop it!'

I gaze across at Harley but I'm so exhausted I begin sinking back into a pool of dreams . . . a pool so shallow that when he kisses my hand, I'm not sure if I really felt anything at all.

Ten

A FAIRY BREAD SANDWICH

I've always marvelled at how quickly the sky can change. An amber sunset burns out in an hour and a half, a charcoal smudge on the horizon. Two days ago, clouds had thundered across the sea, turning a glimmering strip of white sand into the pallid flesh of someone who is dying. Today is pale light, mist on the sea. The ocean's dying swell strokes the sand. The colours we see, the way we perceive the world, all determined by lighting. The sun, it changes everything.

Curled beneath my quilt, I listen to Mum chatting in the kitchen, her words carried down the hall on a breath of salty air.

'Honestly, it's just like when they were kids. One gets hurt, the other knows. Bizarre, isn't it?' She wanders out of hearing, then back. 'Yeah, exactly. Crazy . . . I mean, I spoke to Ben at the hospital, and he swore he knew the second Grace went under, he knew, he felt it.' She pauses, and I wonder who she's speaking with. 'What they have, I don't think the rest of us will ever really understand.'

—⁓—

'Are you certain you're up for it? The school won't mind if you take another day off . . .'

'It's been three days, Mum – I'm *fine*.'

Fussing as if it's my first day of school, she hands me my lunch inside a brown paper bag, *Grace* written on the front in black texta. 'Call me if you need anything.'

'Thanks, Mum.'

She hugs me, and as her breath rolls over my shoulder, tumbling down my back, I wonder about the fear that forever circulates, like blood, in a parent's veins.

At school, I take a seat in my biology class. Two girls from my pastoral care group stop at the edge of my desk with 'get well' wishes. Jake slithers up beside them, brushing his hand against one girl's arse. She tucks a strand of hair behind her ear, blushing a little, flashes a cheeky smile and says, rather unconvincingly, 'Hey, don't . . .'

Harley and Ben stroll in, chatting. I lean down to my bag, unpacking my books and pencil case as the chair beside me is pulled out. As I look up, Harley sits down beside me. Ben stands in the aisle, searching for another seat, his usual one now taken. His eyes flick between Harley and me, his smile faint but ever present.

Mr Johnson waltzes into the room and stands in front of the whiteboard. Jake pulls out the chair beside him, motioning to Ben. 'Sit here, bro,' he says.

'Good morning, class. Hope we are all feeling well? Today we will be moving on to our next organ, the heart.'

Unlike Ben, who only takes this class so that Mum can help with his assignments, I love biology, and I'm usually attentive in class but today is different. I think about the cells that make up my arm, resting beside Harley's on the smooth, cool tabletop and the muscles that tense as he touches the back of my hand. My skin tingles, my breath shallow. He takes my hand and our fingers entwine. A hot river pours down my arm. A current of electricity heats my bones.

'The heart is one of the first organs to grow in the womb,' Mr Johnson says, then directs his attention to Ben and me, explaining that, being twins, by the time we first heard outside voices, we would already have been listening to each other's heartbeats.

Mr Johnson instructs us to flip to page 150 of our textbooks. Harley lets go of my hand, opens his book and slides it into the middle of the desk for us to share. Leaning over the illustration, shoulder to shoulder, I can almost feel his own heart pulsing in his temple.

'Although it is common knowledge that the heart is constantly responding to orders from the brain, what most don't know is that the heart is actually sending far more signals to the brain!' Mr Johnson explains that the rhythm of our heart changes according to our emotional state and affects cognitive function. With a heart that races, my mind wanders.

Harley nudges me. 'What kind of lab partner are you? Have you even been listening?'

'Sorry, I think I missed the last bit.'

He smiles and turns the page. 'We're doing this exercise.' Harley reads out the instructions, but I am caught on one word, *we*.

⌣

I meet Mia at her locker before our lesson in ancient history. It's the first time I've seen her since Sunday afternoon when I got back from the hospital and found her waiting for me with her mum on the verandah. She had hardly said anything; she'd just hugged me for a really long time.

As we walk off to class, she tells me how she's finding Greek history to be such a bore and how much she's dreading the class. Never before has she seen learning as a chore. I swallow hard, wishing I could have foreseen the future, like an oracle at Delphi predicting the attack on a great warrior, wishing I could have stopped us from going that night.

At lunch, Ben finds us in the crowded hallway. Mia is clutching a huge pile of papers she's picked up from the school office and books, her bag slung over one shoulder. 'Want me to carry some of those?' he asks, stretching out his arms, but she shoves him out of the way.

'Stop feeling sorry for me. Pity looks ugly on you.'

He stands in front of her, blocking her exit from the building. 'I brought you something.' Ben holds up a paper bag with a fluffy kitten sticker on the front.

'What is it?'

'A fairy bread sandwich.'

'Fine,' she sighs. 'You can take these.' Mia off-loads the pile onto Ben in exchange for the paper bag. Stubborn as anything, she purses her lips to suppress a smile.

'What are these anyway?' Ben asks, eyeing off the stack of papers.

'Posters. For the school fair. Year twelve run it, remember?'

'Yeah, but why are you advertising it now? I thought it wasn't until spring.'

'I brought it forward so it's not so close to exams.'

'*You* brought it forward? I thought the student council was a team effort,' he teases.

'Well, I'm the school captain. That makes me the boss.' A grin cracks her lips for the first time in weeks.

⌒

Wearing one of my old wetsuits, Mia wades across the sandbank as we paddle alongside her. Diving under a wash of whitewater, she surfaces with hair slicked back, squealing as the icy ocean seeps through holes in the wetsuit's worn-out shoulders.

It's the first blue sky we've seen since the storm, and although the winter undercurrents remain frightfully cold, half the town is in the sea. Every man and his dog are celebrating this glorious Sunday morning, floating on kayaks, bodyboards, longboards, shortboards and surfboats. Two teenagers lounge in inflatable doughnuts.

I sit back on my single fin surfboard, close to the tail pad, allowing Mia to loop her arms over the board's nose, her feet dangling in the tides. We rest like this, rising and falling with the tender swell for almost an hour, chatting and giggling while the boys muck around on playful waves.

Suddenly, Mia's grip around my board tightens and her jaw drops. 'Oh my god.' Mia dunks her head underwater. Spinning, I spy a pack of boys, shoulders hunched as they stroke out to the line-up. Eric Rockwell leads the pack. I reach down and yank Mia to the surface.

Gasping for breath, veins bulging, she panics. 'What do I do?'

Before I suggest it, she starts kicking toward the beach, arms thrashing the water, as Ben turns from his conversation with Jake to see what's going on. Noticing Eric, twenty metres away, Ben's jaw clenches. His eyes narrow and he paddles over to the group of twenty-year-olds, Harley and Jake in tow.

'You've got some nerve showing your face out here.' Nostrils flaring, Ben sits up on his board.

Salt on my lips stings.

'Excuse me?' Eric scoffs.

'You heard me—'

'Look,' Eric interrupts, paddling up beside Ben. 'You think you're high and mighty because you're Ben *Walker*, but I think you need to watch your fucking tongue, mate. Seriously, what's your deal?'

Cold undercurrents pull at my ankles.

'First of all, I'm not your *mate*,' Ben spits. 'Secondly, Mia Ellis, remember her?'

Eric laughs as he glances around his group, his friends joining in on the joke. 'Mia Ellis? Are you serious?' he puffs his chest. 'She was begging for a root.'

Before Eric's last word lands on the water, Ben has leapt off his board, his closed fist smashing Eric's nose. I've never seen Ben hit anyone before, never even seen him fight. Blood streams from Eric's nose, clouding the crystal water.

The boys jump off their boards and swim at each other. Limbs flay, lash, and smack, red water splashing high into the sky. Marlow's older crowd paddle in from every direction, yelling and yanking. As they tear the boys off each other, I pull onto a wave and ride it to shore.

On wet sand, I gather my leg-rope as Ben washes in, throwing his board down on the beach. I wonder if he's noticed the dent someone has punched in the deck of his favourite board.

He hurries toward Mia and throws his arms around her trembling body, holding her.

Skin, sand and bone.

He holds her in a way he's never held anyone.

Eleven

BLOSSOM

'So,' Jake says as we sit under the pine trees. 'My birthday is in three days, does everyone know what present they're giving me?'

'My divine presence . . .' Ben mocks.

Ignoring him, Jake reveals his birthday plans. 'The festival of Jake will be kicking off Friday arvo. We'll bender into my birthday on Saturday. Bring everything you need for the weekend, and of course, my presents, because you won't be leaving until Sunday night.'

'Does your mum know about this?' Mia asks.

'Doesn't need to. She pissed off last night with the new toy boy. Got a note saying she'll be back in a few weeks – oh, and one hundred dollars. Enough for beer, ciggies, bread and some sausages – right, boys?' Jake turns away and looks across the yard, his words lacking their usual punch.

'Sorry to hear that,' Mia says. 'About your mum, I mean.'

'Don't be sorry,' he says, hurling a pebble at the base of the pine tree. 'Fuck her.'

'So what's the plan?' Ben says. 'What's happening at this party?'

As they chat, I munch on my crackers, recalling the times when Jake would stay at Toby's house, or with us, when we were all kids, sometimes for weeks at a time. I think of how we'd be excited by it, never quite understanding why his enthusiasm always fell short of ours. There were the times Ben had teased Jake for his nightmares, for wetting the bed, the times Jake was bruised.

'So it's decided.' Ben claps his hands together. 'Tents, sleeping-bags, the whole shebang.'

'Fairy lights,' Mia adds.

Jake negotiates with her. 'You can only have fairy lights if you bring the bedsheets with the psychedelic prints *and* let me hang them in the trees.'

'Deal.'

'We'll even have a bonfire.'

Mia frowns. 'You could burn the house down.'

Jake snorts. 'Who cares? I doubt it's worth more than a bag of firewood.'

'No one's burning the house down,' Ben says. The alpha male. 'We'll bring the empty barrel from our house for a fire.'

'Sounds good,' Harley says, his eyes wandering around the circle, coming to rest on mine like the sky on the sea. 'Can't wait.'

⌒

The sun dips behind the hills as we wander into a dream. In a few short hours, the yard has been transformed. Jake's small weatherboard house, known to the group as the *Fibro Majestic*, sits on the outskirts of town, with a huge yard backing onto the bush. Wildflowers glimmer beneath fairy lights. Glow-in-the-dark paint drips from the bark of gum trees, streamers hang from branches, and colourful vines sway with the ocean breeze. We've set up the tents in a circle, with the fire pit in the centre, a bunch of logs and camping chairs surrounding it and bedsheets draped over the doorway to each tent. Inside the tent Mia and I are sharing, her toy kangaroo is nestled between pillows, quilts and fluffy blankets.

Toby and Harley collect kindling and wood for the fire, then use newspaper to light it and lay a grill over the top of the barrel. Orange flames dance on their faces, in his eyes.

'Yew! That's what I'm talking about!' Jake shouts, walking in through the side gate with Ben, carrying an esky and a tray of raw sausages.

Before long, tails of smoke curl up toward a thousand distant suns. Mia and I drink apple ciders from the farmers markets that are sweet on the tongue and filling in the stomach. Ben tells Mia and me to stay away from the hotplate, that turning sausages is a man's job. Mia, wrapped in a blanket on her camping chair, kicks her feet up on the esky. 'Fine by me.'

When the sausages are almost done, Ben suggests we each take a roll from the bag. 'There's tomato and barbecue sauce,' he says.

Everyone, bar Mia, takes a sausage. Then we drizzle sauce over the top, and take our seats once more to feast.

When he's finished, Jake licks the remaining onion juice and barbecue sauce from his fingers before picking up a bowl and scissors and chopping grass between his fingers. From it he rolls two joints, laying one to rest in the bowl at his feet, lighting the other with a match. He draws back on the filter end and exhales a cloud of smoke, the smell pungent.

Inhaling again, he breathes out this time through his nostrils like a dragon, a cheeky grin plastered on his cheeks. 'Happy birthday to me.'

Ben stands and starts to sing, waving his arms extravagantly as he conducts the rest of us in chorus. We clap and chant *happy birthday* while Jake drinks a beer, throwing the can into the fire when it's empty.

He hands the joint around the circle. Ben reaches for it first, draws smoke deep into his lungs, holds it for a moment and then exhales, blowing smoke rings in Toby's face. Passing the joint on, Harley, Mia and Toby each take a toke or two, sucking lightly. When it reaches me, I glance at Mia and she giggles. I bring the filter end to my lips; hesitate.

'I only turn eighteen once,' Jake prompts.

'Okay, well, I'm only doing *this* once.'

I suck on the now soggy filter end, the smoke filling my lungs, tickling, I start to cough. The boys crack up, teasing.

'That's my girl!' Jake cheers.

My chest is tight, like someone is sitting on it. Breathing out, I can't feel my fingertips, and I drop the joint.

'Nice one, ya got dirt on the doobie,' Jake says, picking it up and dusting it off. Ben cracks up and before long we're all laughing, as if this is the most hilarious joke ever told.

'Not my fault,' I say, but the words stick to the roof of my mouth like peanut butter.

'Grace has cotton mouth!'

Chuckling, we sit together around the fire, enveloped in its yellow haze, as blue dusk fades into the night. It's our own little world, where colour drips from trees, owls hoot and parents don't abandon their children, a haven at the end of the street, a hundred miles away.

Pink embers glow in the barrel as the birthday boy smokes a second joint alone. He stubs it out on the ground, littered with half-eaten packets of lollies and chips, then turns on a torch and shines it up at his face, eyes glistening, cheeks flushed. 'Let's play spotlight.'

Mia, chewing on a sour worm, says, 'What are we? Seven years old?'

Jake shines the torch in her eyes. 'My birthday, my decision. Everyone up, we're playing spotlight.'

The fact that I can't remember how many ciders I've had might explain why I'm hardly able to walk straight.

'I'll count to forty,' Jake says. 'Rules are, you have to stay on the block. Everyone go hide!'

Giggling at my buckling knees, I stumble down the side path and out onto the street, climbing over the fence into a neighbour's front yard and ducking under a hedge.

Waiting, it smells of mulch and fresh turf. I hear a rustle of leaves and hold my breath.

'Who is that?' a voice whispers. 'Grace?' Harley falls in a heap next to me.

We hear footsteps nearby, someone walking down the road toward us. White torchlight filters through the leaves. I shuffle over so we can both fit beneath the hedge, giggling still.

'Shh,' Harley whispers

Jake wanders further down the street, until we can no longer hear his footsteps. Blind in the shadows, I smell honeycomb chocolate and musky sweat. Harley's fingertips trace my jaw, his cool palm cupping my cheek. As he presses his forehead to mine, clouds of hot breath hang between us like a summer sea beneath a black sky.

'FOUND YOU!' Ben yells, the two words slurring together. A burst of light; Harley drops his hand immediately.

Crawling out from under the bush, we follow the others down the street in search of Toby, guided by the wandering light of Jake's torch.

Where we touched, my skin stings.

⌒

Someone presses play on an iPod and 'Wake Me Up Before You Go-Go' by Wham! starts blasting through the speakers. Then I hear Ben's voice busting out the opening verse.

Toby groans, rattles off a string of expletives. My eyelids are stuck together with sleep, my head heavy as a brick. The air inside the tent stinks of sweat and morning breath, and I don't know if it's the volume of the pop song or Ben's tone-deaf singing that's worse.

Toby climbs out of his sleeping-bag and crawls to the door. Unzipping the flyscreen, he hurls a shoe at Ben, who's dancing around the yard.

Something moves, *someone* moves. Hot air brushes the nape of my neck, hot *breath*. I peel sleep from my eyes and look down. I'm in my pyjamas, in my sleeping-bag, with the dead weight of an arm draped over my waist. A tan leather bracelet is wrapped around the wrist.

I roll, look over my shoulder. Harley, in his own sleeping-bag, is cuddled up to me. Pulling me closer, he opens one eye, the stroke of blue brilliant in the green shade of the tent. He grins. 'Good morning.'

As I rest my head back on the pillow, he holds me tighter still.

Outside, Ben wails and I hear Mia's laughter as rich as a kookaburra's.

My stomach grumbles, and I whisper that I'm going to start making breakfast. Harley squeezes me to him again then lets me wriggle out of my sleeping-bag. I pull on my ugg boots and join Ben at the hotplate, where he is frying eggs.

With a bacon and egg roll in hand, I climb into the hammock with Mia. In the morning light cutting through the tall gums, she looks alive, blue flames dancing in her eyes, her body weightless. The air at the edge of the forest is crisp. Wild birds chat in the trees above.

'Did you kiss him?' she says, a cheeky smirk on her face.

'Shh!' I whisper, looking back at the tent.

She kicks me. 'Relax. He won't hear us. So, did you?'

'I don't know.'

'You don't know?'

'I mean, we were drunk . . .'

Mia rolls her eyes.

I peer into last night's shadows and confess, 'No, I didn't. Almost, I guess, when we were playing spotlight. But he slept in the tent . . .' I blush. 'He spooned me.'

Mia giggles, clapping her hands together, silent applause.

'Where did you sleep, anyway?' I ask.

Mia glances at Ben. She starts playing with her bracelet, her rings.

'Don't make it a secret,' I say and her face softens.

Mia tells me they kissed in the dark and that he held her all night. She tells me how in the morning, he brushed pink hair from

her face, tucking it behind her ear, touched his lips to her cheek
and whispered, 'Wake up, Sleeping Beauty.'

I blink and tiny tears slip free, a warm, wet trace.

'Are you mad?' she says.

I shake my head, finding no words for this feeling.

Twelve

SUNSET

We stand with chilled bones and red skin, exhaling white clouds through teeth that chatter, the ocean, in all its glory, just waiting for us.

We sprint across grass, wet sand, and then launch ourselves above the tide. Hands grip the rails of our surfboards and for a brief moment in time our bodies fly over a roll of vanilla foam. Our torsos land on wax, we stretch our arms forward, we dig down and draw back, pulling ourselves through the cold morning milk.

White wash approaches and in unison we lunge forward on our boards, pushing deep beneath the turbulence. We ride up through the dark belly of the wave and emerge through its shoulderblade. With air expanding our lungs, this day is born.

We reach the line-up, the cold pinching every place our wetsuits cannot conceal: our wrists, our Achilles tendons, the napes of our necks. We sit up on our boards and, without passing a single word between us, float effortlessly. We have red-glass eyes and cheeks that sting, licked by the tongue of the winter sea.

As the sun catches fire on the horizon, Ben looks across at me and smiles.

Together we dance on waves of molten gold until our stomachs bring us to the shore, hungry for breakfast. Collecting our boards, wrapping our leg-ropes around our fins, we stroll across the sand.

Beneath the outdoor shower, I rinse conditioner from my hair and jump out, wrapping my body in a towel. Ben washes coconut soap from his torso, turns off the tap, dries his face on his towel.

'Mia is asleep in my bed,' he says. 'She told me she loved me last night.'

'What did you say back?'

'I said I loved her too.'

⌢

Once, this field was inconceivably huge. Wafts of salted popcorn, hot toffee and vanilla made mouths water. The Ferris wheel rode so high I was convinced it would touch the sky. Battered fish and chips with tartar sauce were a twice-a-year delicacy (the only other exception being Christmas). The fireworks, though deafening, entranced us. They were a kind of supernatural phenomenon.

Now, I can see across the oval to the school gates, knowing it's only two hundred metres or so. I notice the spots where the clowns missed their make-up, and the hairlines of their fake wigs. I notice the rust on the arms of the Ferris wheel. Everyone grows up. Yet standing in a candy stall, serving festival treats to wide-eyed youngsters, a sense of the enchantment we felt as children filters through the years.

Jake waltzes up to my stall, leaning against the popcorn machine.

'I know what this fair is missing,' he declares.

'What?'

'A kissing booth. I would easily make the most money for the school.' Grinning, he leans over the counter and grabs a lollipop. 'Where's Ben?'

'He's driving with Mia down to Port Lawnam to pick up the hampers for the raffle.' Slipping my hand into my pocket, I touch the raffle ticket Harley bought me. If my ticket was drawn, would I find the confidence to kiss him, wrapped in the glee of winning?

'Trust.' Jake smirks, sucking on the lollipop, propping himself up to sit on the counter. I push him off but when Harley wanders over, both of them climb over to my side of the counter, reaching for treats.

'My stall is not going to make any money with you two eating all the stock.' I slap Jake's sneaky hand and snatch a bag of fairy floss out of Harley's. They laugh, stealing back their treats. 'Don't you two have your own stall?'

'No one wants to play with water bombs in the middle of winter . . .' Jake says.

Harley agrees, wrapping his arms around my waist from behind, hugging me tight.

'Yuck, are you serious!' Jake winces. 'All this flirting is really making me feel sick.'

'Maybe it's the four cupcakes you've had in half an hour,' I tell him.

Jake shrugs, climbs back up onto the counter and whistles at a group of passing girls.

Suddenly, I feel blood drain from my head, and my knees buckle. Harley's hold keeps me upright.

'What was that?' he says, hands gripping.

Tiny yellow stars sparkle. 'I don't know.'

'Are you okay?'

Goosebumps prick my skin. 'I feel really faint.'

Sitting me down, Harley grabs a water bottle from the cooler. 'Grace, your face is white.'

Jake looks over his shoulder. 'You look like you've just seen a ghost.'

Beads of sweat gather on my upper lip, my brow. Harley uses his sleeve to wipe my damp hairline. 'What did you have for breakfast?' he asks.

'Cereal.'

'Was the milk off?'

I shake my head. 'No, I don't think so. It tasted fine.'

Harley, seeing me gag, is quick to grab the bin. A putrid mix of hot dog and chips fills the bucket. Jake apologises to a customer and asks them to come back in fifteen minutes. Harley offers me some more water, and I slush it round in my mouth and spit it into the bin.

'Where are Mia and Ben?' I say, my eyes darting around the fair.

Harley tilts his head to one side, his brow creases. 'They've gone to Port Lawnam, remember?'

'Yeah, I remember, but where are they? They should be here by now.'

'It's a Saturday,' Jake says. 'There's probably traffic. Maybe they had trouble getting the hampers.'

'No,' I stammer. 'They should be here by now.'

'Okay.' Harley combs cool fingers through my sweaty hair. 'It's fine, we'll just call them.'

Jake hands me my phone, yet with hands trembling so madly I can barely maintain grip, let alone punch in the numbers.

'Let me,' Harley says, taking the phone and dialling Ben. He hands it back to me as it starts ringing.

'No one's answering,' I say, tears escaping. 'I'll try again.'

It rings four times, then someone answers. 'Hello?'

A man's voice.

I hesitate. 'Who is this?'

'Constable Griffin from the Port Lawnam Police Department.'

His speech is slow, articulate – the way someone speaks when they want to make sure you're listening. In the background, voices shout, words I can't make out, words muffled by the wail of sirens. I hear a woman shriek and I drop the phone. Harley grabs it from the grass and brings the speaker to his ear. 'Hello?' he says, straight faced. 'Who is this?'

'What are they saying? Who is it? What's going on?' Jake pulls on Harley's shirt, scratching for an answer.

When he hangs up, Harley puts both hands on my shoulders. 'Grace, where are your parents?'

'Here . . . somewhere. I don't know!'

'We have to find them. We have to go.'

'Who was that? What's going on?' Jake is red in the face. 'Where are we going?'

'Port Lawnam Hospital. I'll drive, we just have to find your parents,' Harley says, taking my hand, squeezing it. 'There's been an accident.'

~

As Harley turns onto the country road connecting Marlow to Port Lawnam, Dad reaches from the front passenger seat into the back, placing his hand on Mum's thigh. 'It's going to be okay, Mel. We can't jump to conclusions. We don't have any real information yet.'

'If it was fine, the policeman would have said it was fine.' Jake rubs her back as she sobs with her head between her knees. Harley presses on the accelerator.

Outside, green hills blur together, a wash of sap green. Seabirds soar above rocky orange headlands. My head, spinning, begins to ache.

As we near the outskirts of Port Lawnam, I feel a cool flush, an emptying, as if blood is draining from my body. In silence, I beg him to *hold on*.

Fifteen minutes later, we turn onto Roma Street.

~

Sound and light travel at different speeds, I learnt that in science, and yet I've never quite gotten over seeing this phenomenon in real life. Like how you see the crowds, people collected on the footpaths, in their front yards, the flashing lights, red and blue, well before you hear any of it. There's a moment of disbelief in between, where you think maybe you're seeing things, maybe this isn't real.

~

Harley pulls to the kerb and we break from the car.

Dad reaches for my arm but I sidestep, slip past, and sprint into the chaos. There is police tape, a crying neighbour, a camera crew. Two cars, bonnet to bonnet, airbags blown, glass like confetti sprinkled across the bitumen, ambulance trolleys. There is the smell of antiseptic, of blood on concrete.

'Hey!' a woman shouts and I feel a man grab my shirt. He wraps thick arms around my chest, holding me back.

I writhe and twist, trying to get free.

Two paramedics peer through the driver's side window as firemen work to cut the door open. 'Wake him up! Wake him up!' the girl driver screeches.

That's when I notice the windscreen, a hole in the lower corner, cracks shooting out in every direction, like fissures around a bullet hole. A smear of red. A head protruding through the hole. Hair matted, his face mutilated, unrecognisable.

I vomit green bile all over the street.

I'm jerked off my feet and carried into the back of an ambulance. Someone drapes a blanket over my shoulders.

My pulse, though thumping in my temples, feels as if it's slowing.

The rhythm becomes irregular.

His beat, the first sound I ever heard, fades, until his heart lies still and the world is suddenly a frightfully quiet place.

Thirteen

DUSK

I'm trudging on a deep seabed. Blues and reds of medical monitors glow like purple shades of dusk filtering down through water.

In weeks to come, I won't remember that her room number is 15C or that the floor is polished smooth. I won't remember the smell of citrus disinfectant, plaster or antibiotic creams. What I will recall, in acute detail, is the shaved patch of hair on her scalp where the stitches are. The right eye, swollen shut. The wires cascading over blackened limbs.

As I stand over her, Mia opens her left eye. I swallow hard at the sight of blood around the iris, mucus in her eyelashes. A single tear slips over her bruised flesh.

'He's gone.' The words cut her dry throat. 'Isn't he?'

I peel back the hospital blanket and climb over the bedrail to lie down beside her. Her right wrist is frozen in a cast, slung around her neck. I interlace my fingers with those of her free hand.

She squeezes so hard, blood pulses in my fingertips. 'I don't want to go to sleep, Grace.' She shudders. 'I don't want to go to sleep because when I wake up, for a moment, I'll have forgotten.'

Fourteen

THE GREY

The sky falls silently into the sea.

I don't know how many bodies have gathered. Hundreds. A thousand, maybe. They spill down the grassy hill, crowd the car park, all wrapped in woollen jackets. Some wander across the rocks and line the perimeter of the ocean pool. The majority stand here in wetsuits, on the crushed bones of the earth.

Some shiver in their black skins, others carry white flowers. All around puffs of breath cloud the air. Young girls, no older than ten, huddle together with purple lips, boards decorated with frangipani stickers at their feet. One of them I have babysat, Ellie, and I think of how she will go home after all this, to a hot shower, and her mum will make her hot chocolate with marshmallows as a treat to warm her up.

The icy, dry sand burns my skin raw. My muscles tighten around my throat.

Several men step aside so Dad can find the centre of the circle. Mum hangs from his side like a dead arm. He takes my hand and draws me to his other hip. A friend passes him a megaphone. Dad presses the wrong button and a high-pitched siren wails in the sea of still bodies. The friend leaps back to his aid.

There are some faces I don't recognise, yet they all seem to know me, and I realise that grief is a colour – beneath the eyes, a stain on my skin. For years we attended the big surf comps and none of them saw me. Now they've flown from all parts of the country, and suddenly I'm the one to watch. A celebrity yet the envy of no one.

'I would . . . we would like to thank you.' Dad lowers the megaphone to clear his throat. 'I don't know that there are words for a father to use when he says goodbye to his son. I guess it's meant to be the other way around.'

In every direction, grey tears bleed from pink eyes.

'All I know is that I am honoured to have raised a son who could have drawn you all to the waves. To know that he has inspired and touched the lives of so many people is everything to me . . . to us.'

Dad squeezes me against his ribs, so tight I fight for my next breath, and hands the megaphone to Mum.

Her hands shake so heavily, she can barely grip the speaker button.

'Anyone who was graced with his presence knew there was never a dull moment with Ben. He was our light, our energy, my sun, and I cannot imagine the next hour, let alone tomorrow, without him.' Dropping the megaphone, she falls in a heap among clumps of dead seaweed, and two girlfriends rush to help her back up.

I hold the urn against my chest, close my eyes and kiss the lid, as if my heartbeat could somehow inspire his.

At the water's edge, surf club members wearing lifesaving caps and leis around their necks drag a jet ski off a trailer into the frothy tide. Dad carries Mum in his arms across the wet sand and sits her down on the back of the jet ski while a lifeguard climbs on and revs the engine. Mia is coming with us and her dad and Jackson help load her into an IRB, her broken wrist wrapped in a plastic bag to protect the plaster cast.

Dad takes the megaphone. 'If you are participating in the paddle-out with smaller children, please make sure you keep them close by. Lifeguards are wearing red and yellow caps – please don't hesitate to ask for assistance if you need it. Thank you all from the bottom of my heart.'

Dad kisses my forehead, takes Ben's ashes from my arms and hands the urn to Mum. The boat and jet ski's engines spit, kick into life and fly forward over the first roll of white wash. The crowd follows.

Jake and Toby are at my side as we pick up our boards. We each wear a party shirt of Ben's over the top of our wetsuits.

The boys clench the stalks of white roses between their teeth as we wade out together, sliding onto our stomachs when the water laps our waists. I duck-dive my first wave, water stripping back all that is left of me. As I surface, I can taste my own tears mixing with salt on my lips.

The ocean swell is small, the waves weak. We paddle through water as smooth as silk, past the pool and the rock shelf into the deep. The sky and the sea fuse together and I can no longer distinguish the horizon. From the cliffs, seabirds swoop down from their nests and glide across the ocean – a sheet of grey glass.

When we reach a place far beyond the break, I glance over my shoulder and struggle to take in the sheer number who are joining us. Friends and strangers paddle on long and short boards, stand-up paddle boards, kayaks, a rowboat and boogie boards. I even spot the bobbing heads of those who have swum. As the crowd collects, people paddle into position and link hands. The floating circle stretches hundreds of metres, with the boys, Dad, Mia in the boat, Mum on the jet ski and me in the centre.

I look across at Mia, her eyes pink, tears flowing down her face. A thousand words are said with silence.

Then, like a winter storm, voices cry out, thunder clapping over dead water. Some slap the water; others throw it into the sky. The waves of Ben's life ripple through the deep.

Mum raises the urn from her lap and the cries become deafening. She removes the lid and tips a part of me into the sea. Passing the ashes to Dad, she unravels, breaking down in tears, covering her face with her hands. Dad sits up straight on his board and tips up the urn. A coarse powder of dust and broken bones pours out, clouding the water. His face contorts, an ugly, bitter mask of grief and whatever it was that held his sorrow at bay until now is washed away with the tide. As Dad dissolves with his son into the ocean, colour drains from his cheeks, as if it is escaping in his tears.

Splashes of water and flowers fly through the air.

I draw a breath deep into my lungs and exhale slowly as I take the urn from Dad, my feet dangling in the water, Jake's hand on my shoulder.

I feel time beginning to slow, until the last of him is grey powder on the sea and time stops altogether.

Fifteen

SASHA

Pale sea. Silver dust on the horizon.

Someone knocks on my door and I roll over, shoving the crumpled, damp tissues under my pillow. 'Hey,' Jake says, leaning against the doorframe. In the middle of winter, he wears a thin white T-shirt and grey trackies. He steps over the mess on the floor and climbs onto my bed, lying down beside me. 'My mum came back.'

We're still, shoulder to shoulder.

'Without her boyfriend,' he adds.

'That's good, isn't it?'

He shrugs.

My room smells of sweat, dirty laundry.

'Have you seen Facebook?'

I shake my head.

'Everyone is writing on his wall. I swear some of them weren't even his friends. So stupid. It's not like he can read it.'

Waves take huge mouthfuls of sand from the shore, feasting. I don't know how long we lie here before Jake takes my hand, starting to sob. 'I really miss him.'

There's another knock at the door. Aunt Kate pokes her head in the room. 'Grace, honey, you really need to eat something.'

She repeats herself twice before Jake and I climb out of bed, trudging down the hall into the kitchen. Kate pours me a bowl of cereal with almond milk, garnishing it with blueberries and fresh banana slices. Spooning it into my mouth, the flavours are bland. I force a swallow, my stomach churns and I fight to keep it down. My aunt offers Jake some but he declines.

Kate leans across the bench to ask Mum, 'What about you, Mel, some porridge maybe?'

No more than ten feet away in the lounge room, it's as if Mum hasn't even heard her.

Kate sighs as I slide the bowl back to her and admit I'm not hungry.

'Love, you need to eat something.' Kate passes the bowl back, turns to Uncle Mark and adjusts his shirt. He says the car is packed and that the girls are dressed and ready to go.

I look at Daisy, in her frilly pink socks and hair in piggy plaits, lying with Monty on his doggy bed, playing with her dolls, then notice Rachel, uncomfortable on the couch. We make eye contact and she quickly turns away.

They arrived the morning after the accident, driving down from the city. Kate immediately took charge, organising the necessary events, making the phone calls, addressing the press, all the things Mum refused to do.

Daisy had asked where Ben was, and when Kate said he was gone, Daisy said 'oh', then asked where her gumboots were. She wanted to go outside and splash in the puddles.

Rachel, only three years older, clung to her dad's side. She didn't dare speak to Mum, Dad or me, terrified that she would say the wrong thing. In the two weeks since they arrived, Rachel has read four books, burrowing her face into pages of distant lands where dragons and fairies fly so no one will notice her wet cheeks.

Kate lays a slice of honeycomb on my cereal. I bite, gold syrup oozes. It all tastes the same.

Outside it is overcast, the light dull. The earth is dank, flowers droop. I hear the first drop hit the roof, thick and heavy, then a second and a third in quick succession. For the millionth time this week, the clouds clap, and it pours. Kate is at the sink by the window, washing Daisy's and Rachel's breakfast bowls. She turns to Mum, who's slumped in an armchair with a bed quilt draped over her lap, loose strands of hair straggling over her shoulders.

'You know what?' Kate says. 'All this rain, I bet it's the angels crying with laughter. Ben's telling another joke.'

Mum makes a strange sound, primal and disturbing. Her body rumples in the chair and she bursts into tears as Kate throws down the tea towel and rushes to her side. 'Oh, Mel, honey, I didn't mean to.'

Jake nudges me. 'The shed?' he suggests. I shrug, leave my virtually untouched bowl, and follow him out through the downpour.

In the shed, my teeth are chattering, as we scurry under the woollen rug draped over the mouldy couch. Settling in, Jake draws a pack of cigarettes from his trackpants. He strikes a match, inhales, then offers me one. For the first time, I accept, drawing out a cigarette. He exhales a thick cloud and then strikes another match, holding it out to me. I suck on the filter, smoke fills my lungs and I choke. Jake almost giggles, patting me on the back, and tells me to try again. I do, and by the fourth inhalation, I have pins and needles in my toes and birds flying around my head.

Jake finds the remote under the couch and flicks on the old TV set. We play Nintendo, Ben's character racing around the track with us, computer simulated. It crosses the line in first place. Jake says, 'Fucker, he's not even here and he's still winning.'

We play two more times, until Jake crosses the chequered finish line in first position. He doesn't do his usual gloating dance, just hunches forward and flicks off the TV, then offers me another cigarette. We sit back and, without saying a word, watch grey tails of smoke curl in front of the black screen. Above, raindrops drum on the tin roof. I feel the heavy rhythm in my blanched bones.

'When do you think it will stop?' he whispers.

I rest my head on his shoulder and squeeze my eyes shut.

We stay there, a sheath of silence draped over our shoulders for nearly an hour until the rusty roller door screeches as Toby lifts it. He and Mia scamper into the shed like two drowned rats. Wet cotton socks strangle their ankles. They dump soaked bags and fall back on the second couch. Wearing their school jumpers, each carries the odd scent of damp synthetic wool.

'How was it?' Jake asks.

'We went to physics,' Toby says. 'Mr Davis started talking about inertia and—'

Mia interrupts. 'I told him to fuck off.'

Jake blinks and offers her a cigarette. Mia removes her beanie, exposing the shaved scalp and bandage patch, and for the first time in *her* life takes one too. With her right arm still wrapped in a sling, she struggles with her opposite hand, dropping the cigarette into her lap. Jake retrieves it and holds it to her lips, lighting it with a match, a fleeting flame. Like me, she coughs and splutters at first, then sinks back into the upholstery.

'He'd *die* if he saw us smoking, Grace,' she says.

A second passes. I swallow, my heart beats, and I breathe out. In the uncomfortable silence, Mia starts to laugh. The sound is crude and horrifying and magnificent.

I start laughing too, and then Jake, and Toby, louder than the thunder in the sky. And soon, I'm not sure if I am an angel laughing or if I am simply rain.

⌒

Back in the house, we watch a mindless reality TV show, all four of us piled onto the same lounge room couch, because Ben hated reality TV and somehow that makes us think the contestants' banal conversation won't remind us of him, but everything does.

Uncle Mark and the girls are on their way back to the city, but Kate has stayed behind. She arranges a cup of dandelion tea, a flower and some biscuits on a tray and climbs the stairs, taking them to Mum, who has gone back to bed. By the end of the TV program she returns with the tray. I watch her tip the tea down the sink and brush the half-eaten biscuits from the plate into the bin.

'I'm going to heat this up,' she calls out to us, holding up *another* lasagne. The freezer is full of food the neighbours have brought around. 'Or do you want a casserole? I think this one is fish.'

When I don't respond, I hear the words, 'Lasagne it is,' escape under her breath.

As we watch another episode in the TV marathon, the rich aroma of baked cheese floods the kitchen and flows out through the living area, until Kate draws the lasagne from the oven, serving it onto warm plates. She offers one to each of us, then sits in the armchair with a slice for herself. Shovelling pasta, bolognaise and warm, gooey cheese into her mouth, she nods her head, swallows and says, 'This one has some merit, good flavour – I wonder who made it.'

'Mum's is better.'

She looks at me. 'I know, baby.' Coffee bags beneath her eyes. 'We'll have her cooking again. Promise.'

On the TV, one of the celebrity contestants has a meltdown because her tailor has messed up an alteration the day before the big event. Chewing the stringy cheese until it is soggy mush in my mouth, I watch her hunt in designer boutiques for a new gown, an emergency replacement, her grief a futile cry, contained behind a screen. I wish mine was that simple.

A while later there's a wary knock at the door, so quiet I'm not sure I heard anything at all. The second knock is louder. Kate calls, 'Come in.'

Harley opens the door and slides in. He's wearing a jacket over his school shirt and pulls the hood down, eyes fixed on the tray in his hands. 'My mum made these – she's at work, so I thought I'd bring them round.'

'Hey,' Jake says, but Harley's eyes look past him, past them all, until they land on me, blue electricity burning my skin.

Kate jumps up and thanks him for the flatbread and dips. She tries rearranging some of the bowls and containers in the fridge, then the freezer, before turning to him. 'Looks like we're out of room – this doesn't need to be refrigerated, does it?'

He shakes his head, not breaking his stare.

'Okay, great,' she says, placing the tray on the kitchen bench next to the plate of muffins, a box of biscuits and the platter of sandwiches. 'What's your mum's name?'

'Nila.'

'I'll tell Mel.'

Eyes lingering on mine, Harley says, 'I should go.'

Jake turns to him. 'Nah, dude. Stay. We're watching hot dumb chicks.'

He shakes his head, pulls his hood up, says goodbye and slips back out into the rain.

'What was that all about?' Mia says over her shoulder.

I shrug, turning my attention to the woman on screen in the glamorous emerald dress, its scooped back, the gold necklace, the fake eyelashes, desperate for a detail to distract me from Harley, from the way he'd just stared at me . . . a stranger.

⌒

Come the weekend, the front door flies open, swinging on its hinges. I look up to see a hot pink pair of gumboots step into the house. 'Where's your father?' Sasha asks, taking off her yellow raincoat. 'There's no ute in the driveway.'

It's the first time I've seen her since the funeral. She's left Pa in his nursing home in the city and come down to give Kate a hand in the fight to revive my mum.

'He's at work,' I say, mixing chocolate powder into a cup of milk.

'On a Sunday?'

'He's always there.'

Sasha glances at Kate. Putting on the kettle, Kate answers with a kind of *I'll tell you later* purse of the lips.

My grandmother, who refuses to be called *Nan*, has wild white hair and wears bright red lipstick. She unwraps the orange sequined scarf from around her neck and dusts her hands together. 'Right, well. Where is my daughter?'

'Bed,' Kate admits.

'*Still?*' Sasha huffs, rolling up her sleeves. 'She needs a reason to get up. A bloody good one.' Striding into the kitchen, she pulls out half the pantry, along with bacon, eggs and sausages from the fridge. For almost an hour, I watch her parade around the kitchen, mixing, blending, chopping and frying, throwing herbs and spices in every direction. Finally, she plates up a monster breakfast – baked beans, toast, marinated mushrooms, hash browns, poached eggs, hollandaise, sausages, grilled tomato, avocado on toast and crispy bacon, with a side of pickled vegetables and a freshly squeezed fruit juice. To top it off, she paces out into the rain, returning with an auburn banksia flower to lay on the platter.

'Breakfast, like I keep telling you lot, is the most important meal of the day,' Sasha declares, before picking up the tray and marching her seventy-six-year-old legs up the stairs.

Kate plops a marshmallow in my half-empty chocolate milk, and we sit down on the couch. I wonder what Dad's parents would say if they were here, if they hadn't left him all those years ago with tombstones to visit and this big white house on the headland. Would my grandfather have held Dad, or would he have sat in his wheelchair wondering where he was and why he'd been brought here, like Pa had last week? I wonder what Dad's siblings would have done if he'd ever had any. Would they have fussed the way Kate does?

My aunt and I have just started an episode of an old cartoon when we hear music booming from the floor above. It's loud enough to drown out the television, but Kate and I just sit there, watching episode after episode, listening to the stamping of dancing feet and Sasha belting out choruses.

When we reach the credits of the fifth episode, Sasha parades into the lounge room with Mum trudging behind, head down, yet showered, clean and out of her pyjama robe for the first time in two weeks. 'Grace, get dressed,' Sasha orders. 'We're going to lunch.'

~

'I don't want a bloody discount!'

'Mum, please. *Stop*,' Kate begs, tugging on Sasha's sleeve.

'We don't need people feeling sorry for us,' she says and slaps the full amount for the bill *and* a tip on the counter, picks up her bag and charges out of the restaurant.

When we arrive home, Dad's Rodeo is parked in the driveway. He and three friends sit on the verandah steps drinking beer, quiet and still, staring at a silver sea. They each acknowledge us with a nod and slight curl of the lips. Inside, Sasha complains, loud enough for them to hear, ripping into Dad for ignoring his responsibilities as a husband and father.

Then she turns to the pantry. 'Enough of the frozen sympathy dishes – tonight we're cooking our own dinner,' she announces and begins organising ingredients on the bench.

For the next few hours, I sit at the bench with Mum and watch Kate and Sasha juggling spices, chopping vegetables, crushing garlic, wrapping raw tuna in foil. The room is fragrant with lemon and coconut milk and I see Mum breathe it in, a flicker in her eye. With her fingers, she combs her blonde hair into a ponytail, fastening it with a hair band. Like a fish released back into the sea, she takes over the chopping board and sets to work.

As dusk falls, Sasha lays plates on the table and Kate goes outside to get Dad for dinner. Returning alone, she grabs a blanket from the hall cupboard and walks out to the shed where he's passed out and drapes it over his tired bones.

Tonight, Sasha sleeps in bed with Mum, as I imagine she did when Mum was little and had a nightmare.

Sixteen

THE SHRINE

I'm not sure if I'm ever going to get used to the way they stare at me in the halls, in the classroom, in the yard – the poor girl who lost it all. I see, in their eyes, a battle between what is polite – turning the other way – and their intrigue. I see the slant of their mouths, the anxious tapping of their feet, as if my grief highlights the fragility of their own lives. Perhaps tonight they will make an effort at dinner to give thanks for their loved ones.

In the yard, I share my lunch with Toby and Mia, Sasha having stuffed my lunch box to the brim with leftovers from the trays, plates and dishes full of food our neighbours have given us. We eat muffins with raspberry and white chocolate filling and scones with strawberry jam, until the box is empty. With so much inside, we should be full.

'Only one more class and we'll have survived a whole day at school.' Mia's soft voice carries no sense of triumph.

ↄ⌒

Kate is reading on the verandah when I dump my schoolbag at the front door.

'Where is everyone?'

'Sash is out shopping, your dad's at the factory – he left before we woke up this morning – and your mum is inside. She's on some sort of mission.'

I cock my head in question.

'She's cleaning, and cooking, and god knows what else. Hasn't stopped all day. I don't know what was better, lying in bed or *this*.'

Mum acknowledges me in the lounge room with a quick hello before pressing on with the vacuuming. As I walk down the hall to my room, she follows behind, the nozzle at my heels.

For the first time in days, I can see my floor. Every ornament on my bedside table has been straightened, the photo frames aligned, my books stacked in order by size. She has wiped down my desk and dusted the windowsills. I'm suddenly not sure where I am permitted to step.

ↄ⌒

At the end of the week, Mark calls from the city. He's been juggling his business and the girls, but now Daisy has gastro, and she needs her mum. From my room, I hear Kate crying for the first time as she packs her things. Sasha has already left, gone to visit Pa in the nursing home. Dad has taken to sleeping in the shed. When Kate leaves, the house is so clean, so empty, you'd swear no one lives here. She leaves me in a museum.

I first notice the smell when I step out of the bathroom after a shower amid clouds of hot steam. Though subtle, I know something is rotting. I walk down the hall and shiver. Something is rotting in Ben's room.

With each day that passes, the smell becomes more potent, until I have to hold my breath as I walk down the hall.

When I tell Mum, she says I'm imagining it, and for a while I believe her.

It's not until the laundry toilet beside the shed breaks the following weekend and Dad comes into the house to use my bathroom that I learn this stench of decay is not a product of my imagination.

'What the hell is that?' Dad yells over the TV.

Mum steps out of the kitchen, pulling off her oven mitts, and hisses, 'What?'

'That disgusting smell.'

'I don't know what you mean,' Mum says. 'I can't smell anything.'

Cheeks flushed, Dad storms around the house, searching every room until he arrives at Ben's door. 'It's coming from in here.'

I jump off the couch, following Mum as she chases after him. Dad goes to open the door.

'Don't you dare,' she warns.

As he turns the handle and goes in, I shudder.

Mum hurls abuse from the hall until he steps out, minutes later, with a plastic bag. Inside it, a ham sandwich, hairy and spotted purple, green and blue.

Mum grabs at his arm, but he shakes her off. As he carries the sandwich into the kitchen and dumps it in the bin, she follows, screaming at him, pounding his back with her fists, frail arms flailing. 'How dare you!' she cries. 'How dare you!'

I watch helplessly, hands over my ears.

Dad yells something back, the words muffled, and shoves her. She throws a container from the bench, plastic bouncing off his chest, brown rice is scattered like dirt on the floor.

He punches the wall beside the fridge, fist cracking the plaster. 'It's not a bloody shrine!' he bellows. 'Ben isn't coming back!'

Seventeen

BLIND DANCERS

I don't know what aches more, falling asleep and dreaming of him, or lying still in black hours, thinking over and over about how it could have happened differently . . . The *what ifs* are infinite.

One tiny variation – a traffic light, a struggle to find a park, a delay in the office where they picked up the hampers. Just *one* tiny variation to make that day the same as any other.

Pulling my blanket over my head, I think about when we were little and still sharing a room. How we'd swap beds and hide beneath the covers to fool our parents when they came in to say goodnight. How Ben would check under my bed for monsters. I think about the glow-in-the-dark stars we stuck to our ceiling. Ben had used superglue, to Dad's sheer horror. I think of how I'd wake from a nightmare and hear his breaths, slow and even, like gentle waves lapping on the shore, a lullaby to put me back to sleep.

Peeling back the blanket now, I stare out my window at tiny stars burning holes in the skin of the night. Tiny stars, impossibly far away.

⌢

Mia corners me in the hallway. 'Where did you go this morning?' Her cheeks flush red with anger when I play dumb. 'I know you skipped class. We had English first period.'

Students pour out of classrooms, the hallway seems to shrink.

'Exams are in *three months*, Grace.' She pushes her fringe out of her eyes. 'It's fucking hard for all of us, okay? But you don't see me or Toby wagging every second day. You and Jake will fail.'

I look down at my sneakers, at their dirty, loose laces.

Mia sighs and stomps away while I collect my bag, slamming my locker. Two girls jump with fright at the sound and then exchange whispers. I turn and bolt, shoving people out of my way, making for the exit.

The footpath out the front of the school is crowded with students waiting for their buses. I pause a moment, trying to decide what to do, where to go, when I see Jake pull up to the kerb. He reaches across and opens the passenger door. 'Get in.'

We pull away and I reach for a water bottle at my feet. 'This safe to drink?'

He shrugs, knees steering the wheel as he uses both hands to spark a match and light his cigarette.

'Whose car is this?' I ask.

'Mum's.'

'What's wrong with your ute?'

'I've got an empty tank.' He winks. 'Mum won't notice anyway.

Gone away again.' He offers me a cigarette, then smashes his hand against the radio. 'Piece of junk.'

We drift through the backstreets in silence. I don't ask where we're going because I'm not sure it even matters.

When the winter sun falls behind grey hills, Jake pulls into my drive. We pass Mum asleep on the couch, flour in her hair, and a hundred or so muffins neatly aligned in trays on the bench. Jake flops down on my bed, the creak of the mattress the only sound in this empty, polished house.

'There's a party tonight, a warehouse party,' he says. 'You should come with me.'

I reach into my closet and yank a pair of black jeans off a hanger. He plays with the lamp on my bedside table, flicking the light on and off while I pull on boots, a lace top and a beanie.

'Sexy,' he says, his smile teasing in the pervading shadows.

⌐⌐

Jake parks with two wheels on the kerb.

'I don't know how you got your licence.'

'Neither do I,' he laughs and pulls a plastic bag from beneath his seat. 'Supplies.' Jake winks and turns on the light above the rear-view mirror. Holding the bag open, he reveals a bottle of vodka and a saddy of pot, as well as a saddy with a couple of pills.

Jake locks the car, and I take the bottle he offers, unscrewing the cap. The rancid smell already burning my nose, I take a swig. My throat burns. Grabbing it back, Jake takes a swig too, then arches his neck and howls at the moon.

By the time we arrive at the party, music thumping, screams curling in the night, my stomach is hot and legs wobbly. Jake pulls me aside at the warehouse entrance, fumbling in his pocket for the sachet. 'Here,' he says, and I hold out a shaky hand. 'Trust me,' he smiles and I do, taking the pill he places in my hand, popping it in my mouth and washing it down with another swig.

Inside, the roof is barely visible through the haze of blue smoke. Couches line the perimeter; the dirty walls are covered in graffiti, and beer cans and glass crunch beneath every step. When I breathe in, the air is dank with beer, sweat and wet tobacco. I turn around, realise I have already lost Jake.

I sway, knocking into people. I lose myself to the hour. And then it hits me, like a phosphorescent wave in a midnight sea, so cold it almost feels hot. Toxic bliss. Someone pushes me, and I push back, forcing my way into the crowd of blind dancers. The beat grips me, thick and heavy, as a strobe throws light in wild bursts. Faces are contorted, jaws swing loose from ears, eyes are red, half-closed, with astounding black moon pupils. My limbs thrash, my body whirls, my hair whips, and I laugh, an ugly sound, but magnificent, too. I stumble, fall, and a man with rough hands grabs my arm and hoists me to my feet. I loop my arms around his neck and press myself against him as he slides his hands over my hips and grabs my arse, his breath hot against my shoulder. I reach up and cradle his jaw, pull his face to mine, his lips hot and hard. It is my first kiss, fierce and blistering.

The DJ morphs one reality into another and I'm torn away. I see Jake across the room and he grins at me before he's swallowed up in the crowd again. I am surrounded by strangers, alone, anonymous, but it is glorious, a grin stretching my cheeks until they ache, strangers grinning back at me, all of us dancing together, one huge, sweaty, grinding mass.

After a while – I don't know how long – I stumble out of the crowd and collapse onto a couch next to a boy smoking a joint. He pulls out his phone and I lean across to see what time it is. Four hours have passed. I lean back, exhale and wipe sticky hair from my face. The boy slides his phone into his pocket and offers me the joint. I take it and suck. It tastes like damp earth and wood. I cough for a moment. He laughs and cups his hand over my knee.

I feel it first in the crown of my head, a creamy warmth that dribbles down through my body into my boots. We sit giggling, passing the joint between us, until we seep into the couch like butter melting in warm milk.

The music slowly dying, my eyes roll around in my head like marbles as I drift in and out of the passing hours.

A hand shakes my shoulder. Jake's silhouette comes into focus.

'Let's get out of here,' he says, reaching for my hand, peeling me off the couch. We stumble out of the warehouse to find the sun already climbing high above the surrounding factories. The light hurts my eyes. We have defied sleep, and it feels strange, somehow unnatural.

'How about a feed?' Jake's smirk splits chapped lips. 'There's a drive-through at the edge of the industrial area.'

I can't remember the last time I ate a burger and fries. Thanks to Mum, I didn't even taste fast food until I was thirteen years old and we stopped roadside on the bus to school camp.

Jake, eyes glazed, orders three times as much as me and we drive down to a parking lot near the centre of town, overlooking the harbour. Fish scales scattered on the concrete sparkle like glitter confetti. As Jake winds down his window, salty air and the smell of yabby bait engulf the inside of the car, and we devour our food, so greasy its paper packaging is now translucent. At the end of the pier, men in washed-out jeans, flannelette shirts and gumboots cast fishing lines into the sea. When one reels in a catch, gulls flock from every direction. He waves his arms to scare them off, slamming the lid on the esky before any bird swoops on the prized fish.

Jake throws a handful of fries out the window. Within seconds, the gulls have abandoned their efforts on the pier and are fighting over the oily chips, squawking in argument. We notice one that's missing a leg, hopping along behind the others. I toss it a fry, only to see it drop the other webbed foot.

'Little shit,' Jake says. 'I hate it when they do that!' and he hurls half a chicken nugget at the bird's head, knocking his box of fries across the dash in the process. He gathers several, squishes them with his hands and rubs them into my hair. Squealing, I scramble onto his lap and stuff my half eaten burger down the back of his shirt. Pushing me off, my back presses against the steering wheel and the horn honks. Two fishermen turn around, staring.

'What're you looking at?' Jake yells out the window. 'Get a real job.' The men quickly look away. Jake and I exchange glances. Smiles crack and we burst into laughter. I lean against his chest, surrounded by mashed fries. Jake holds me until I am still.

⌒⌒

Mum is still asleep on the couch, in exactly the same position she was in when we left. Monty hobbles up to me as I walk in the door. His eyes are sad and muddy, as if he hasn't been fed in days, and I wonder if perhaps he hasn't. Jake and I fill his dish to the brim with dog biscuits, top up his water bowl and put a few of the muffins Mum made in his bed, a treat for later, an apology.

Jake and I have a shower together in our underwear. I wash dirt and remnants of the mashed chips from my hair, scrub the smell of tobacco and spilt beer from my skin and squeeze extra toothpaste to brush away the grit.

In the shed, Jake looks at the blankets and pillow on the fold-out couch. 'Your dad sleeping in here?'

'Either here, or at the factory.'

'Heavy.'

We kick aside empty beer cans and settle ourselves on the couch with a bag of salt and vinegar chips. Jake flicks on the TV and asks what I want to watch. I shrug and he picks a rom-com, something he would have never watched with Ben.

Jake jokes the entire time about how corny it is, but I'm not really paying attention. Being overtired has made me strangely numb. It's almost enough to stifle the ache inside.

My breath catches when the roller door screeches and I notice Harley stepping into the shed, holding a Tupperware container. 'My mum asked for me to bring this over.' His eyes touch mine as I bite down on a chip, salt and vinegar burning my tastebuds.

'What is it?' Jake asks.

'Harira soup,' Harley says, then explains, 'it's made with tomatoes, lentils, chickpeas and lamb.' Harley reaches into his pocket and pulls out a zip-lock bag with some chopped coriander in it. 'You're meant to put this on after you heat it up.'

'Thanks,' I say, my voice shallow.

He looks at the towel on my head, Jake's wet fringe. 'What have you guys been up to?'

'Went to a warehouse in Port Lawnam,' Jake explains.

'A party?'

'Yeah, we just got back.'

Harley glances at his watch. 'Whoa. It's almost twelve.' He forces something that almost resembles a laugh. 'Must have been good.'

Neither of us answers him, and he shifts his weight, uncomfortable. 'I better go,' he says.

'You can chill with us, bro,' Jake says.

Harley shakes his head, says, 'See ya round,' and is gone.

'What happened there?' Jake says.

'What do you mean?'

'Well, you were basically his girlfriend.'

My throat swells. 'Was not,' I stammer, and turn back to the TV, almost angry now at the girl on screen, the silly girl who fell for a dickhead.

Jake shoves a handful of potato chips into his mouth. 'Whatever. He's lost the plot.'

I laugh from the stomach. 'And we haven't?'

Eighteen

A BEACH VIBE

'You stink,' she tells me. 'Like you actually *stink*. When was the last time you washed this?' Mia takes a bottle of perfume out of her locker and douses my school uniform in frangipani, both of us sneezing.

The bell rings and the crowd dissipates. We hang by our lockers until we're the only ones out here. Mia tells me she went to the police station again.

'I thought you already made your statement.'

'I did.'

The frangipani perfume on my uniform makes my nose twitch. Mia tells me the cops still wouldn't give her any information about what might happen to the woman.

The woman who was taken to hospital with a broken rib. The woman who stole everything from us.

I fall back against the lockers. 'Stop telling me this. I don't want to know.'

'What!' Her voice is shrill, incredulous. 'Still? I mean I under-stood at first, tried to at least, it was fresh . . . but are you serious? Are you actually being serious?'

I shrink beside grey metal, thinking of how Kate had hidden the newspapers. How Mia had shown me anyway.

'My god,' she says, not caring now who can hear her. 'I don't believe you.' She grabs her bag and slams her locker so hard it echoes down the corridor.

A teacher pokes his head out from a nearby classroom. 'Is everything all right?'

Mia storms off, leaving me alone. The teacher asks if I'd like him to call someone. I shake my head, waiting for him to step back inside before I let go of the tears.

⌒

Stepping out of the girls' bathroom, face washed, water dripping from my chin, I almost bash straight into him. 'Sorry,' Harley says, stepping back, then ambles away. It's not until I'm sitting in biology, next to an empty chair, that I realise he had actually turned and walked off in the opposite direction.

I sit alone in biology twice more before I hear Mia ask in the yard why he dropped the subject, the only class he and I had together. Harley shrugs. 'Too many units, I guess.'

I skip my next biology class, instead joining Jake by the rock pool with a box of fish and chips, smoking rolled cigarettes and throwing stones into the ocean, unable to sit in a classroom where *two* people are missing.

⌒

Mr Mitchell, the school counsellor, has a daughter who goes to our school. Young with orange frizz and freckles, she's one of the few girls at Marlow High who wears the school uniform properly, with no fashionable alterations or additions. Her puppy fat makes her a target for the taunts and ridicule of other kids, older *and* younger. I don't know her name, but for years I have seen her in the corridors, always slouched with her head down, trying to make herself small enough to slip through unnoticed, to hide from the girls who gossip and guys that shove. Watching her from a distance, I liked to think that having a counsellor for a father might make things easier for her.

Mr Mitchell gestures for me to sit down, turns on a kettle and spreads an assortment of biscuits across a plate. He holds them up and I shake my head.

'Okay, well, they're here if you want one.' He lays the plate down next to a box of tissues on the coffee table. 'Have you ever seen a counsellor before?'

I shake my head again.

'I want you to know that everything you say is confidential. Nothing leaves this room.'

I shrug, looking at the door, which is covered in a collage of mental health posters and positive phrases scrawled on colourful post-it notes.

'Grace, these sessions will work best if you are able to speak openly to me.'

Leaning back into the couch, a slab of sunshine pressing on my shoulder, I wonder if there has ever really been a time when I have spoken openly.

On the floor, the carpet is ocean blue. I stare until I am swimming in it, deep beneath the surface.

'The school went for a beach theme,' he finally says.

'Excuse me?'

'The room, they tried to give it a beach vibe.'

'It's pretty ugly.'

He smiles, a smooth curve. 'I agree,' he says, handing me a box of tea bags.

I pull out chamomile.

'Good choice,' he says. 'Chamomile is my favourite too.'

⌒

When we were thirteen, Dad took all us kids up to Illuna Bay with the tinny to go fishing. It had been raining, and it was so murky in the shallows you couldn't see your hand when you stuck it under the water. The grand fishing escapade proved not such a grand idea when the racket the boys caused in the boat scared away all the fish. They were stealing bait from Dad's esky and shoving it down each other's shirts. When Jake squished a yabby head against my cheek I squealed and hit him. He laughed and pushed me out of the boat.

I had to take off my soaked clothes beneath the privacy of a towel, and sit, shivering, on the floor to shield me from the wind as we headed back to the boat ramp.

Two days later, my glands were swollen and the boys teased, saying my face was so chubby I looked like a thumb. Mum made herbal tonics and loose-leaf tea, but by the fifth day, I had strep throat, my skin was speckled with pink dots and I was in bed with a raging fever. When I missed Mia's birthday party, Ben brought home a piece of cake in a paper towel and one of the lolly bags Mia had insisted on giving out. I thanked him even though I couldn't stomach any of it.

Slipping in and out of sleep, shaking in a pool of cold sweat, it wasn't the cramps that ached most. I was yearning for the ocean.

Down the grassy hill, waves called, still alive even after they'd reached the shore, pulsing in the ground. Lying in my bed, I felt it, I always feel it, a rhythm as known to me as my heartbeat.

I was in bed for almost two weeks and out of the water for a further five days. It was the longest I'd ever been without the sea, and I remember how when I dived back beneath that blue skin for the first time, it was like coming home.

Now, three weeks after the paddle-out, four and a half weeks after the accident, so homesick my core aches, I pull my surfboard off the shelf in the shed. My wetsuit hugs tight, my neck pulses. I draw two deep breaths to slow my heart, another two for reassurance, walking down the grassy hill toward a body of water Ben is now a part of.

When I step from grass onto the beach, there's someone there, a figure in a wetsuit and a hooded winter jacket, sitting on the sand by the car park. They're too far away for me to make out their face, yet as I meander across the beach to the shoreline, I feel their eyes on my back. I wrap my leg-rope around my ankle with hands shaking.

The first step beneath a wash of foam is cool grey. My skin tingles, almost stings. Lying on my board, I stroke, push beneath. In the second before I surface through thick clouds of turbulence, I feel a bizarre sense of both presence and absence, as if he's here in the water, but the ocean is so huge, so dominating, and he is just one tiny part of it.

On an ordinary day, heads would turn when I reached the

line-up, people would say hi, but then they'd turn away, looking back at the horizon. Today, eyes widen, linger on me.

'Grace, it's good to see you back in the water,' one man says, breaking the silence. He was our coach at Nippers for a couple of years, back when Ben won every board race and Jake thought it was funny to eat sand. I half-smile, rising and falling with the tides.

As the sun slides behind us, blue water turns to orange satin. No one speaks, at least not to me, as if I have a kind of buffer zone stretching around me, as if grief is contagious. A set approaches, but as I paddle, racing for the big wave, men and boys paddle out of my way, out of position. I pull onto the wave, feeling like a foreigner after weeks on dry land, my legs wobbling. My board skids out and I come unstuck, slammed by the breaking lip. This feeling, this lack of conviction, is unlike anything I have experienced. I can't remember a time when my legs didn't dance on water. I never learnt to surf. I never learnt to breathe.

With my heavy arms I paddle out to the line-up. 'Nice wave,' one guy says, a few years older than me.

My brow creases. 'No it wasn't.'

'Sure it was.' His voice wavers. 'Everyone falls off sometimes.'

I paddle around him, my cheeks hot.

Another wave climbs out of the water and I claim this one too, uncontested. This time, I don't stand up, riding down the face and all the way to shore on my stomach.

A breath of night air drifts across sand as the sun sinks behind the mountains. Further up the beach, by the car park, the figure who was watching me earlier stands up and walks toward me. When he pulls down the hood on his jacket I see that it is Harley. I don't stop, walking past him to the outdoor showers, but he follows me.

Turning the tap on, bitter winter water spits from the shower-head, droplets sharp on the skin.

'How was it?' he asks.

I shrug.

He tucks his hands into his pockets, slouches his shoulders. 'I only just got here, thought it was a bit late to be paddling out.'

I turn off the tap hard, my knuckles white, and start walking back to the grassy hill, away from Harley.

Over my shoulder, I call, 'You didn't miss out on much.'

Nineteen

TWO-MINUTE NOODLES

When BBQ dies, lying limp in the coop on scattered chicken feed, I don't tell Mum, scared she'll go and bleach our house.

We bought the chickens on our way back from a surf comp up the coast a few years ago. It was before Mum got the full-time position at St Mary's High School in Port Lawnam, when she used to travel with us to competitions. We'd surfed our finals on a Saturday and had the whole of Sunday to cruise back down to Marlow. Driving a scenic route, we weaved through a coastal town on the edge of an inlet. The main street was lined with bait shops, milk bars and a fish and chip shop with a giant prawn sculpture on the roof. On the sports field of the local school was a farmers market. Mum had her seatbelt off before Dad had time to park the car. There were stalls selling fresh fruit and vegetables, meat, fish, handmade jewellery, clothes made locally out of Australian cotton, a petting zoo and rides on ponies. Ben asked the farmer with the Shetlands if he could ride one and was told he was too big. Laughing, he'd fallen to his knees, hands together in prayer, begging the man in his Akubra, who hardly knew how to react.

We left the markets with paper bags filled to the brim with produce, a few jars of homemade jam and a bag of popcorn for Ben and me to share. It wasn't until we were loading our goods into the car that Mum saw them. A man by the gate had a pen with baby chicks. She passed Dad her bag and ran back toward them. 'Oh heavens, they're adorable! Come look!'

Running around in circles on yellow straw, squeaking balls of fluffed feathers tripped over and bounced off each other. Mum – who loved cooking with eggs but hated the idea of buying them from farms where they kept chickens in tiny cages – saw the chicks as the perfect solution. By having our own chickens, she could ensure they were fed clean, quality grain and were free to run around the yard, sleeping in their coop at night.

Ben and I were allowed to pick one each and sat with them on our laps the whole way home, debating over what we would call them. When Ben suggested BBQ, we laughed so hard warm tears wet our cheeks. When we caught our breath, I suggested Honey Soy. We erupted again and the baby chicks squawked with us. Even Mum giggled, though I'm not sure if it was because of the names we'd given our chicks or at our fits of giggles. Ben and me laughing – it was infectious.

Now, standing on my neighbour, Mrs Brown's doorstep, I ring the bell three times before she opens the door.

'Oh, Grace dear.' She steps out in her slippers, wearing a long floral dress and a knitted cardigan. 'Are you okay?'

'BBQ died.'

'Your chicken?'

I nod, crossing my arms, hugging them tight against my chest.

She sighs and holds her wrinkly hand to her heart. 'Oh, darling, I'm sorry. Why don't I get John and we'll come over.' She steps back into the house and calls out to her husband. Together, the three of us walk back across the road into my yard, where Honey Soy is in the coop, kicking dust and flapping wings, squawking hysterically.

Wearing his gardening gloves, Mr Brown suggests I look away as he lifts out BBQ and lays her in a cardboard box. Mrs Brown takes my hand, squeezes.

'Can you please take her?' I ask Mr Brown.

Standing in his button-up shirt and high-waisted pants, holding the cardboard box, he flushes and glances at his wife, who answers, 'Of course we will, sweetie.'

Mr Brown nods and makes his way back across the quiet street with the box. Mrs Brown, pudgy and soft, hugs me tight. 'Do you need something for dinner?' she asks. 'I've made potato and leek soup.'

'I'm fine, Mum is inside making something.'

She glances at the empty driveway, the house with no lights on. 'Thank you,' I say.

Embracing me once more, she says, 'Well, we're just across the road if you need anything,' and ambles home.

Dragging the bag of chickenfeed out of the shed, I scatter fistfuls of grain on the ground of the coop, refill the water bowl Honey Soy has kicked over and, with darkness creeping across the sea, I pick several heads of kangaroo paw, blooming early this year, from around the side of the house. I coil them through the coop's wire mesh wall, scoop Honey Soy up and hold her until her wings are still, then, tears welling, I place her back down on the straw, knowing her coop will now seem awfully big.

Later, in my pyjamas, I cook a cup of two-minute noodles I find at the back of the pantry. Although I'm sure there's no actual chicken in the chicken flavouring, I throw the sachet in the bin and eat them plain.

With Monty moping around at my feet, I let him drink the soupy leftovers from the cup and fill his bowl with biscuits. I grab a blanket from my room and lie down on the floorboards beside Monty in his bed, remembering how after Ben and I moved into our own rooms, if I had a nightmare, I'd go and sleep in his room. I'd had this undying faith that if we were together, nothing bad would happen.

⌐⌐

Mum taps me on the shoulder. 'Grace, honey.' I wake to the scent of a butter cake baking in the oven. She helps me to my feet and I hobble over to the kitchen, blanket slung around my neck, and observe the bench, covered in bags of flour, spilt icing sugar, half a block of butter, bowls and trays and cake mix on spoons and whisks.

The clock ticks above the fridge. It's after midnight.

'I'm sorry I was so late home. I got held up marking essays, then Mrs Brown called to tell me what happened and asked where I was.'

I prop myself up on a stool. Mum's voice cracks on certain words, but it's the most she's said to me this whole week, so I don't dare interrupt.

When the oven timer goes off, Mum slips her hands into her mitts and flips the cake out onto a cooling rack on the bench, then cuts a piece for me, a piece for herself. We eat until our stomachs are full, with the awkward hope that we will somehow be satiated.

As I crawl into bed, Mum stands at my bedroom door and wishes me sweet dreams, although I sense in her heart she no longer believes in them.

Twenty

THE PALMS

I'm sitting at the bus stop outside the bottle shop, waiting for Jake to buy us our drinks for tonight, when Dad walks up, about to enter the shop. It's only now, with him standing before me, neck red, hair thinning, that it occurs to me I can't actually remember the last time I saw him.

Each of us, awkward at the best of times, stares at the other, mouths gaping, and I'm not sure there are even words to fill a void as wide as this.

Jake steps out, weaving around Dad in the middle of the shop's doorway.

'Hi, Ray,' he says.

Dad ignores him.

'How are you?'

Still no response.

Jake grabs my shirt and drags me away from my dad, just another man on the street.

It's an hour and a half drive to the Palms, the biggest town between here and the city. It's dead during the week but comes alive on the weekend, when the rich people come down from the city to relax, wine, dine and party in their luxurious beach holiday homes.

Turning down the radio, I ring Mum from the car and leave a voice message, telling her I'm staying at Jake's. With no landline at his house, and a mother who can't stay in one place for more than five minutes, it will be near impossible for Mum to check up on me without driving around herself. She stays at school late most days now anyway, distracting herself with marking in the lead-up to her year twelves' final exams, coming home in the dark and baking or cleaning or both until she's too exhausted to climb the stairs and collapses on the couch, sleeping in till midday Saturday.

We pull into the drive-through of a greasy fast-food joint, roadside in a run-down town. Jake tells the lady on the intercom her voice is sexy, and she gasps, giggling as he orders an absurd amount of food.

'Someone's hungry,' she says.

'I can't get enough,' Jake answers.

Eyes watering, I've got my hands over my mouth trying not to laugh.

He specifically requests tight buns and lots of sauce before we drive round to the window. A woman with bleached hair, gold bangles and pink nails has written her number on his cup of Coca-Cola. We're hardly out of the drive before we burst out laughing.

Jake stuffs his face with a burger as we roar up the highway. Holding up the cup, he cracks up again, almost choking, spitting patty, breadcrumbs and rubbery cheese across the wheel and dashboard.

Where we're headed, there are expensive beach bars, fine dining restaurants, and a famed nightclub that regularly hosts the city's most happening DJs. Jake tells me he's got connections through someone he met at the warehouse who can get me in through the back door of the nightclub without an ID. I munch and swallow, my mushed-up burger thick in my chest.

Outside town, we pass a strip of burnt forest. I recognise a wagon, trays of fruit, a man in a Driza-Bone. 'Do you know someone lit that fire?' I ask. 'I saw it on the news.'

Jake shakes his head, chuckles. 'Don't be stupid, Grace. I don't watch the news.'

'One person, with a tin of petrol and one match. Look how much they destroyed.'

'Yeah, it's fucked up.'

My phone buzzes.

'That message tone is so annoying,' Jake says.

'Mia keeps texting me.'

'Don't tell her where we're going.'

'I haven't . . . *obviously*.'

'She'll lose her shit.'

I read the message. 'The hearing's next week.'

Jake focuses far ahead, hands tightening around the wheel, his knuckles white. I turn my phone off and chuck it onto the back seat.

I picture the woman in her chair before a magistrate, lawyer at her side, shirt ironed, hair slicked. I consider her, just sitting there, air in her lungs, colour in her cheeks.

The very thought of looking at her, alive and intact, makes my stomach churn. 'I don't want to go.'

Jake takes a deep breath. 'Neither do I.'

⌐

We reverse into a parking bay, by a quieter strip of beach south of the Palms, then take the blankets out of the ute's cabin and climb into the tray. We lie back against pillows under the blankets and pop open our first drinks, finishing off the last of the fries as the ocean turns deep indigo.

Nudging me, Jake points up at the sky. 'That first star, it's not really a star. It's a planet. Jupiter or Venus, depending what time of the year.'

I rest my head against his shoulder.

'My dad told me that,' he says. 'Probably the only good thing the man ever said to me.'

He offers me a toke of his joint and I stretch my mind to those planets, to the stars beyond, across the unfathomable lengths of the universe. Jake coughs and I snap back to earth in an instant, like an elastic band returning to its original shape. I realise I am awfully small in the grand scheme of things, and yet I am here, aching, and that is just as real.

I take a swig from the bottle of bourbon. 'My mum told me that some stars are already dead, but they're so far away that the light from them will still be flying through the universe for millions of years.'

Jake closes his eyes, leans his head back. He smiles.

⌐

By the time I'm sitting in the ute, the cabin lights on, trying to do my make-up in the fold-down mirror, I'm seeing double and wondering if this is really the smartest idea. Jake and I get changed in the empty car park behind the ute. In a dress and heels, found in my hand-me-down bag from Mia, I stumble under a streetlight, slurring, 'Do I look eighteen?'

'No, not really,' Jake laughs. 'But you look sexy as hell.'

'Piss off.'

'I'm serious!' He takes my hand and we make our way to the street, where Jake hails a cab to take us to the main strip in town.

I've never seen the beach promenade at night before. We surfed in the state titles when they were held here a few years ago, but at this hour, it's a whole other world.

There are guys with stubble and beanies leaning against walls smoking cigarettes. Girls with clutches in stilettos and tiny skirts stand in the club lines in tight groups. The ones who strut and show off their cleavage are permitted to skip the queue. On the kerb, several police stand in clusters, eyes surveying the crowd. Music pumps out of narrow entrances, guarded by frowning security.

'This way.' Jake grabs me by the elbow and leads me down a side alley. A couple, half-undressed, grind against each other between a garbage bin and a brick wall, so drunk they don't notice us pass.

We stop at a heavy metal door. Jake knocks twice before someone answers. A man steps out, clean-shaven, hair gelled, wearing a designer button-up, smart jeans, flash shoes and an earpiece, cord slipping down his neck under his collar. Introducing himself as Aiden, he steps aside and motions for us to come in. My heart thumping, I follow Jake into the back staffroom of the club. On a shiny aluminium bench, two men dressed like Aiden are scraping powder into lines with a credit card.

I take Jake's hand as one turns to ask if he wants a line.

'Sure.'

'What about your girl?'

'Oh, she's not *my* girl.'

'Your loss, mate.' Aiden chimes in, his eyes sliding down my legs. He smiles at me. 'So, beautiful, should I line one up?'

Jake squeezes my hand, shoots me a glance. *You don't have to.*

'I'd love one,' I say.

I watch Aiden empty enough powder from the sachet for two more lines. He hands me a tiny gold tube. 'Ladies first.'

I take it with shaking fingers.

'Relax, darling,' he whispers, leaning over me, so close his breath touches the nape of my neck.

I saw this done in a movie once and thought it was revolting. Now, like the Hollywood woman had in her red satin dress, I bend down, hold the tube to one nostril, cover the other with my finger and inhale. My eyelids flare open as Aiden runs his finger over the bench to pick up any leftovers. 'Here,' he says, holding his index finger out in front of my face. I open my mouth and he bites his lip, running his fingertip along my gums. His eyes, dark as a black hole, slide all over my body.

After Jake has had his share, rubbing the leftovers on his own gums, Aiden asks that we follow him. He leads us out the door and onto the dance floor. Bile burns the back of my throat, my mouth so numb I feel like all my teeth have fallen out.

Twenty-One

THE LUCKIEST

Electric currents flow through my body. My spine lengthens, my muscles twitch, my senses feel fine-tuned.

Beams of purple, yellow, pink and blue cut through the dark. Light slants against my black dress, my olive skin. I push past a group of girls, making for the bar. At the counter, a man makes room for me. He smiles, his eyes slipping from my red lips down over my collarbones. I realise I'm smiling back.

The barman turns to me. 'What can I get for you babe?'

'Pina colada,' I say, noticing my voice is louder than usual.

He winks. A pina colada is the only cocktail I'm sure I know the name of. It's the one from that song my parents played when they were teenagers and later sang to each year on their wedding anniversary. The song they sang when they were happy.

A hand wraps around my hip. It is Aiden, his breath hot against my cheek. Turning to face him, my lips linger just centimetres from his, close enough to taste vodka on his breath.

Minutes later, when the man behind the counter places the drink in front of me, Aiden shoots him a glance, head cocked, and the man nods, moving on to serve the next person. We walk together from the bar, Aiden stopping beside the glass wall at the front of the club, overlooking a deep purple sea. He slips an arm round my waist, pulling me tight against him. I let my lips brush his, then lean back and take a sip of my drink. 'Thank you,' I say. 'It's delicious.' I slide free from his grasp and wander off to the dance floor.

Bass pumps from speakers, so deep it alters my own rhythm. Some girls bob and sway, clinging to their drinks and purses. Others throw their hair and thrust their hips back and forth. I push closer to the girls with wilder performances, trying to copy their dance moves.

One dress strap slips off my shoulder as I dance, exposing the side of my bra. I see Aiden weaving through the crowd toward me and let the loose strap dangle, teasing, then slide it back up a moment later with a delicate brush. He takes me in his arms, holds me close, hips pressed hard against mine. Leaning in, he speaks into my ear. 'Thought I'd lost you.'

I laugh and drink the last of my cocktail, parched like never before.

He flashes a line of straight, pearl teeth, takes my hand and leads me off the dance floor. At the end of the bar, a bouncer stands at the entrance to the VIP area. The man gives Aiden a grin, unhooks the velvet rope and steps aside. Aiden ushers me into a red leather booth and slides shut the privacy screen. As he pours us each a glass of champagne, I reapply my lipstick, sliding it back into my purse as he passes me the drink. Tiny pink bubbles dance around the glass.

'Another line?' he asks, placing his drink on the table, drawing a sachet of white powder from his wallet. I nod.

I inhale with the gold tube, then pass it back, and Aiden does the same.

He rubs the leftovers on my gums and I bite his finger. A moan sounds deep in his throat as he lifts me from the couch and plants me on his lap. I move freely as if I'm in the ocean. His hands hold my waist, the gentle push and pull of the tides and suddenly it doesn't seem to matter that I'm small or thin. I reach for the two champagnes. We clink glasses, chilled, fruity bubbles bursting on our tongues.

In the dim red light, I run my hands down his chest, tugging on his ironed shirt. His breath is hot and heavy. His hands tighten around my waist and he pulls me toward him, kissing my neck, biting it. He takes my dress strap in his teeth and draws it off my shoulder, bites my collarbone.

Suddenly the screen is flung open, coloured light from the strobe bursting through. It's Jake, with one of Aiden's friends from the staffroom. Both have bloody noses. There are three security guards behind them and everyone is talking at once, shouting over the music. 'What the fuck is going on?' Aiden says. I can barely make out the words. *A fight. Two dealers. Police.*

Aiden helps me to my feet, kisses my cheek. One of the security guards leans in. 'Aiden,' he says, 'we gotta move.' Jake wipes blood from his nose, his upper lip trembling. He takes my hand, squeezes it.

We're escorted through the club back to the staffroom. Sudden white light takes away the glamour and Aiden is just a man with panicked, bloodshot eyes. A guard thrusts open the metal door and we escape into the darkness of the alleyway, Aiden and his friend still with us. In my heels, I stumble on the uneven gravel as we make our way around the building, spilling out onto a backstreet.

A cab turns the corner and Jake flags it down. Jumping into the back, he slides across to make room for me.

Standing on the bitumen beside the cab, Aiden whips out his phone, offering it to me. 'Give me your number.'

I reach out, but at the last second, I pretend to fumble, letting the phone fall. It bounces on the street. 'Oops,' I giggle and slam the car door shut.

As the cab drives off, Jake lies down across my lap, laughing. 'Grace, you're a fucking player!'

Dropped off at the car park, I take off my stilettos, my dress and slip into trackpants and a winter jumper lined with sheepskin. Inside the ute, Jake and I examine his nose beneath the cabin light. 'It's definitely not broken,' I say.

'Obviously,' he grins, picking up a fry from the dashboard, popping it in his mouth. 'I'm unbreakable.'

Outside, we climb into the tray, lie back beneath a sheet of stars and pull the blankets up to our necks. I find his hand beneath the quilt. 'What was that all about, anyway?'

He draws a deep breath. 'Don't ask questions you don't want to know the answer to.'

⌒

Someone jerks my shoulder, and I hear a rough, disgruntled voice. 'Excuse me!'

Eyes opening, I wince, a bright blue sky burns my retinas. I sit up, pull my matted hair back into a ponytail. I stink of alcohol and men's cologne.

The ranger leans over the tray, waves his hand in front of my face. 'Excuse me!'

I look down at Jake, still passed out beside me, his nose swollen, puffed eyelids bruised purple. I shake his shoulder to wake him.

With the sun high in the sky, I look around at the crowd that has gathered on the beachfront: two men in wetsuits, several women in expensive exercise gear and designer sunglasses, a couple with a dog that yaps, and a bunch of giggling children with ice-creams.

'Morning.' Jake grins at the ranger and sits up.

'Actually, it's midday.' The ranger wipes sweat from his forehead.

Jake glances across at me, snickers.

'Here,' the ranger says, stretching out his arm, two tickets in his hand.

'What are these?'

'Fines.' The ranger shakes his hand, encouraging Jake to take them.

'Oh, no thanks.'

'They're yours,' he says through clenched teeth.

'But I don't want them. Honestly, you keep them.'

I laugh as Jake pats the ranger's hand and says, with a warm smile, 'Thank you for being so thoughtful, but I'd like you to have them.'

The ranger slams the tickets down on the tray. 'Look, buddy, you're sleeping in a beachfront car park, you're parked across two bays, and you've been parked here for almost five hours in a two-hour car park without buying a ticket.'

'Okay, *buddy*.' Jake snatches the tickets.

'You're lucky I only fined you for two offences.'

Jake sighs, his smile falling off his face. 'Yeah . . . the luckiest.'

Twenty-Two

EIGHTEEN MONTHS

I'm at my locker with Jake when Mia comes striding down the corridor toward us, Toby in tow, clutching his schoolbooks to his chest. The only time I've seen Toby outside of class in the last few weeks has been in the library when I returned textbooks for one of my teachers.

'So we went round to your place Friday night, Jake,' Mia says, arms crossed. 'And yours.' She glances at me. 'Strange, you weren't at either.'

'Stalking us?' Jake smirks, his eyes still black from the blow on the weekend.

The crease in Mia's brow doesn't soften. 'I'm serious – I don't know what you're doing, but you both look sick.' Her eyes blur with tears. 'Have you been reading *any* of my messages? The hearing is *tomorrow*.'

I begin to wilt. Jake slings his arm around my waist, holding me upright.

Mia's face twists with the sour taste of silence. 'And what is this,' she snaps, grabbing my scarf. 'It looks ridiculous.' Mia yanks it off, revealing the dark lovebites Aiden gave me that stain my flesh. Jaw dropping, she looks to Jake, to his hand on my hip, and then to me.

She leans in close, so close I can almost taste the vanilla bean perfume on her collar. My face scrunches.

'Who *are* you?'

I shrug. She shakes her head, tears dripping from tired eyes, and grabs Toby. They leave us floating in their wake, Jake and me not knowing whether we will sink or swim.

'You okay?' Jake says, brushing my hair off my face.

When I don't answer, he looks over his shoulder to see what I'm staring at. Harley stands in the middle of the hall, students moving around him like water around a stone in a river. He looks at my neck, at Jake's hand. His gaze drops and, just like that, the stone comes loose from the riverbed and is carried off by the rapids.

'You're better than him,' Jake says but I can see his smile is forced.

'Whatever,' I say. 'Let's get out of here.'

Jake wraps one arm around my shoulder as we walk out of the school building. He begins telling me how a girl from the warehouse party won't stop messaging him but as the deep blue in Harley's eyes crosses my mind, I interrupt Jake mid-sentence. 'Can you please stay with me tonight?'

'Are you asking me on a date, Grace Walker?' he jokes.

When I don't laugh, Jake sighs and holds my body tight against his.

⌣

'It's okay! Grace, you're okay.' I'm in Jake's arms, panting, covered in sweat. 'It was just a nightmare.'

I bury my face in his chest, sobbing, unsure what is more terrifying – the nightmare I just woke up from, or the nightmare I've woken up to.

Mum, having heard the commotion, comes rushing in from the kitchen. The sea and sky outside are still ashen, waiting for the sun to rise, yet she is already dressed for the hearing in her finest clothes, make-up done, hair blown dry, combed into a neat ponytail, loose strands pinned back. Mum seems relieved that both Jake and I are wearing pyjamas, choosing to ignore the bruises on my neck. She doesn't tell me off for having him in my bed on a school night, or for having him in my bed at all. Maybe she finds comfort in knowing someone is lying with me in the abyss.

I look at her closely now and can see, beneath the make-up and hair spray, her eyelids sagging, her strands of grey hair and the deep creases in her forehead. I look at my mum who has aged ten years in eight weeks and suppose she is simply too tired to fight.

She half-smiles. 'Would you like something to eat?'

Jake and I follow her into the kitchen. There is a cake with raspberry jam and whipped cream spread between the sponge layers and a tray of blueberry muffins. She pushes them aside, making room so she can start breakfast. I don't have the heart to tell her I'm not hungry.

'Could I please have some cake?' Jake says.

Mum stares blankly.

'Breakfast is the most important meal of the day, Mel,' he says, forcing a smile. 'You taught me that. I think cake's worth getting up for.'

Tears run down her cheeks leaving black trails of mascara as she rounds the breakfast bar to embrace him.

I cut three pieces from the cake, ice Jake's with chocolate butter and sprinkles and serve them on colourful plastic plates I find at the back of the cupboard. We take them out onto the verandah and sit down, the three of us, on the day bed, pulling the rug over our legs. Monty wanders out and lies beneath us. I drop crumbs down the side for him to munch on as we watch the sun creep into the day.

Mum swallows her last mouthful. 'Please, Grace,' she says. 'Please come with me today.'

I imagine the woman and my cake sticks in my throat. Tears well as I shake my head.

'I can't do it on my own,' Mum sobs.

'I'm sorry, Mum,' I say, my body aching, bones brittle, cheeks wet. 'But I can't. I just *can't*.'

I take the plates and carry them inside, then hover at the door. Jake tries to get Mum up but she brushes him off. Monty climbs onto the day bed and she sits there with him, stroking his head, gazing out at the horizon, until the sun has risen well above the sea and a car pulls into the driveway.

Mia's parents climb out and make their way to the verandah. Mum doesn't look at them, keeping her eyes fixed on the horizon. Louise places her hand on Mum's shoulder. 'Mel, it's time to go. We have to be early so we can avoid the press.'

Mum nods slowly. William and Louise help her off the day bed, down the steps and across the grass to their car. I walk out onto the verandah to stand beside Jake, watching William open the front passenger door for Mum.

In the back, I spot Mia, her door closed, window up, arms crossed. Her eyes are like pink glass.

William walks round to the driver's door. Lingering a moment, he tells me it's not too late for me to change my mind, there's still room in the car. I grab Jake and walk back inside the house.

⌣

I was ten years old the first time I really felt it; anger.

We'd been to our first interstate surfing competition. When I won in a pool of three girls in my division, Mia said it was the lucky origami frog she had made for me to take away that had brought good fortune. Rummaging through my show bag, a sunburnt smile stretched from ear to ear. I had blocks of bubblegum-scented surfboard wax, a shell necklace, a key chain in the shape of a kombi van and a packet of lollies. When Ben collected his first-place prizes, he sat next to me on the grass and pulled out, among other things, a set of headphones and a limited edition pro surfer MP3 player. I didn't mind – he promised we would share them and it was a promise he upheld. On the way home, we took turns listening to the songs preloaded on the MP3 player through the headphones, each hugging our trophies on our laps.

A week later we arrived home from school to find a huge cardboard box on the verandah. Sprinting across the yard, we bounded up the steps toward it. Monty, then energetic and agile, nipped at our heels. The box was as high as my ribs and wider than my arms could reach. On the top, it read: *Mr B. Walker, 11 Walker Street, Marlow.*

Neither of us had ever received a package before, so this was surprising. We didn't know whether to open it. I wanted to, but

Ben was cautious. 'What if it's actually for Dad?' he said. 'Maybe it's just a mistake. I think we should wait till he gets home.'

Arriving back from work, Dad sat us down and explained that a big surfing label had decided to sponsor Ben. He encouraged Ben to have a look in the box.

'No.'

Dad stepped back. 'What do you mean, *no?*'

'Does Grace have one?'

'I'm sure she will sooner or later.'

'I don't want it.'

'Don't be ridiculous.' Dad tore open the box. Smells of synthetic rubber and wax flooded the room. Suddenly, Ben jumped up, pulling out a wetsuit, T-shirts in individual plastic packaging, a pair of sunnies, skating shoes, tie-dyed socks . . . It was more than anything we'd ever received for birthdays and Christmases combined!

My cheeks flushed crimson. I couldn't watch. I couldn't *not* watch. My eyes felt watery and I retreated into our bedroom before anyone saw my tears fall.

It is only now, years later, that I realise anger is nothing. Anger is hot and sticky and uncomfortable, but rage, true rage, chokes.

⌇

Mia lifts the roller door with such force I feel the walls of the shed shake. 'She admitted it! Admitted she was texting!' she screams.

I am in the shed with Jake. We've been there all day, ever since Mum left.

'You know what she got?' Mia cries, flailing her arms. 'A fine and eighteen months!'

Acid bubbles in my stomach, stings the back of my throat.

'And where were you? Not supporting your mum, or me!' She notices the bowl of chop, red film over our eyes and a dozen half-eaten blueberry muffins between us on the couch. 'Just sitting in the shed, high as fucking kites!'

There's quite a lot you can do in eighteen months. You could do half a university degree, fall in love, fall out of love, travel the world, have a child, have your heart broken, witness something majestic, realise your passion.

I wonder what she will miss out on – birthdays, Christmases, holidays. I wonder who will abandon her, who will stick by her.

But then I think of Ben, and the years she stole from him. Eighteen months is less than a heartbeat.

I lean over the couch, emptying my insides onto the floor until there is nothing left.

Twenty-Three

TEA AND TIM TAMS

I'm a twin. It has always inspired jealousy. The fact I was related to Ben Walker came second to the fact that I was a twin.

It's not until a crowd from Port Lawnam turn up that Nick Fisher starts to think that throwing a house party while his parents are away was possibly not the best idea. He tries to turn them away at the front gate, but they outnumber him ten to one, pushing past and marching up the driveway. Sitting on the front verandah, smoking a cigarette with Jake, I catch one guy's eye as he walks past and smiles with closed lips. He winks and follows his friends around the side of the house to the party.

I swallow the last of my drink, stub out my cigarette and throw the butt on the lawn, turning to Jake. 'I feel like dancing.'

He shrugs and jumps up. 'I should warn you, though, you dance like a clown.'

I punch his arm. 'Speak for yourself.'

In the backyard, a DJ has set himself up on the patio, the garden having been transformed into a dance floor. Jake takes my hand, lifts my arm and spins me underneath. We giggle at our clumsy rendition of the tango.

A girl who was in the year above us at school grinds against him from behind. She is blonde and wearing clothes that are far too small for winter – Jake's type down to a T. I motion for him to seize the opportunity. Turning, his hands drift around her waist, over her hips, groping her arse as she shakes it in her absurdly short denim skirt. In mere seconds he has gone in for the kill and is kissing her.

I move into the middle of the crowd, most of the kids too drunk to tiptoe around me as they would in the corridor at school. Closing my eyes, I surrender to the music, letting it beat my body, rattle my bones, until a hand touches my hip. I spin to greet the Port Lawnam gatecrasher from the front yard. Someone knocks me, I stumble, and the gatecrasher catches my fall. Grabbing his shirt by the collar, I draw him from the crowd, down toward a couch by the back fence. As we sit down he slips an arm around my waist.

He introduces himself as Dave and I tell him my name's Grace.

'Gracie?' he says with a grin.

'No, just Grace.'

'Well, *just Grace*, tell me something about yourself.'

'What is this? Speed dating?'

He laughs, offers me a sip of his drink, and says, 'I'm serious – it's always funny to hear what the first thing someone reveals to a stranger is.'

I shrug. 'I dunno.'

'One thing,' he persists. 'Like, what's your favourite colour? Do you have any brothers or sisters?'

'Blue, and yes, I'm a twin.'

He runs his hand through sun-bleached hair. 'Epic, I've always wanted to be a twin. Do you look the same?'

I trip over my tongue. 'Kind of, wait, no . . . I don't have . . . I dunno.'

'You don't know?'

'No, I mean we *did*, sort of. I guess.'

'But not now?'

I shake my head, throat swelling. 'I don't have any brothers or sisters,' I say.

'You're a wigger.' He laughs. 'How many drinks have you had?'

I hear Mia's voice, shrill. 'Grace?'

I look up at her, a white strobe light cutting her face. She wears dark jeans, an overcoat, her Docs and a black beanie.

'Are you all right?' she asks, surveying this stranger's hands snug around my waist. 'What are you doing? You know Harley is here.'

Dave smirks. 'Who is Harley?'

Ignoring him, I face Mia and force the words out. 'So? We were never together.'

She looks back toward the house and I see him, standing with a group only a few metres away. He is looking right at us, but when he catches my eye he turns away.

⌒

'It says here you've missed almost forty per cent of winter term.'

Arms crossed, I shrug.

'Given the circumstances, there will be some leeway, but if you continue at this rate, you'll be lucky to pass.'

I look down at the packet of Tim Tams on the table. 'You've upgraded.'

He chuckles. 'The school buys the home brand assortment I had last time. They taste like cardboard.'

'Do you have any milk?'

Mr Mitchell rocks back in his chair. 'Not up here, but there's probably some in the staffroom. Want me to pop down?'

'Sure.'

He ducks out of the room and returns a minute later with a carton of milk.

I pour myself a mug. 'Have you done this before?' I ask, biting both ends off a Tim Tam, using the chocolaty biscuit as a straw to slurp up the milk.

'Of course I have. That trick's a classic,' he teases. 'My grandfather taught me when I was younger than you!'

For the first time, I giggle in this shoebox of a room. 'Really?'

He laughs. 'No, not really. My grandfather drank scotch, not milk.'

I reach for another Tim Tam, kick my feet up on the coffee table. 'So is this all we do in these sessions? Eat biscuits?'

'Pretty much.'

'I should be a counsellor.'

Mr Mitchell slurps milk through another Tim Tam like a five-year-old. 'You can make these sessions into whatever you want.'

'I'm happy to stick with Tim Tams for now,' I say, speaking through a mouthful of chocolate mush. 'You know they make ones with white chocolate in the middle now? You should definitely get those next time.'

'You have good taste.' He notes my request on a pink post-it.

I inhale deep, sinking into the couch. 'Are my friends okay?'

Mr Mitchell's forehead creases.

'I know you've been seeing them too, Mia and Toby. Grief counselling or whatever you're calling it.'

'Why don't you ask them yourself?'

In the quadrangle, the bell rings for recess. I sit up straight and sling my bag over my shoulder. 'Can I take one with me?'

Mr Mitchell picks up the Tim Tams, offering the packet. 'Have as many as you want.'

I slip one into my pocket and take another two in my hand. 'Thanks.'

Walking out, I leave behind a mug of milk, soggy crumbs floating on the surface.

⁀

'She has a kid.' Mia leans against her locker beside me as I pile my books onto the shelf.

'Who?'

'The woman. *The* woman.'

I shut my locker door. 'How do you even know that?' I ask.

She shrugs. 'Does it matter?'

A girl shrieks, just down the hall. It's Maddie, a pretty, popular girl two years below us. As she crouches to pick up the books she's dropped all over the floor, three boys kneel to help her. One of them is Harley. I take a swig from my water bottle, pretending not to notice.

Books collected, the boys stand. Two go their separate ways, but Harley lingers. Maddie brushes her hand along his forearm, and although I'm too far away to hear what they're saying, I watch his lips move as he makes conversation, laughing and smiling.

As they walk away together, I cough on water in my throat, spraying it all over my school shirt.

Mia slaps me on the back a few times. 'You all right?'

I splutter, finally nodding as I catch my breath.

'I thought you didn't care.'

'What?' I say, my nostrils stinging, wiping the water that drips from them on my sleeve.

'Grace, I'm sorry, and you know I love you, but you can't get upset if he flirts with someone else. You're doing the exact same thing. It's not fair.'

I push shut the padlock on my locker. 'Fair?' I scoff. 'Nothing's *fair*.'

Twenty-Four

YOUNG AND TRAGIC

Jake and I climb a gum tree behind the school oval at lunch. Cockatoos sit on branches around us, squawking, flaring their yellow feather Mohawks.

'Maybe I should get a Mohawk,' Jake says.

My brow crinkles.

'Seriously, cockatoos are killing it. They're so boss.' He leans across to my branch to pass me the joint. I draw on it and feel my limbs start to sway with the tree. There is a light breeze, unusually warm for the end of August. Leaning back against the trunk, the smell of eucalyptus reminds me of dry summers in the schoolyard and Christmas beetles in the bubblers.

I pick pieces of bark. 'This probably wasn't the best idea.'

'What do you mean?' Jake says, exhaling smoke the colour of a bushfire.

My mouth feels as if it's filled with cotton. 'How are we going to get down?'

He hoots. 'You're so stoned!'

I snap off a twig and peg it at him, missing by a mile.

We hang up here talking garbage until our stomachs churn and rumble and we climb down. A metre or so off the ground I slip and land flat on the grass. Winded, I wait for Jake to pull me back up, but he doesn't. I roll onto my side to see him strolling off, already halfway across the oval.

⌒

I remember the first time I left school when I wasn't supposed to. Thirteen years old, Jake had forged a note for Ben, pretending to be Dad, giving him permission to leave early, but he said he could write a new one if I wanted to come with them. It was the last day of term and they were going to the skate park. I pictured them riding on ramps, imagined the smell of spray paint, dry bush and gravel, the sound of wheels on smooth concrete, metal trucks on metal bars. I saw myself sitting in class, a fan clicking above, my hand sore from taking notes, listening to our history teacher drone on, and I winced.

'Make up your mind, Grace,' Jake had said. 'Are you coming or not?'

I hesitated, torn between where I *could* be and where I *should* be, then gulped. 'I'm coming.'

Jake scrunched up the note he'd written for Ben and wrote one to excuse both of us, saying we were leaving early for a family holiday. He didn't write one for himself, saying it would be too suspicious if we all handed one in. I wasn't sure if his carefree attitude was brave or just idiotic.

On the way to the skate park, one of the boys suggested we go into the corner shop and get some food to take with us. With the little pocket money we had, we each bought a slushy and some gummy lollies, which we put into the cup and mixed with the frozen drink to make them tough and chewy. At the park, we skated until dark, our tongues blue from the slushies. Rebellion was fizzy like a sugar high – but like any high, it was followed by a comedown.

Walking in the front door, Ben said hi to Mum and asked her how her day was. She didn't answer – she didn't even look up. Ben and I glanced at each other, wide-eyed. We retreated to his room and played Nintendo until Dad got home.

Over the sound of our characters racing on the TV, we heard Dad's ute mount the kerb, coming to an abrupt stop in the driveway. We heard the screen door slam shut, footsteps stomping down the hall. Ben's door flew open, and without turning the TV off, Dad tore the electrical cords from their sockets, yanked the TV set and Nintendo console off the TV stand and marched out the door with it, wires trailing behind his ankles. Putting it in the shed, he locked the door and told us we were banned from playing it for the whole school holidays.

A friend of Mum's had seen us in the corner store and called her. Ben argued that we had only missed one class and that it was the *very* last class for the year, so no one did anything anyway.

'I don't care if it's one class or a hundred classes,' Mum said. 'You still skipped school.' It was the only thing she said to us that night.

Now, walking through the streets of Marlow with Jake in the middle of a school day, I watch the way people glance at us, turning away almost immediately. They hide behind their shopping trolleys, phones, newspapers, acting casual, pretending they're not witness to our truancy. Nobody wants to be the one to call Mel or Ray

Walker and inform them their daughter is acting out. No one wants
to add to my parents' stress.

'Should we?' Jake snickers, stopping outside the Marlow Hotel.

'Should we what?'

'Go inside, order beers and burgers or something, pretend we're
old and tragic.'

'Yeah,' I laugh. 'Instead of young and tragic.'

The pub is gloomy with few windows, dated wall lights,
burgundy carpet and dark wood balustrading. It smells of stale
beer-sodden coasters. We take a seat at the bar. I order a burger
and chips, Jake orders a beer and a steak with mash. The barmaid,
a friendly woman with acrylic nails and a rough Australian accent,
has a daughter who goes to our school. She knows I'm not eighteen
but takes the order out the back to the chef anyway.

Our food arrives and we hoe into it. We joke about how sophis-
ticated we are, the masters of fine dining. Beetroot juice dribbles
down my chin as we giggle, staining my skin pink.

All of a sudden, Jake goes silent. He looks down, swearing under
his breath. Slowly, I peep over my shoulder.

I drop my burger into my lap, it bounces and falls to the floor.
The barmaid grabs a dustpan and brush and rushes to clean it
up. I get off my stool to help her, picking up lettuce and sliced
cheese. By the time I turn and look around the pub again, Dad
has already left.

～

'How long have you been with your wife?'

'How do you know I have a wife?'

'You're wearing a wedding ring.'

Mr Mitchell looks down at his hand, stretches out his fingers, playing with the wedding band. 'I still find it funny how this little piece of jewellery says so much. Like someone knows a part of your story just by looking at you.'

I take a bite of a white chocolate Tim Tam, thinking of the way everyone looks at me. That colour beneath my eyes, the way my bones show, the smear of grief. Just by looking at me, anyone can tell a part of my story, and it's a part no one likes to read. I remind them that nothing lasts. I remind them no one is safe.

'So how long have you been together?'

He shifts, folds one leg over the other.

'Can't I ask questions? Why do I have to be the only one talking?' I ask. 'It's not like I'm going to tell anyone. You said nothing leaves this room.'

The kettle reaches boiling point, whistles. He swivels to turn it off and pours the water into his coffee strainer. He gives me a bashful smile. 'Thirteen years,' he says.

I watch him add three sachets of sugar and full-cream milk to his coffee.

'Does she complain about that?' I ask, pointing to the mug.

'What?' He chuckles. 'The sugar?'

I nod, trying to hide a grin.

'She loves me more than she complains.' Joking as he leans back, 'At least I hope she does.'

'Is she the only person you've ever loved?'

'No,' he says, stirring his coffee. 'I had a girlfriend before, when I was in my early twenties.'

'Did you stop loving her?'

He sips his coffee, eyes closed, pondering.

'Sorry,' I say, arms crossed, tilting back on the couch. 'I just don't really get it.'

'Get what?'

'How people can just fall *out* of love.'

Twenty-Five

A PERFORMANCE

Knocked up or just fat?

Scrawled beneath the question on the crumpled paper Jake has passed to me is a grotesque drawing of Ms King, her stomach blown severely out of proportion. He wears a devilish grin. I laugh, snort and our teacher whips her head around from the whiteboard.

She hesitates a moment, something teachers often do now before addressing my poor conduct. She walks a fine line between her responsibility to correct bad behaviour and her fear of further upsetting a girl already wrestling with loss.

'Is there something funny, Grace?'

Seeing the note in my hand, she struts down the aisle and plucks it from between my fingers. Opening it, her brow furrows, and she breathes through her nose, nostrils flaring.

'And who was the artist behind this masterpiece?'

'Uh, that would be me.' Jake smirks, raising his hand.

Again she hesitates, taking in the smears of grey beneath his eyes. Her face flushes red as she looks back at the note.

'It's an excellent likeness, don't you think?' Jake says. 'I was especially pleased with the double chin. So which is it? Knocked up or just fat?'

Ms King just stares at him then points at the door.

'Get out!' she says, her voice harsh.

His smile is dry. 'You can't fire me. I QUIT.' Jake strolls out of the classroom, laughing.

It takes a moment for any of us to react. Mia is the first to move, chasing him out into the hall, Ms King and me in tow. Looking over his shoulder, Jake sprints, bursting out the fire doors onto the quadrangle, and we follow.

'Jake, are you serious!' Mia screams as she catches up with him, slapping his chest. Ms King is already looking puffed and blotchy and has no idea who to yell at. She whispers something to herself.

'I quit! I quit! I quit!' Jake taunts, shoving Mia away from him.

'It's one month till exams. ONE MONTH! You're stupid if you leave now!'

'I don't care!' He stretches his arms wide, proclaims it to the world. 'I DON'T CARE!'

Mia falters. 'Jake, please.' She's begging, tears spilling down her cheeks.

'What does it matter? Seriously, what does *anything* matter?' he says, quiet now as he steps away from everything.

⌒

He's waiting for me on the steps when I get home, crouched, his head hanging between his knees.

'That was quite a performance,' I say, dropping my schoolbag on the verandah. I sit down next to him, kick off my sneakers and sling my arm around his shoulder.

He raises his head and gives me a wan smile. His eyelids are puffy and he looks tired. 'Ben would probably tell me I was a freaking idiot.'

'Ben always told you that.'

As he buries his face in my shoulder, Jake's body quakes, and I'm not sure if he's laughing or crying.

'It's the way they look at me, at you,' he mumbles. 'Every teacher, like they're just waiting for us to crack.'

'Screw 'em.'

Jake laughs. 'Screw them all with their high pants, ugly blouses and fat ankles!'

'We're going to end up screwing everyone.'

Jake's smile finds balance on his lips. 'I've always been good at that.'

Above, the fig tree stretches its limbs, swaying in a light offshore breeze. The jasmine wrapped around the verandah's banisters is nearing bloom. Its scent, once beautiful – redolent of spring, beach barbecues and picnics on the grass – now makes my heart ache.

I gaze around the yard. Ben doesn't exist and yet I see him everywhere. I see him on the grass we ran on as toddlers, naked beneath the sprinkler and a burnt summer sun. I see him hanging from the Hills Hoist we used to swing on, Dad having to fix its rusty arms each time we broke them. I see him in the flowerbed, stepping on the roses, picking hydrangeas to give to Mum with her breakfast in bed on Mother's Day. I see him sitting on the roof of the shed, the day he discovered he was tall enough to climb up, me standing on the ground, arms crossed, cheeks puffed, still too small. I see him in the fig tree, remnants of our cubbyhouse, branches we claimed ownership of, our names carved into the trunk. I see tiny pods hanging from twigs, baby fruit starting to grow. Figs we ate in the cubbyhouse. Figs Mum poached and served with our porridge. Figs Mum made into jam and spread across our sandwiches for school.

I pull off my socks and pad to the top of the yard, leaning against the wiry old gate, sinking my toes into the soil, wondering just how many times the soles of his feet touched this earth.

Jake wanders up beside me. 'Surf looks all right.'

I shrug.

'There's hardly anyone out,' he says. 'Won't have to deal with pricks asking how we are.'

⌁

Jake, having practically lived at our place for years, finds one of his old wetsuits in the shed. I grab mine from the rack and we suit up.

The tide's low, rocks exposed. We carry fat boards for the tiny waves curling around the point. Seagulls flock to the sand, fighting over leftover chips someone has thrown. There are piles of seaweed on the shoreline, hauled onto the beach by an east swell. The scent of rotting seagrass makes our noses twitch, and as we wade through the thick tides, weed gathers in my leg-rope, pulling like an anchor dragging behind a boat. By the time we're in the line-up, the water is clear and we uncoil the seaweed from our ropes. Jake throws a clump at me, scratching my face.

He laughs and laughs and laughs until each of us realises we've been waiting for a voice to defend me.

Jake turns to face the horizon; I watch him shudder in his black skin.

Twenty-Six

HEY, GRACIE

I wake in the night's darkest hour, throat dry and lips cracked.

I wander in socks over the floorboards, eyes adjusting to the shadows, and pour myself a glass of water in the kitchen. As I sip, words cascade down the stairs from Mum's room.

'Dear God, *please* . . . teach my baby girl to stand on her own.' Faint sobs interrupt her prayers. '*Please* . . . teach me to live in a world without sunshine.'

Leaving the glass on the bench, I stumble out the front door, tripping down the steps, landing in a heap on wet earth. Damp seeps through my pyjamas and I shiver, my heart heavy and swollen. I don't want it, I don't want any of it. Tears drizzle down my cheeks.

And then I see it, beneath a silver moon, my surfboard left on the grass after today's surf. Stripping naked in the yard, I yank my wetsuit off the line and wriggle into it. It is still cold and wet, but I am numb, immune to winter's bite. I pick up my board, drag my fingernails through wax, crosshatching lines for grip. Running down the grassy hill, my moon shadow chases after me.

Blinded by black tears, I cut my feet on clumps of dried seaweed, broken shells and sticks of sea wood, the sand like grains of ice. My feet are as heavy as my breath. At the water's edge, whiffs of fish and seagrass lift from silver foam.

It's not until I take my first step, my toes sinking in wet sand, a gentle wave washing over my feet, that I become aware of where I am and what I am doing. I feel the water suck out, drain away from my skin, and know another wave is approaching. I hear it, smell it. Leaping forward as it laps the shore, I land on wax and glide through the water, stroking, arms digging deep. I hear the spill of a second white wash and push down. I'm a moment too late and am slapped in the face. Turbulence whips me from side to side, spits me through the back of the wave. Coughing and spluttering, I wipe hair from my face.

As I paddle, I slowly discover the way the tides sway beneath me, gentle pushes and pulls so subtle the movement goes unnoticed during the day. As a third wave approaches, I lean down on my board, driving it beneath the foam, this time too early, and I pop back up in the thick of the cloud. Spun and yanked before ripping through the wave's skin, I fight for breath.

A fourth wave tumbles before me. This time, I stop paddling, lie still on my board and listen. The sound of this surge is as individual as my own voice is to me, the way it gasps, spits, laughs and cries. As it rolls closer, I grip my rails, and when it whispers, I push down. Swooping beneath the turbulence, I fly up and burst to the surface like a bird into the night sky.

When I reach the line-up, stars rest on a black silk sea.

With the horizon impossible to distinguish, I surrender and close my eyes. Palms on the surface, I feel ocean currents moving like blood through veins, drawn by the moon in all its silver glory. I feel the rise and fall of my board with the rise and fall of tides. Pulses of swell have the rhythm of a heartbeat. I hear the ocean breathing.

The water pulls beneath me, and a wave climbs out of the depths. With my eyes still closed, I read the water's surface like braille, paddling to its wide shoulder, stroking over the edge.

I slide to my feet as it grows beneath me, the drop unexpectedly steep. Opening my eyes as I pull into a bottom turn, I ride back up to see a thousand stars, sparkling crystals on the wave's dark face. Again, I underestimate its build; the lip curls, flips my board and I plunge into the water. I surface with a smile that splits cracked lips. Tasting blood, caught on this high, I forget momentarily just how much my bones ache.

Returning to the line-up, skin tingling, moonlight dancing on the water, I notice a figure, a hundred metres away, sitting on a surfboard. My arms hang limp in the water.

The figure's silhouette is broad, strapping. His head turns and a wash of foam knocks me clean off my board. As I climb back on, stars fall from the sky. My arms shake, fingertips tingle, and after several heaved breaths I paddle toward him.

I sit up on my board, only metres away, staring at the ray of moonlight slanted against his cheek. Even at this hour, swathed in darkness, his smile beams like the sun.

'Hey, Gracie.'

I'm sinking, my limbs swaying. There's a wild drumming in my ears.

'Cat got your tongue?' he says.

I can't bear to look at him. I can't tear my eyes away.

'It's okay,' he says.

Okay? I almost topple off my board again in indignation.

His laugh lands on the water the way it always has. 'It's okay, I'm here.'

'No. No.' I shake my head. 'This isn't real.'

'I'm here.'

'No, you're not.' Tears pour down my cheeks.

'I'm here, Gracie.'

'Stop saying that!'

'Trust me.'

'STOP SAYING THAT!'

I'm hysterical now, wild sobs shaking my body. A dark mountain of water looms and I paddle to meet it. Jumping to my feet, I swoop down the face, laying into a turn, sweeping around the wave's belly, shooting up to carve around its shoulder. But again, my surfboard rail bites and I come unstuck, falling off, plunging into the sea. I am thrashed beneath the surface, my body thrown up and down, back and forth by the rush of water.

When I surface, I climb back onto my board, feeling as if the beating has scoured my mind, my thoughts clearer now, more rational.

Calm down, he's not real.

I take two deep breaths.

Maybe I just want him here so badly, my imagination got the better of me.

Paddling toward shore, I suddenly remember the heaviness of my feet as I walk on land, the oppressive weight of my head on my shoulders, my lungs in my chest. Out here, I'm not straining to breathe. There's a kind of ease in the way I move.

A wave approaches, ready to take me back to shore. At the last moment, I duck-dive under it and head back out toward the horizon.

Back in the line-up, alone, I rest my hands on smooth silk and close my eyes. For a moment I wonder if I've missed my chance – the chance to be with him again – before I remind myself it wasn't real. He wasn't real. Ben doesn't exist.

'No offence, but that wave was shithouse.' He laughs.

'Piss off,' I say, jaw clenched.

'No.'

'I want you to piss off!' I say again, as if I can reason with my imagination.

'Well, I'm here whether you like it or not. I'm here for you, Gracie.'

'You're not.' Blood simmers and I begin to shout. 'You're not here! You left me! You left me all by myself!'

He weeps, a silver stream on his cheeks. 'I'm sorry, I'm *so* sorry, but I'm here now. I won't leave you again.'

'This is fucked,' I mumble to myself. 'I've lost it. *Proper* lost it.'

He tells me he loves me.

'How can you, Ben? You're dead.'

I swivel as the next wave forms, paddle over the shoulder and ride it all the way to the shore on my belly, washing onto the sand like a beached sea creature with no idea how to get home.

Twenty-Seven

FAR, FAR AWAY

Mr Woodlow isn't teaching anything new this week. With exams only three weeks away, we're spending our lessons revising coursework and fine-tuning our essays. Mia takes shallow breaths and I soon understand I've forgotten to put deodorant on. I'm also not wearing socks. I couldn't find any clean ones, so now my feet are sweating in my sneakers. I wonder what smells worse.

Fans click overhead, pens scribble on paper. Mr Woodlow calls me up to his desk and I bring with me my tattered notebook. He pulls a chair over for me to sit on and clears his papers and laptop to one side of the table. Sitting down beside him, I wonder if he can smell me too.

'Okay,' he says, his voice hushed so he doesn't disturb the rest of the class. 'What have we got to work with?'

I put my notebook down on the desk and flick through. The dates written at the top of each page skip days. Some skip three or

four in a row. I stop on today's page, revealing a few loose notes
and a paragraph scrawled in purple texta.

He sighs. 'Well, it's a start.'

I think about how, before all this, I'd wanted to score ninety
on my HSC, because my lucky number is nine and there are
lots of university courses you can pick with that score. I didn't
know which course I wanted, but I figured it would be nice
to at least have a choice. Mum said the HSC wasn't the be all
and end all. She said there are always other ways to get what
you want.

Mr Woodlow turns to a fresh page and begins to map out an
essay plan. I watch his pen draw and write and circle but soon his
words are just ink on paper.

I'm sinking into a dark sea. *Hey, Gracie.* I think of Ben's silhouette, the moon resting on his cheek.

Mr Woodlow reaches under the sea and pulls me to the surface.
'Grace, I'm trying to help you, but you need to concentrate.'

He lets go and I sink straight back down. I think of Ben,
how he said he was there for me, out in the water, and consider
what Mum told me; how there are always other ways to get what
you want.

Perhaps this is how I get him back.

I'm waiting for Jake on the kerb out the front of school at recess
when Mia meanders along the path and sits down beside me.

'Please don't go,' she says softly. Her skin ashen with dark marks
beneath tired, sinking eyes. 'I've eaten recess by myself every day
this week.'

'What do you mean? Where's Toby?'

'In the library, studying. The only time he comes out is to go to class.'

A magpie eating crumbs off the road narrowly misses getting hit by a car.

'So he goes to the toilet at his desk?'

Mia crosses her arms. 'Don't joke. His mum was talking to Dad the other day, and she said Toby studied for eleven hours straight on the weekend. That's not normal.'

Jake pulls to the kerb, winds down the passenger window. 'Ya coming?'

I stand, dust dirt off my school skirt and sling my bag over my shoulder.

Mia tugs on my sleeve. *'Please.'*

'You can come with us,' I suggest as I open the door and climb in.

'Yeah,' Jake laughs. 'There's room. Grace won't mind sitting on the gearstick.'

Mia rolls her eyes, her feet planted firmly on the ground. 'Disgusting,' she mumbles and we drive off, leaving her to choke on black exhaust, alone.

⌒

I wake up on a bed of milk crates between a grimy wall and a garbage bin, cradling a kebab, plastic digging into my skin. Sitting up, I wipe dry, crusty drool off my chin.

Jake is sitting with his knees tucked up, arms wrapped around them, his back to my crate bed. His head hangs down between his knees and I lift it by the hair to make sure his lips aren't blue, to make sure he's alive.

My tongue is cardboard, my teeth are chalk and I've got a cracking headache. With Jake, Fridays dissolve into Sundays and soon I can't remember who held me tighter, whose hands got closer to my underwear or which name belonged to which guy. I look around the dank alleyway. *Where are we?*

I unzip my fly and take a peek to make sure I've still got underwear on.

'Don't worry,' Jake says. 'We were together the whole night.' He spies my kebab. 'Can I have a bite of that?'

'Are you serious?'

He smiles, reaching across and stealing a mouthful of cold meat wrapped in stale, flaky bread.

'Wow,' I say, eyes wandering around the grimy walls. We're surrounded by bags of trash, graffiti and broken glass. I wonder how many rats slept with us. 'Low point.'

He shrugs, smirks. 'Well, what do you expect?'

Glancing at my watch, I swear. 'Shit. I'm meant to be in class in twenty minutes.'

Jake laughs. 'Good luck with that.'

We find our way back to the car eventually and drive home, even though I tell Jake he shouldn't.

⌒

Monty licks dirt off our legs as we climb the three steps onto the verandah. In the shower, we stand in our clothes, slowly peeling off wet fabric, shedding skin. In my room I charge my phone. I don't know if I'm relieved or concerned that there are no missed calls; that Mum didn't even register I wasn't here last night.

We smother crackers with peanut butter and sink into the couch, neither one of us bothering to turn on the TV. Jake lights a cigarette and I don't bother to remind him he's not allowed to smoke in the house. I just close my eyes and doze off, barely breathing.

⌐

A slap to the cheek – my eyelids burst open and I gasp.

Mia stands over me, hands gripping my shoulders, shaking, jolting. 'Wake up!'

I feel my eyes roll back in their sockets. My neck flops, my head sags. She holds me upright, slaps me again.

'I'm awake, I'm awake,' I mutter, rubbing my eyes, peanut butter stuck to the walls of my mouth. The light is pink; it's late afternoon.

'Take a look at this.' Mia shoves her phone in my face. It's a picture, posted last night, of Jake and me sitting in a gutter with two boys, slices of pepperoni pizza and kebabs in our hands, beer cans littering the street, vomit pooled at my feet. I vaguely recognise the face of one boy and scratch my brain trying to recall the other.

Posted 3.27 a.m.

'Is this a joke?' Mia says as Jake reaches across me to take a look.

'Legends,' he says. 'They shouted us pizza!'

She slides the phone into her pocket and crouches, putting both hands on my knees.

Her words are hushed. 'Come home.'

'I *am* home,' I tell her.

Shaking her head, she stands up. 'You are so far from it.'

⌐

I don't know if I'll ever get used to the silence, the heaviness
between a wave breaking and a gust of wind, the void where his
voice should be.

Alone in the house, I crank the stereo and turn it full volume.
I rummage through the fridge and pantry, pulling out food that
has been here since Sasha and Kate left. Piling a bag of frozen
peas, carrots and corn and half a litre of clumpy orange juice into
the blender, I blitz it at the highest setting. I flick the TV on as
I make some toast but it burns, setting the smoke alarm off. I'm
up on the breakfast bar, flapping a tea towel at the ceiling, when
I hear someone call my name.

'Grace!'

I turn to see Harley through the flyscreen. The smoke alarm
stops beeping, I flick off the blender and climb down to let him in.

'This is for you,' Harley says, holding a tray of food. There is
a dish of olives, some bread and a bowl of a creamy coloured soup
topped with a swirl of olive oil and a sprinkling of cumin. Nestled
between the dishes is a small bunch of daisies, tied together with a
blue ribbon. His hands shake, and I notice the tan leather bracelet
around his wrist, the one I used to think was so trendy. I see it
now for what it really is, a strip of hide, dead skin.

Harley edges forward. A stitch knots in my abdomen. I take
half a step back.

'Tell Nila thank you, but I think we've had enough.'

His body shrinks, ever so slightly. 'I'm sorry.'

'Are you?' I say.

As Harley steps away, I watch a brilliant blue flare burn out,
dashing any hope of rescue.

Twenty-Eight

ANYTHING

On clear nights, a stream of moonlight pours through my window, plating my body in silver. This bedroom was the one thing that truly inspired jealousy in Ben. His window overlooks the yard, out toward the street – our veggie patch, Mum's flowerbed. Mine overlooks our fig tree, wild kangaroo paw and bottlebrush, our rickety fence and the smooth, sloping grassy hill. It faces the sea – her majestic blue body.

Dad and two friends built a dividing wall when we were ten, splitting our room in two. We played scissors paper rock to see who would get the ocean-facing room. I won the first round and Ben said *best of three*. When I won the second round, I remember feeling more surprised than joyful that I was the lucky one.

Sitting in our rooms when we were grounded, we'd play knocking games, communicating through code rhythms of knuckles on plaster. When we each received stereos for Christmas at thirteen, we'd turn our music up and up, trying to drown out the sound of the other until it was so loud the wall between us vibrated. Often, Ben hid in my cupboard, jumping out to scare me, frightening me so badly I would burst into tears and he'd feel truly sorry – until he did it again.

And then there were the times he would come into my room and we'd sit on my bed, gazing out for hours, mesmerised by the sea. I'd open my window and we'd listen, enthralled by the conversation between the ocean and the earth.

Now, I wake on clear nights to the cold tide of moonlight, no knuckles on plaster behind the wall, no heart beating between ribs. I lie, paralysed, in a soundless dream, one that I desperately want to wake from.

Tonight, though, the early October air is warm enough for me to open my window before I go to sleep. When I wake in the night, I hear breakers singing, and though I shiver, I can almost hear him, too, in the rhythm of the waves knocking on the shore. I start to wonder – is *something* better than nothing? Is a figment of the imagination a cruel trick, or a gift?

Climbing out of bed, goosebumps prickle my bony back. Hunched, blind, I sift through my drawers until I find a bikini and creep through the house, out into the yard. As I draw the side door of the shed open, it creaks, and I pause, checking Mum's window. Inside, I shake sand off my wetsuit, scramble into it in the shadows, fumble, stub my toe, lower my board off the rack and emerge, draped in moonlight.

My moon shadow, a stranger, stalks me as I tread down the hill.

I leave footprints in the wet grass; sand burns my toes like dry ice. Arriving at the water's edge, air slices my lungs. Lunging into the shore break, water cleanses my skin. Like last time, I'm knocked off my board. After the third wave, I remember what it is to surrender. Digging deep, I close my eyes.

I listen to the tumble of each white wash, feel the pull of tides, the bubble of undercurrents, taste the salt and smell the foam. I imagine all the creatures alive beneath the surface. I imagine all the creatures that have lived and died in this blue body.

The wash becomes stronger. I'm ripped and tossed in the thick turbulence. I hear waves crunching, chewing, and as I duck-dive, my board scrapes the ground, fins slicing the sandbank.

I'm close to the line-up, but not close enough, as I hear a wild roar. Panting, thrashing my arms in the water, I race out to sea. Tides beneath me suck out, drawing water off the shallow bank, and I know something big is approaching. It gurgles as it stands. I throw my weight down, pushing as deep as I possibly can, but it's not enough. Its lip cracks on my back, its hands ripping me off my board, jerking my body in all directions. Whips of sand scratch my face. Water shoots up my nose.

Remembering, again, all those years of training, I curl into a ball, sink under the cloud of turbulence, touch the sandbank, plant my feet and jump up, shooting through the back of the wave. I pull on my leg-rope and climb onto my board, breathless, with sand in my ears, nostrils, mouth, all burning.

I stroke into the line-up, weak with jelly limbs, sit up on my board and wipe matted hair from my skin. My feet dangle from my board, swaying with the gentle currents. Tonight a crescent moon rests on dark water.

I sit up on my board and look around but Ben's not here. The sky and sea blur together. I rest my palms on chilled black milk, breathe in, but my lungs don't seem to expand. It's as if someone has carved out my insides, and even if I were to drink the entire ocean, it would not be enough to fill me up.

I drift in dead water, alone, warm tears on my cheeks. Maybe I missed my chance. Maybe it was my imagination.

'Pretty fat out here. Some fun ones on the inside, though. They're really jacking up.'

Breath catches in my throat. I twist and there he is, among floating stars, perched on his board.

'Told you I'd be here.'

Moonlight paints silver leaf on his cheek, neck and shoulder. I splash water. It sprays his chest. He splashes me back. Water sprays *my* chest.

'Impossible,' I whisper.

'I hate to say I told you so, but—'

'Impossible.'

'Give it up, Gracie. I'm here.'

Words roll off his tongue, landing on the water the way they always have. Impossible, and yet they do.

Ben reaches out his hand. 'I'll prove it.'

I kick back, out of reach. If my imagination has brought him here, pulled him up from the bottom of the ocean, I won't let my skin break the spell. Anything is better than nothing.

'You've really fucked everyone over,' I say at last.

'What? By dying?' His laugh is a clap of thunder, a crescendo in the sky.

My body is neither hot nor cold and yet my teeth chatter. Water begins to suck as a wave climbs out of icy depths. I lie down, closing my eyes to paddle into position. The wave picks me up, carries me on its shoulder. I glide to my feet, swoop, fly, hovering for a moment before swooping once more. I open my eyes to see streaks of molten silver twisting with black liquid and ride until the wave spikes on the sharp sandbank. I catch a rail and am hurled from my board into the tide. Standing up, my knees buckle, and I tug on my leg-rope. Although I'm sure I should head toward land, I leap back onto my board, stroking the sea, pulling back to him.

'You know,' he says, as I reach him again, 'this whole night surfing business, I don't know whether you're brave or just stupid.'

Floating in a ray of moonlight, I shrug.

'I don't want you to get hurt,' he says.

Hurt? The very idea makes me laugh out loud.

'I'm serious,' he says, lips slanted. 'I'm worried about you . . . you *and* Jake. You're going to kill yourselves.'

'You can't lecture me.' My voice cracks. 'You're dead.'

'Gracie.'

I sit, legs swaying, eyes fixed on his, and for the first time the silence between us is not quite as heavy.

'How does it feel, being dead?' I ask.

He swallows hard, shifts his weight on his board.

'Come on. If you're really here, a ghost or whatever, tell me what it's like.'

'It's everything and nothing.' Ben's smile is weak, his lips curling the way they used to when he didn't want to hurt my feelings. 'It's like the absent moment between night and day.'

Twenty-Nine

HIDE AND SEEK

Sitting in biology, I spread my books, pencils and loose study sheets out over both tables so the seat beside me doesn't seem quite so empty. I try to concentrate on my notes but my eyes keep sliding in and out of focus and I see double. I wonder if people saw double when Ben was alive.

You don't have to look the same to be two parts of the same thing.

Someone in the front row burps and several girls giggle. Pencils scrape against rulers, ballpoints stain paper, and when I hold my breath, I can almost hear a boy biting his fingernails.

In the muggy air, my eyelids sag until my head tumbles down my chest and I wake with a quick, shallow breath. Sweat has gathered at the nape of my neck and I loop my hair up into a ponytail. It's like dry seaweed, crispy with salt from last night's surf – my third surf with Ben this week.

Anything is better than nothing.

Above the whiteboard, a clock ticks. I cover my ears with my hands, muffling the seconds, as I close my eyes and imagine being back there with him, sinking into a secret place where time does not exist.

Mum arrives home with takeaway Chinese as the blue sky fades outside. 'I got short soup and honey soy chicken, want some?'

I nod and help her plate up the food in sticky silence.

After dinner, I disappear into the shadows, strip in my room and climb into bed with my laptop, sliding beneath sheets that haven't been washed in weeks. Flashing advertisements surround most of the blog posts. *Lose Six Kilos in Ten Days!*

The first woman writes about how we stay around for seven days after we die. She says that some people stay longer if they have unfinished business, if they're connected to someone who's still alive. *It means that they miss you, or that they're trying to tell you something.*

Another man shares his experience of seeing his other half. *Sometimes, when someone dies unexpectedly, they can visit us.*

I'm halfway through the notes when I choke on mike69's post. *This page is a load of ●●●t. When you die, you're dead. Finito!*

⌒

Mr Mitchell corners me in the school corridor.

'I've got Tim Tams.'

'I'm not hungry,' I say.

'They're a new flavour, caramel.'

I don't budge.

'And chocolate milk,' he persists. 'Double whammy.'

I sigh, roll my eyes. '*Fine.*'

In his room, Mr Mitchell gently closes the door behind him, takes a seat and tilts back with an earnest smile. 'Please, sit.'

'They've changed the couch.'

'Nice observation,' he says.

The new couch smells of a vacuumed showroom, the fabric bright and synthetic.

His smile slackens. 'I've had three different teachers inform me you've fallen asleep in their classes.'

I shrug and shift my weight.

'Weight loss, dark circles beneath your eyes . . .'

'Nice observations,' I say.

'You know, there are a number of ways we can address insomnia. There are exercises, strategies, even medications.'

Reaching across the coffee table, I pour chocolate milk from the carton into a mug, rip open the packet of Tim Tams and sit back, slouching as I bite both ends off a biscuit. Fudge softens in my mouth; caramel coats my tongue. I slosh milk between my cheeks and biscuit becomes gooey chocolate. Swallowing, I lick my lips, wipe them on my sleeve. 'Do you believe in ghosts?'

Mr Mitchell reaches down for a Tim Tam, bites into it and rocks back on his chair, munching on my question.

'Like do you think clairvoyants are legit?' I ask. 'Or are they just hallucinating?'

'Well,' he says at last, 'I have never seen a ghost.' Sipping chocolate milk, gazing out the window, he continues, 'But that doesn't mean they don't exist.'

The bell sounds for the end of the period and I shiver. 'Can I stay a little longer, please?'

He nods and I take another biscuit.

'Ghosts always look so scary in cartoons, but what if they're not? What if they're good?'

'Like I said, I've never seen one.' Mr Mitchell swirls his Tim Tam around in his mug. Crumbs float on a rich cocoa sea. 'But from a psychologist's point of view, I'd say seeing a loved one, for example, could help someone to work through their grief.'

My skin is hot; I loosen my collar and tuck my hair into a bun. 'So it's possible . . . It wouldn't mean you're insane.'

'Wow,' he chuckles. 'You're throwing out the hard ones this morning.'

I smirk. 'You're the one who made me come in here.'

'Everyone has their own truth, Grace, and that means illusion and reality are sometimes impossible to distinguish.'

I think of the horizon at midnight, the sky and sea blurring together.

Mr Mitchell folds one leg over the other. 'Can I ask why you're so interested?'

Planting my mug on the table, I grab my schoolbag and make for the door, turning at the last moment. 'You should ask for your old couch back. This one's shit.'

～

There's a line in the girls' bathroom. Several year tens are clustered in front of the mirrors with tubes of lip gloss and mascara brushes. I dive into the depths of my brain for the name of the blonde standing in front of me but find nothing. We've had class together since kindergarten.

Nearing the front of the queue, the nameless girl turns and sees me. 'Hey, Grace,' she says, waiting for a hand dryer to turn off before continuing. 'How are you?'

Leaning against cool tiles, sticky with hairspray, I realise I've reached *that* point – the point where people are no longer afraid to ask me how I am and aren't going to kick themselves for asking when they realise what they've just done.

'Fine,' I say. We're at the front of the line now. As a girl flushes and walks out of a cubicle, I motion toward it. 'That one's free.'

'Oh, uh, thanks.'

Another door opens and I rush in, sitting down, slumping on the toilet seat, fully clothed. There are dirty shoe marks and ripped toilet paper littering the tiles and a sanitary bin filled to the lid. I rummage through my bag for my phone and Jake picks up on the third ring.

'Hey,' he says, his voice croaky, as if he has only just woken up. I check my watch – 11.42 a.m. – and assume he probably has.

'Can you please come and get me?'

<hr>

The night is so still the sea has turned to glass. As I dip my toes in the water, a wave kisses my ankles. I close my eyes as I wade through time and my mind starts to drift with the tides. During the day, we see ourselves relative to others. We know our place. But out here, cloaked in shadows, my place in the universe is impossible to define. I am stardust, and yet I breathe.

He's waiting for me out in the line-up.

'Hey, Gracie.'

I sit up on my board, the swell rocking my body like a baby in a cradle, stars freckling my skin. Ben asks me about my day, and even though I'm sure he already knows, I tell him about Mr Mitchell and the new flavour of Tim Tams. I tell him about my ghost research.

'Well,' he laughs. 'Are you a sceptic or a believer?'

I shrug. 'Does it matter?'

Basking in moonlight, he smiles. 'I'm a part of you.' Then he asks me where I was last night.

I tell him I was at Jake's house, and that I let Mum know – that much is true. Then I tell him how we watched a thriller and ate a pizza we found in Jake's freezer, still in its box. 'The use-by date was three years ago,' I laugh, 'but we figured it would be fine, being frozen. Plus that shit has so many preservatives . . .'

'I don't believe you.'

We rise on a swell and sink back down. I look back to shore, the whole town still, as if under a spell.

'Jake hates thrillers,' Ben says, 'and his DVD player is broken.'

I smirk, considering how pointless it is telling lies to Ben, whether he's a figment of my imagination or an all-knowing ghost.

In truth, I was high last night before I even got to Jake's house. I spent most of the evening wedged on the couch between two guys with greasy hair, stubble and ripped jeans – guys I'd met at some point at a house party or in a garage or alleyway.

Jake didn't know where his mum was, so we sat in his lounge room with the curtains drawn, dropping ash everywhere and spilling beer on the floor, clouds of green smoke filling the hours. When we heard scratching coming from the ceiling, Jake found a flashlight and with a wicked grin suggested we investigate.

The walls of the attic were like stale bread, flaking and covered in mould. There probably hadn't been anyone up there since the house was built. Where I touched wood, I left handprints in the dust. After a few minutes, we found the trespassers – a mother possum with raised hackles, backed into a corner, guarding her two babies. 'Aw,' Jake giggled with bloodshot eyes, crawling toward them. 'Come here, poss, poss.'

She hissed and growled, trying to ward him off.

Suddenly, we heard a crack, a split, and Jake and his torch disappeared through plaster. He landed with a thud so heavy it shook the house, and as my hands clenched around a wooden beam, I held my breath.

Moments later, laughter ripped through the house. 'I'M ALIVE,' he shouted.

I heard him crawl across the floorboards, calling for us to jump down through the hole. Falling, I landed in a pool of hysterics. Jake shone the torch on his face.

'I'm naming the possum Hercules!' he declared. 'Grace, you get to name the kids.'

Between bouts of laughter, I managed two names. 'Connie and Button.'

Ben looks across the water at me, his face twisting, teasing. 'Button? What kind of a name is Button!'

'It's cute!' I argue, splashing water at him.

As ripples fade, he looks at me seriously. 'You're scaring me, you know.'

'Scaring *you*? Ben, you're dead. Shouldn't I be the one who's scared?'

'But you're not scared – you're not scared of anything. Maybe that's the problem.'

'Stop it,' I say, glaring.

'Stop what?'

'Stop talking to me like this.'

'*Fine*,' he says, and asks me what else is new, as if he's just been away on holiday and is checking in on the latest gossip.

I try to think of my life on land, of the heaviness, the slog. It's like trying to recall a dream, summoning only dribs and drabs, but he listens with a keen ear as I jump from one story to another, skipping foggy details, unable to explain the in-between.

I remember Mia once telling me a story about a woman with a disorder that made her switch between two personalities. She would talk and act like a five-year-old child, even responding to a different name, until she switched back to her adult self. As her illness worsened, she spent more and more time as the little girl. I wondered at the time what it would be like to be her. I wondered what it was like when the surreal became her reality.

I feel the currents tugging on my ankles and clench my hands, grabbing fistfuls of sea and salt, for a moment believing that if I grip the ocean tight enough, I'll stop the tides from pulling me to shore.

I press my eyes hard against his skin, the slant of his jaw, the scar at his hairline where Jake tackled him and he split his head open on a stick.

I look at Ben's lips and wonder if Mia's memory is failing her. I wonder if she wakes in the middle of the night in a panic because she's forgotten the shape of his nose, or how his arms felt around her.

My heart pulses in my throat. What if I really am insane? When I start to heal, will these delusions fade away? Will I too start to forget the way his tongue bends around certain letters, his laugh?

I scrutinise every inch of his torso and broad shoulders, his cowlick, the curve of his eyebrow and the position of the mole above his collarbone, checking to see that his earlobes are the free hanging kind that cut up slightly like mine and Mum's, not the ones that attach completely to the jaw like Dad's. I pocket every detail, locking them away.

Ben cocks his head to one side with a crooked smile and eyes like the sun, as if his head never flew through a windscreen, as if this night has become day and my life on shore is nothing but a nightmare.

'I just don't understand,' I say at last, stars falling silently around me.

'What?'

'How you're here, how I can see you.'

'Do you remember when we used to play hide and seek with everyone when we were younger?' he asks. 'How we'd always find each other first, how we always knew where the other was hiding when no one else could?'

I nod, a lump wedged in my throat.

'Well, I think it's like that.'

Thirty

THE PADDLE

This night is cool for October. A northerly breeze earlier in the week has brought in undercurrents, chilly like dark blood.

'Your first exam is in five hours . . .' Ben says.

'I know,' I say, rolling my eyes. 'I'm not *stupid*.'

He scoffs. 'You haven't done an hour's study. Probably not the smartest decision.'

Kicking, I pivot my board; lie flat on my belly and stroke toward an oncoming wave. As I paddle over the lip, I hear him call out, 'Good luck!'

'Luck?' I say under my breath, rising to my feet, swooping down the face.

I don't believe in luck.

⌣

In the kitchen, Monty licks salt crystals off my calves. Mum rushes down the stairs in a floral-patterned dress and stands on the spotted gum floorboards wriggling her legs into a pair of stockings.

'Pop some toast into the toaster, please, love.'

I cut two slices of Turkish and put them in to toast before hopping up to sit on the bench, a bowl of cereal in my lap. The milk tastes a little sour, so I try to scoop flakes of wheat bran up off the surface without any liquid.

'Your hair's wet,' she points out. 'Did you go swimming?'

'Nah, just showered.'

'Didn't hear the shower.' She pauses for a moment, then pulls her hair into a ponytail, shrugging off my comment, and scuttles to the front door to fetch her shoes. 'How'd you sleep? Nervous?'

'Toast popped,' I say and watch her hurry back to grab her breakfast. She smears butter across the bread, collects her stack of books from the end of the bench and dashes toward the door, then halts and spins, running up to me and planting a kiss on my cheek.

'Good luck, honey. Sorry I can't drop you, I'm already so late!'

I look down at my cereal. The bland flakes are now soggy and sinking in a sour pond. I hear Mum's old Range Rover pull out of the driveway, the clutch grinding, and just like that, my mum is gone.

Hopping off the kitchen bench, I pour my breakfast down the drain and wonder how different this morning might have been.

⌒

They've converted the school assembly hall into a huge exam room, perfect lines of desks and chairs standing to attention. We wait by the doors at the back of the hall while our teachers lay exam papers on each of the desks. All around me, students cling to their study notes, eyes running back and forth over their essays and quotes, scratching words into the bone walls of their skulls. One girl whispers to another, 'I drank four coffees last night, didn't get to sleep till 3 a.m.!'

Several students are gathered around paper sheets tacked to the wall, checking their seat numbers. I weave my way through the cluster to check mine, scrolling down through the list to W. The paper is crumpled and has fingerprint stains on the corners and suddenly I notice they're the same sheets that were tacked to this wall for our trial exams several months ago. Nobody has bothered to print new ones. His name is there in bold above my own – Ben Walker, row 9, seat 11.

'Ouch!' a girl whines as I push past, as I step on a guy's foot, as I charge into someone else's shoulder.

'Grace!' Harley grabs my sleeve, pulls me close.

I slap his chest, shoving, grunting, 'Get off me!' I make for the hallway.

My laces have come undone and strands of hair fall in my face as I bash and kick on Mr Mitchell's door. He opens it and immediately steps aside. 'Come in, come in.'

I collapse on his ugly couch, my body folding in two, head dropping between my knees. Hot tears drip onto the carpet. 'Please, don't make me, tell them I can't sit it, tell them I can't, I can't do it.'

'Grace . . .'

'No. No. I can't. Please don't make me, please!'

He waits as I sob, my chest heaving, shoulders shaking. He waits until there is nothing left inside me.

'I won't make you do anything.'

He waits until I sit myself up, elbows on knees, palms cupping my wet face.

'Can I get you something?'

Shaking my head, I watch him sink back in his chair as he acknowledges that Tim Tams and milk won't even touch the sides of this ache, not today. I wrap my arms around my body the way I used to when I was small and my stomach hurt. Above, the ceiling seems to press down. 'Can we please open a window?' I ask.

He jumps up. 'Of course.' The sky outside is grey and a cold breeze blows in.

Mr Mitchell pours me a glass of water and places it on the table in front of me. 'How 'bout this,' he says. 'You surf. Imagine how the tide touches your feet.'

My lips quiver, but I close my eyes.

'Imagine you've got your board and you jump into the water, how you duck-dive, how amazing that feels.'

I frown.

'Bear with me,' he says. 'I want you to imagine paddling out the back, all the waves that thunder toward you, and how each and every time, you dive deep beneath. You know you will surface, inevitably.'

I can feel the ocean combing through my hair as he continues. 'No matter how many times you have to dive beneath, you'll keep paddling, okay? That's how you're going to make it through.'

I open my eyes and he smiles at me.

'That's how you survive.'

⌒

Jake is waiting on the verandah when I get home. He sparks a match, the tiny flame curling around the end of his joint. 'How was it?' he says as I flop down beside him, landing in a heap.

I tell him how I wrote my name in the boxes on the front sheet in lower case and they're meant to be in upper case, so I had to be given a whole new exam booklet and how that seemed like such a waste. I tell him how I finished forty-five minutes before the end of the Advanced English exam with a three-paragraph essay and a half-page creative writing piece and had a nap on the desk while everyone else scribbled away.

'What'd ya write about?'

'A girl with an imaginary friend.'

'Your hair is salty.'

'Went swimming. Before school.'

From the way his eyes touch mine, I know he can tell I'm lying, but he just lies back on the wooden slats of the verandah, unfazed by my fib. As I kick my shoes off, Jake passes me the joint and I lie down beside him, eyes closed, drawing smoke into my lungs, as if breathing something else will make this life less real.

We lie there until dusk envelops us in shadows and I wonder if Mum will be home soon. Inside, Jake has brought with him peanut butter, choc-hazelnut spread, mini-marshmallows, sprinkles and a loaf of white bread. Licking our lips, we make sandwiches and end up with the kind of dinner you'd expect to indulge in somewhere far away, in a land where unicorns gallop through pink meadows made of fairy floss.

When Mum finally trudges through the front door, I don't know if I'm more surprised that she doesn't care about the spread of sweets across the kitchen bench, or that she takes a slice of white bread, slathers it in peanut butter, garnishes it with sprinkles and comes to join us in front of the TV.

With choc-hazelnut butter spread across the roof of my mouth, I watch the flickering blue light of the TV illuminating Mum's flesh like lightning on grey clouds. I catch glimpses of the wrinkles carved deep into her skin in the bright bursts, in the electric moments before she disappears in black shadows.

As the credits roll, Mum asks how the exam went.

'Fine,' I answer.

'That's good,' she says, and I look for a smile on her lips. Hoping, maybe.

Leaving her plate on the table, Mum says she's going to bed, wishes us goodnight, and drags herself upstairs to her bedroom.

I sink back between the cushions. They still smell of Ben. Even after all these days, they smell of him. I close my eyes and picture him, idle, waiting for me beneath the moon's silver rays.

'I think you should go home now,' I whisper.

Mountains of cushions move as Jake rises like a sleeping giant, waking after seasons underground. 'Seriously?'

I don't answer him. I just lie there, saying nothing.

'Fine,' he says, scrambling off the couch, shoving his feet into ugg boots. 'Fuck you.'

⌒

On Saturday afternoon, my papers are sprawled across the dining room table. I've coloured in with highlighters a few paragraphs of the essay Mr Woodlow essentially wrote for me, underlining words like *disenfranchised* and *upheaval* and *human condition*. I sit back in my chair, spine straight against the hard wood, sipping on my orange juice, satisfied with the supposed progress I've made.

Mum pulls up a chair beside me, laying down two plates of overripe, brown avocado on toast, sliding one across the table to me.

'Thanks, but no thanks.'

Ignoring me, Mum leans across my shoulder, eyeing my essay. 'Sounding good.'

'I wrote it myself.'

Whether Mum believes me or not, she draws her phone from her pocket and shows me a photo she's taken of a store window in Port Lawnam. 'Saw this on my way home from work the other day.'

I glare at the mannequin in the window and wonder if she's embarrassed to be wearing that dress.

'Pretty, huh?'

'*Pretty?*'

'Okay, fine – there are other dresses in the shop. I thought we could drive down today, pick one out. Don't want to leave it to the last minute.'

'How do you know I even want to go to the formal?'

'Doesn't matter, I've already bought you a ticket.'

'I don't have a date.'

'Neither did I.'

I've seen photos of Mum when she was seventeen and highly doubt she went to her formal alone. But looking back at my notes, lines of fluoro pink, purple and yellow blurring together, I cave. '*Fine.*'

As we drive through farmland and bush down to Port Lawnam, I don't think she's excited to go formal dress shopping with me but rather relieved she's got something to fill up her empty day.

For the first time in living memory, my chest is tight in a size six. I cup my hands to my breasts; they really are growing. I am growing. I am growing up.

'That one looks great,' Mum says as I step from the change room.

'You've said that about all of them.'

'Well, it's true.'

The shop assistant holds up another dress. 'How about this one?' She has a slick black ponytail, fake eyelashes and a belt tight around her waist.

Inside the change room, light bulbs frame the mirror, like in Hollywood green rooms. Yellow light hits my body in all the wrong places. Behind me, the curtain is thick red fabric, imitation velvet – an artificial sense of luxury in this damp harbour town.

Shimmying into the dress, I stand up straight to face myself.

It's not until the shop assistant calls out, 'How's it going in there, babe?' that I realise how long I have been standing here. The dress cascades down my body, smooth arcs and gentle curves, all the way to the floor. The fabric is as smooth as the ocean at midnight, as deep blue as my eyes. A smile curls my lips as I step out, telling the shop assistant, 'I don't mind it,' not wanting to give her the satisfaction of knowing it's perfect.

Afterward, I sit in a cafe with the dress in its shopping bag held tight between my feet, sipping on a vanilla milkshake, sharing a banana muffin with Mum.

⌒

'Today's my last exam,' I tell him.

Ben says he's proud of me, that he loves me.

Only a few hours later I am sitting at my desk in the assembly hall again, looking down at the Extension English exam paper. The first section requires short responses to an excerpt from a novel and a quote from a poem. The second is multiple-choice questions. I fill in the half that I know and then go back to the beginning of the pamphlet to colour in my guess answers. The final section is an essay and I write down the parts I can remember from my practice essay.

Then, while everyone else races toward the end of their exam booklet, I try to work out what the odds are of getting the answers I guessed in the multiple-choice section correct. When I'm done with that, I take a nap.

A bell wakes me for the end of the exam, for the end of my schooling, the end of the paddle. I've reached the line-up.

One ring of a bell and it's all over.

It's as if the room lets out one big exhalation, and I try to imagine the relief I would have felt.

⌒

At home I find a balloon tied neatly to the front doorhandle, and I yank at it, snapping the string.

CONGRATULATIONS! it reads, the block letters printed in rainbow colours. *Love Dad* is scrawled in black permanent marker on the balloon's side. He has always had shit handwriting. I dig my nails into the balloon until it bursts, sending the lorikeets in the fig tree into a frenzy. Tearing it apart, I notice another gift and assume it's also from Dad. Daisies are tied together with a blue ribbon on the day bed. Grabbing them, I march with the flowers and the shredded plastic out into the street, where I chuck the

plastic in the bin and rip the heads off the daisies, hurling them
into the air. Then I spit on the mess, jumping and stamping until
it's nothing but a blemish on concrete skin.

~

Mum arrives home with pizza, somewhat soggy in its cardboard
box because she bought it from a takeaway joint in Port Lawnam.

'Congratulations, bub.'

As she lays the box down on the table, I don't know what's more
foreign – the greasy pizza in her kitchen, or the way Mum ruffles
my hair when she kisses my cheek.

Thirty-One

THE LEGEND

I find Jake in the skate park, smoking cigarettes and swearing at eight-year-olds wearing helmets, kneepads and wrist guards, who are riding the ramps on scooters.

'Piss off, you little shits – it's called a *skate* park for a reason. Kooks.'

One boy's ears turn pink and I wonder how hard he's trying not to cry.

'Finished my exams.'

'Cool.'

'Want to be my date for the formal?'

'No.'

Jake drops down the ramp, narrowly missing two of the eight-year-olds. I plonk myself down on the concrete slab and wait for him to skate back up. He deliberately avoids the slab for almost half an hour, grinding rails on the other side of the park before finally riding back up to land next to me.

'Fine,' he says, sitting down, offering me a cigarette. 'But I'm not wearing a suit.'

⌒

Because he has decided to wear black skinny jeans, black Converse and a white T-shirt with a black bow tie drawn on with texta, Mum makes him at least shower and wash his hair, which Jake does only after an argument.

'I'm obeying,' he calls from the bathroom. 'But only because you're a MILF, Mel!'

Mum is attempting to style my hair with a curling iron. 'A MILF?' she whispers. 'What does that even mean?'

I giggle. 'You don't want to know.'

By the time Jake emerges from the bathroom, Mum has sprayed my hair into place. The fumes make me cough.

'Are you sure you're supposed to use that much?' I ask.

Mum laughs, opening the window. 'Um, not sure. That's what it says on the can.'

Jake knocks on the door.

'Don't come in! Not ready yet!'

As his footsteps tread back down the hall, he mocks, 'Women!'

Holding up a mirror, my hair is not quite red carpet Hollywood, but it's just about as good as it's ever looked. I thank Mum as she helps me apply eye shadow and mascara and brush my cheeks with bronzer.

It is the closest our bodies have been in weeks.

My dress has a low back with two strings to connect the straps above my shoulderblades. Mum ties them together in a loose bow. 'All done.'

My steps are slow and measured as I walk down the hall, careful not to trip in Mia's old heels. Jake is sitting at the kitchen bench munching on pistachios and looks across to me as I enter the living room. His face softens around the eyes.

'Wow.'

'Shut up,' I say, and he laughs.

Mum picks up her phone. 'Photo! On the verandah, maybe?'

Outside, draped in November light, I discover that when someone has died, being told to smile is twice as awkward.

⌒

The upstairs hall of the surf club is used on occasion for elections, local council meetings, charity auctions and yoga classes, and, every year since I can remember, the year twelve formal.

Ben was one of the few from our year group who was taken to the formal last year. Jake mocked Ben's date, saying she was a cougar, but we all knew how jealous he was, how jealous all the boys were.

Girls in frocks of all colours with make-up even more blatant than mine gather out the front of the club on the grass, posing for photo after photo. Jake and I sneak past, creeping into the boys' public toilet, where we light a joint. I only take one toke, careful not to let watery eyes make my mascara run.

'*Seriously?*' Jake says. 'Never thought I'd live to see the day when Grace Walker doesn't want to wreck her make-up.' Laughing, he smokes the joint right down to the filter, while I down a plastic bottle of cheap wine mixed with orange juice and stash a flask of vodka in my purse. I've cut a hole in the actual lining of the clutch and slip in the flask so it's concealed.

'You're a genius.' Jake laughs, kissing me on the cheek.

I unlock the cubicle door.

'Just a sec,' he says, reaching into the back pocket of his jeans and pulling out two pills wrapped in cling wrap. 'Let's save 'em for dessert, ay?' He winks and shoves them back into his pocket, taking my hand, leading me to the surf club's entrance.

As we cross behind a group of students, Jake photobombs their winning shot before helping me climb the stairs to the club in my heels. Our year group supervisor, Mrs Harold, is standing by the door with a security guard, who is actually someone's dad dressed in black. I watch the colour drain from her face as she spies Jake in the queue.

'I don't think so,' she snaps.

'Tough luck, I've got a ticket,' he says, waving it in front of her face.

'Fine. But one wrong move, Jake, and you're out. Do you hear me?'

'Loud and clear.'

The security guard asks me to open my clutch, which I do, revealing my phone, ticket and a stick of lip balm. 'All good,' he says, and then pats down my waist and hips.

'Hey!' Jake jokes. 'Hands off my lady.'

Mrs Harold glares. 'One wrong move. Remember that.'

After Jake is patted down too, we're permitted entry. He shows his ID to one of the mums inside and is given an over-18s' wristband and a free beer. He grins. 'Score!'

Gazing around the hall, I see silver streamers tacked to the walls, along with pictures of our year group at school camps, sports carnivals, discos. I spot a picture from the school fair, from the day night fell at noon.

White tables are positioned around the club's perimeter with a space for dancing in the middle. There are candle centrepieces and silver glitter sprinkled on each table. Overhead, white balloons with silver strings dangle like fragile moons.

I spot Mia and Toby on the other side of the room, each holding a champagne glass filled with soft drink. 'Some ploy to make the under-18s feel included,' Mia jokes when we get close. Eyeing off Jake's outfit, she chuckles. *'Really?'*

Jake pretends to adjust his drawn-on bow tie. 'Tailor-made.'

'Very handsome,' she says, raising her champagne glass.

He laughs. 'Fucking oath.'

Her face, naked of make-up, relaxes. 'I'm really happy you both came.'

Jake surprises her with a smile. 'Me too.'

Letting go of his hand, I excuse myself to get a soft drink, the taste of cheap wine and orange juice foul on my tongue.

A woman wearing a modest blue dress with a pink cardigan serves me. I can't remember whose mum she is but her timid smile tells me she knows exactly who I am. 'Here you go, honey,' she says, passing me a plastic champagne glass filled with pink lemonade.

Turning, I narrowly miss stumbling into someone. 'Sorry,' I say. 'My bad.'

'No worries.' Harley steps back, eyeing me from head to toe. 'You look so beautiful.'

As I look down at my feet, I wonder if he can see the pink in my cheeks beneath this make-up.

'Hey,' a girl says and I glance back up. It's Maddie, the girl who dropped her books in the hallway. She walks up to Harley, loops her arm through his. Her dress would have to be the shortest here, the plunging neckline screaming for attention.

'Excuse me,' I stutter, pushing past.

I grab Jake. 'Gotta show you something,' I say, pulling him away from Mia and Toby, leading him to the end of the hall, into the shadows, where I reach into his pocket and pull out the ball of cling wrap. 'Why wait?'

Swallowing the pill, it's like watching a storm roll over the horizon. You see the whitecaps racing, the shadows moving across the sea. You hear the clouds growling and feel the temperature plummet. Burning sand beneath your soles begins to cool. You watch the storm thundering toward you and you brace yourself. You know it's coming and that is as thrilling as it is terrifying.

Everyone is called to sit. Our names are written on cardboard cut-outs in metallic pen, placed on each dinner plate. Jake and I stumble around the tables in search of our seats. Pulling out a chair, I plant myself down.

'Excuse me,' a girl whispers, patting me on the shoulder. 'You're in my chair.'

I close one eye, and the name tag comes into focus. *Gemma Wilkins.*

Jake, giggling, hoists me up, and we continue our search.

'Over here!' Toby calls and we stagger to the table, flopping down in our seats. Mia pinches my cheeks and hisses, 'Are you on something?'

'No,' I say and smirk at her as Mrs Harold, standing at the front of the hall, sings out for Mia, school captain, to join her at the microphone. Looking across the hall, I spy Harley, sitting with Maddie on the furthest table from us, and I'm positive Mia put him all the way over the other side of the room on purpose.

'Hey everyone, welcome,' Mia says. 'Food is about to come out, we'll kick off the awards in half an hour and then Byron is going to DJ.' Standing in the spotlight she looks beautiful, her curls plaited and twisted like pink vines, pinned into place with flower clips. Her dress is white lace, as delicate as her skin. My heart aches. I wish Ben could have seen her.

Everyone claps and the parents who have volunteered to help tonight start carrying out the food. Local fruit and vegetable farmers, Margie from the bakery and Rob from the fish shop have all chipped in to cater the event. I'm served a plate of roast veggies with a piece of grilled bream, a slice of lemon and sourdough. I say thank you, my speech a little slurred, and pick up my knife and fork with unsteady hands. That's when I see it. I glance across at Jake and know he can see it too. The storm is coming, closing in on us.

With cheap wine already filling my insides, I can barely stomach my meal. Instead, I hold my soft drink under the table, pouring vodka into my glass as Mia strolls back up to the microphone with two prefects to give out the class awards . . . as Maddie touches his cheek across the hall . . . as Harley laughs.

I see whitecaps, racing across the sea. I see a smile stretch Jake's lips.

'The first award is *biggest flirt*.' Mia steps aside so one of the prefects can announce the winner.

'Gus Kelly.'

I feel the temperature drop.

'*Most likely* not *to remember this formal*.'

'Luke Palmer.'

'The next is for the *best looking*,' Mia says.

Another prefect leans in. 'Starting off with wet pants on the oval in year one, Harley Mathews is getting this award for his tremendous improvements.'

As Harley wanders up to collect his award, a guy calls from the back of the hall, 'How is that even an award? This is a stitch-up! The formal committee's all girls.'

Mia leans into the microphone and smirks. 'Piss off, Dave.'

Harley collects the certificate, laughing, and that's when the storm breaks over me, in a sudden turbulent rush.

I hear Mia say, '*Class legend.*'

'George Collins.'

And then I hear Jake . . . 'Are you serious?' he bellows. 'No offence, Georgie, but fuck that.'

Hopping out of his chair, Jake stumbles toward the prefects, pushing Mia out of the way as the parents watch on in horror, paralysed.

Jake takes the mike and rips it off the stand. 'Testing, testing,' he says, bashing his fingers against it. Mia lunges for it and they wrestle before he overpowers her and she staggers back, tripping, falling – landing heavily on hardwood with a painful thud. 'Now,' Jake says, his voice blaring through the speakers, 'Georgie boy might tell a joke or two, but let's be honest. He's LAME.'

Mrs Harold screams, 'JAKE! HOW DARE YOU!' as she marches over to him.

'Hold up, missy, I haven't finished yet.' He climbs onto a chair. 'I think we all know who should be getting this award.' There is a pause; the room holds its breath. 'Ben Walker!'

Everyone chokes, and the next thing I know, the five dads dressed as security guards are charging toward Jake, yanking him off the chair, tackling him to the floor.

'HEY!' I yell, kicking off my heels and climbing out of my seat, over the table, my feet squelching in fish fillets, stamping on crusty bread, mashing potatoes. 'GET OFF HIM!' I fall off the end of the table, thump the floor, clamber to my feet and lurch across the dance floor to Jake, pinned to the ground by two of the guards.

Leaping onto their backs, I punch someone's dad in the back of the head. That's the only thing I remember before I black out.

Thirty-Two

PINCH AND A PUNCH

Walking along High Street, I pass our old primary school, just two blocks down. Kids with blue caps, scuffed shoes and backpacks far too big for their little frames spill out onto the kerb. Gertie, the lollipop lady who has overseen this pedestrian crossing for as long as I can remember, beams at them, her eyes disappearing between wrinkles as she smiles. A current of children, skipping and holding hands, flows across the road, bringing the traffic to a standstill. They are followed by mothers with prams or dogs on leashes and teenagers picking up their younger siblings.

Sitting on the ground, backs against the school's white picket fence, kids wait in clusters for their buses. I remember how Ben and I caught the bus for a term in year four, although it was hardly necessary. Living on Walker Street, the first left after the main shops, we barely had time to sit down before pressing the button for the second bus stop. Nevertheless, I wrote my name on my bus pass, decorated the front side with frangipani stickers and gave it the front card space in my sky blue wallet. After a month or so, the novelty wore off. Ben and I returned to skating or riding our bikes to and from school.

Arriving now at a cross street, I lean against a telegraph pole, sunlight hot on my shoulders. Parents drive out of the school's pick-up zone, and I wait for a clean break between cars, wiping sweat off my upper lip. Two kids race each other to the kerb, their mum calling out behind to make sure they don't leap onto the road. One of them, a girl with a low pony and gangly arms, barrels into me. The other, a boy wearing his school cap backwards, catches up to her, pinches her on the arm, punches.

'Pinch and a punch for the first of the month. NO RETURNS!'

Squealing, her tiny hand curled into a tight fist, she lunges back at him, narrowly missing his arm.

'I said no returns!' he yells. Crossing his eyes and pulling his ears, he jumps up and down like a monkey.

There's a break in between cars and their mum takes them by the hand, apologises to me for their cheekiness, and leads them across the road. A car horn beeps and I glance up. A driver is waiting for me to cross, but I can't. I'm stuck here, glued to the spot. I motion with my hand, encouraging her to drive on. She glares, shakes her head, and pulls out onto High Street.

Several minutes pass before I finally peel myself from the telegraph pole and cut through the procession of cars. A station wagon comes to an abrupt stop to avoid hitting me, a horn blares. I start to run, feet pounding the pavement, blood pounding in my temples. Tears blur my vision, but I don't slow, I don't stop, not until I am in our yard, kicking off my shoes and climbing high into the fig tree, perching on his branch, panting, skin red and sweaty.

The first of the month. December. Summer. Grevilleas, mulberries and fresh lemonade. Afternoons that stretch out forever. Cicadas, blue skies and honey bees. *Our* birthday.

Sitting in the tree until the sun sinks behind burnt orange clouds, I think I am finally starting to understand it.

They called his time of death, but it was not an end; it was a beginning. The afterlife is not so much a place but rather what happens to me, to the others left behind, after *Ben's* life.

Beneath me, at the base of the trunk, Christmas flowers are beginning to blossom. Days are growing longer, grey sea waves will turn turquoise, and as much as I want to stay close to him, the world carries on, dragging me further away with every hour.

⌒

'Yeah,' I say, 'Mia's coming over soon. She went back in to school to pick up her art major work and talk to Mr Mitchell.'

'The counsellor?' Mum says, shoving undies and toiletries into a bag.

I nod, leaning against her dresser.

'How did it go with him?'

'He's nice.'

Mum zips up her bag. 'I have to go or I'll miss the train.' She still hasn't looked me in the eye. 'You and Mia will be at her house, like you said.'

'*Yessss.*'

'I don't want you two here alone,' she says.

Shifting my weight, palms clammy, I tell her, 'We're watching a movie in town – I think her dad's coming.'

'Oh yeah, what's on?'

I pause for a moment. 'Um . . . Knowing them, we're probably seeing something foreign.'

Mum almost smiles, pulling on her coat. 'A bit of culture won't do you any harm.'

'Yeah, but I'm too slow for the subtitles,' I complain, adding texture to this fabrication.

She gives me an awkward peck on the forehead – no hug – and grabs her bag. 'I'll be back Sunday night. If I don't pick up my phone for any reason, you've got Kate's mobile and the number at her house.'

I follow Mum down the stairs from her bedroom, through the house, and onto the verandah where Monty stands at my feet.

Mum waves, but our eyes still don't meet.

It's been three days. Three days since she looked me in the eye and smiled and took my picture on this verandah – the day I wore curls in my hair and a midnight dress. Now she's retreating to the city, and sending me to Mia's place.

As she pulls out of the driveway, a thin cloud of dust rises above the gravel. I watch Mum turn in the cul-de-sac, waiting for the Range Rover to drive out of sight before falling back and lying down on the verandah steps. Monty rests beside me, relaxing his head on my abdomen. On the beach, waves pulse against the shore, rhythms beating through the earth. Pulling my phone out of my pocket, I punch in Jake's number.

'Hey, Mum just left. You can come over now.'

⌒

Chucking his skateboard on the ground, Jake stands over me on the verandah. Opening one eye, I peer up at him, squinting in the afternoon light. He lowers a string of saliva, slurping it up at the very last moment. I sit up, whack the backs of his knees.

Laughing, he plonks himself down beside me.

'You're gross,' I snicker.

Unzipping his backpack, Jake slaps a bag of cinnamon dough-nuts and white chocolate chip cookies onto my lap, still warm, condensation beading the plastic packaging.

I grin. 'You're forgiven.'

'I thought you'd say that,' he says. He has already taken out a bowl and scissors, a bag of herb, cigarette papers, ready to start rolling a joint. 'Oh, and I got this.' He reveals a chocolate coconut bar.

'OH, JAKE!' I say, eyes wide and hands on cheeks, like a woman who's just been proposed to.

'Ha, ha . . . shut up.' He knocks me with his shoulder, lights the end of his joint, steals a puff and then hands it to me.

After three tokes, my head is butter cream running down my back, soaking my singlet. Grabbing the bag of treats, I take Jake's hand and wander through the yard, through the rickety gate, giggling down sloped grass, along the rocks, coming to sit, at last, beneath cracked cliffs. Tearing open the bag, I bite into a cookie, gold crunch and gooey centre. White chocolate droplets turn to milk on my tongue.

Resting my cheek on Jake's chest, I close my eyes, breathing deep his musk of sweat, tobacco and butter biscuit. His shirt, stiffened by salt crystals, grates against my cheek with the rise and fall of his chest. A wave devours emerald rocks, sand crabs scurry, foam spits.

'Today's the first of December,' I say. 'We turn eighteen in three weeks.'

'Shit,' Jake says. He brushes the hair off my face, wipes a stray tear from my cheek.

I begin to sob, my body shaking. 'I don't want to grow up.'

He laughs. 'I've heard there's some great anti-ageing creams on the market.'

I grin at him through my tears. 'You know what, screw it. If I'm turning eighteen, it's going to be how he'd have done it . . .' I jump up, skipping across the rocks to the edge of the shelf. Raising my arms, I scream at a wispy grey horizon, 'With FUCKING STYLE!'

Jake jumps onto the rock beside me, hurls half a doughnut into the sea. Gulls swoop, diving for cinnamon delight.

I turn to him. 'Jake . . . I'm going to throw a birthday party.'

A grin creeps across his face. 'Fuck it, why wait three weeks? Why not have a party tomorrow?'

Thirty-Three

WHEN SHE SINGS

We drive to Port Lawnam with the hundred dollars Jake's mum has left him. He's not sure where she's gone or who she left with, but if Jake cares, he's hiding it well.

Arriving before the bottle-o is even open, we hang in his ute, filling the cabin with smoke until the owner, tired and balding, traipses up to unlock his shop. Jake swings open the driver's door, loses grip of the handle and falls from his seat flat onto the concrete. We both laugh, almost in hysterics, as he staggers toward the store.

He returns a few minutes later with our supplies, wheeling them into the car park in a trolley. As he piles it all under my feet and on my lap, I eye off the hoard. Three packets of cigarettes, a case of beer, five bottles of bubbles, two flasks of vodka, several packets of chips and salted nuts, and two casks of white wine.

As he climbs back into the driver's seat, I turn to him. 'You got all that for a hundred dollars?'

Ignoring me, Jake turns the key in the ignition as the door to the bottle-o flies open and the shopkeeper charges out. His bald patch shines as violet as his neck. 'HEY!' he screams. 'YA LITTLE SHIT!'

'Oh, crap!' Jake sniggers, throwing the car into reverse. Revving the engine, he changes into first and we speed out of the car park in a cloud of brown exhaust.

A guy with a nose-ring and a black rose tattooed at the base of his throat leans his head in the driver's side window. 'How many do you need?' he says with a sly grin.

Jake looks across to me. 'It's your birthday . . .'

I sink my gaze into the dealer's murky green eyes. 'How many can you get?'

He winks and tells me not to worry, he'll get it sorted.

'See you tonight, man,' Jake says, slipping the car into gear, and we drive off down the street, weaving between abandoned factories and shabby, broken-down houses.

By the time the DJ has set up his decks on the verandah, I'm lying in a hammock strung between the fig tree and the fence, cradling a bottle of bubbles. I'm barefoot, with smoky eye make-up, dressed for the occasion in a black lace G-string and one of Jake's grey T-shirts as a dress. Cigarette between my fingers, I watch a group of guys from Port Lawnam transform the yard – guys I've met in warehouses and at parties but never before seen during the day. I watch one of them spray-paint *HAPPY BIRTHDAY GRACE* onto the lawn and I clap, applauding his efforts.

The DJ plays his first set as everyone lounges on tattered couches under the fig tree, sinking beers until sunset, when dusk bleaches the sky and I send the first text. Like wildfire, the invite spreads.

By the time tiny fires appear in the sky, there is a whole bottle of bubbles in my stomach and over a hundred people in my yard. Fairy lights curl around the verandah banisters. Speakers throb and bodies bend like branches in a storm. There's a tinny fishing boat at the base of the driveway, filled with ice, filled with alcohol, glass bottles. A strobe cuts through the night and as I weave through the crowd to dance, I notice guys sitting on the roof of the shed, guys sitting on the roof of the house.

A stranger slips his hand beneath my dress. 'Hey, sexy.' He grips my arse. Then I see his nose-ring, his black rose tattoo. He grins as he leads me from the crowd, behind the house.

'Here,' he says, pulling a zip-lock bag from his jacket pocket, packed tight with pills. 'Take your pick. They're complimentary for birthday girls.'

I wash one down with my cup of cask wine and cough with the bitter taste in my throat. Leading him back toward the party, I stop at the corner of the verandah. 'Help me get up there?'

From the roof, I watch chaos unfurl. Music thuds, bottles smash, someone screams. Jake climbs up, crawling across tiles to sit beside me, our legs dangling over the edge. He hands me a flask of vodka and I take a swig, drawing a cigarette from his pack. Together, we bask in the anarchy, knowing that tonight we're not alone in this vicious dream.

Soon I spot Mia, shoving her way through the crowd. It's eight-thirty and there are two or three hundred people here, no doubt even more drinking in the street and on the grassy hill. 'Oh shit,'

I say, nudging Jake, pointing her out among the dark sea of swaying bodies. We watch her climb onto the arm of a couch, supporting her weight with one hand on the fig tree's trunk as she scans the party, looking for us.

Spying me on the roof, Mia charges to the verandah, where two guys help her climb the banister. Wriggling over the gutter, she shouts, 'So your mum called my house to check up on you!'

I lie back on the tiles, looking up at the stars, wondering how many have already exploded, wondering how many are simply light that is only just reaching us. My eyes roll loose in their sockets. I almost smile.

She's screaming at me, but I don't know what she's saying anymore, can't make out the words.

'PISS OFF, MIA!' Jake fires back.

'I'm calling the COPS!' she shrieks.

I sit up, close one drunken eye to focus on her, suck air through my nose, pull phlegm from the back of my throat and spit at her.

Mia bursts into tears, her body quaking as she retreats, climbing back down to earth.

⁓

Five minutes later, they're here. Whether she called them or not, they're here – with their boots, their pepper spray, blaring sirens and flashing lights – but with every adolescent from here to the other side of Port Lawnam swarming in my yard, the police are severely outnumbered. They sit out front and wait for backup from our neighbouring harbour town.

Jake and I jump from the roof, landing in Mum's jasmine bush, sprinting around the house to the back door. There are people everywhere, mud on the floor, upturned furniture, and then I see it, the door to Ben's room, wide open. Jakes sees it too and I race in behind him, furious, not stopping to think. I am suddenly standing on the clothes he never picked up off the floor, beside the bed he never made, under the roof we used to share. On his mattress, on top of the sheets he lay beneath with Mia in the days before the accident, a couple is now half-naked and dry-humping. Jake tears the girl off, and she falls to the ground.

I look at Ben's desk. Sitting on it, sitting on his *handwritten* pages, two guys are smoking and laughing at the girl on the floor, high as kites. I bellow, 'GET OUT!' and punch one of them in the stomach. Behind me the guy on Ben's bed leaps off, tackling Jake into the wall. They wrestle and the girl in her bra and undies screams for them to stop while the guy I punched gasps for air and his friend shoves me so hard I trip and slam my head against Ben's wardrobe.

The next thing I know, glass shatters. Jake has thrown the guy out Ben's window and leaps out after him, taking the fight out onto the grass. I crawl over to the window and pull myself up to see policemen rip them apart. The policemen yank Jake's arms behind his back, fastening handcuffs tight around his wrists. I reach for the paper bin under Ben's desk, hurling into it, wine and vodka and champagne and whatever else is in my stomach.

'Ew,' the girl beside me on the floor complains. 'Gross!'

Wiping my mouth, I clamber to my feet and barge through the throng of teenagers who've gathered in the doorway to watch the commotion. Thundering blind down the hallway, I ram into the flyscreen and fly out the back door, stumbling across the lawn, struggling over the fence. My feet thud one after the other down the grassy hill to the beach, not stopping until I'm far enough away for salt waves to drown out the sirens and screams. I sink into the sodden sand and scream at the ocean until there is nothing left, my cries peeling flesh from the walls of my throat.

The moon bulges above a bitter sea and I wrap my arms around myself, shivering violently, though I feel nothing of the night's chill. Starved and empty, I wonder how the moon rises each night.

That's when I see him, out to sea, paddling into a wave. His drop is effortless, so much grace and yet so much power, spraying the night sky with flecks of silver as he rises and turns.

As he kicks off the back of the wave, I stand and wade through the shallows toward the sandbank. When I'm close enough, Ben throws his board aside and starts shouting.

'What the hell are you doing? Look what you've done to the house! You spat on Mia! Jake just got arrested, for fuck's sake!'

A wave smashes between us, knocking me down.

'You're an idiot, Grace! An absolute IDIOT!'

'FUCK YOU!' I shout, struggling to my feet. 'You left me! This is ALL YOUR FAULT!'

I push past him, kicking, swimming and punching through waves toward the line-up, leaving him behind. I swim until I can't touch the ground.

For months, I've trodden water. Now, beneath a swollen moon, my heart softens, my limbs go limp, one final exhalation and I sink. My back touches the seabed, the sand a pillow for my head.

On the surface, fractured moonlight and broken stars.

I close my eyes and my tired body comes to rest.

I'm out of my mind, and yet so present, breathing under water. It's everything and nothing.

For a moment, I feel as if I'm truly with him, in that absent moment between night and day.

Then I hear her, the ocean – singing. My body sways in purple sea currents, as her melody, a cradlesong, serenades me. I feel my heartbeat, though weak, ripple through the deep. I feel blood pulling in my chest like the tides and remember I am still alive. *I exist.*

Gently touching my feet to the seabed, I push to the surface, rising, reborn.

My lungs expand. And though my heart aches, my inner rhythm is loud and real, and that is worth fighting for.

Thirty-Four

TO SWIM AGAIN

The house looks like someone left every door and window open in the middle of a hurricane.

'Where the hell have you been?' Dad roars.

I'm dripping wet with slick hair, muddy feet and bleeding skin. 'Are you serious?' I scoff. 'Where have *you* been?'

Backup police have arrived, driving the rioters out of our yard. I see one girl, a goon bag in hand, giving a policewoman lip. The girl is given two warnings before she's loaded into the back of a paddy wagon, already packed with disorderly teenagers.

'You're a disgrace,' Dad says. 'Piss off. I can't stand to look at you.' He goes back to the living room, just out of earshot, to talk to the police. I wonder if he'll tell them he hasn't been living here, that he couldn't have possibly foreseen all this, making it impossible for them to fine him.

In bed, naked and covered in mud and salt, I lie on my back, staring up at the ceiling, an empty sky, remembering the glow-in-the-dark stars Ben glued to the roof. Why had we taken them down? Did we think we were too grown-up?

My pupils are dilated, my heart racing. I won't be falling asleep anytime soon, so I reach into my dresser for the plastic bag Jake stashed in there a few weeks ago. Rolling a joint, I crack open my window and light the end, inhaling and exhaling until one drug counteracts the other and I can close my eyes and escape.

⌒

I hear a car mount the kerb, the crunch of bottles and the screech of its handbrake as it comes to an abrupt halt in our driveway. Rolling onto my side, I sit up. Sunlight splits my head open and I wince. I see my desk pushed up against my door and start to remember.

My limbs are encased in dry mud. It cracks as I stretch my arms and roll my wrists in slow circles. Knees buckling, I hobble to my mirror. Smoky eye make-up has smudged my cheeks black and there are clumps of seaweed in my hair. I hear the front door fly open, slamming into the wall. I wonder if she's broken the hinges.

Mum barges straight down the hall to my closed door. 'GRACE!' she screams, rattling the doorhandle. 'God damn it! Let me in!' She throws her weight against the door again and again. A framed picture of Ben and me on our first day of school topples off my desk, the glass shattering.

I slide the desk away from the door just as she charges it again, and she crashes through onto the floor. I stand there, immobile, as she clambers to her feet and slaps me square in the face.

She stares me right in the eye. 'How *dare* you,' she says, and stomps out.

I feel as if I'm lucid dreaming, aware of my surroundings yet paralysed.

Finally, I wake up.

I trudge out into the kitchen to see Sasha standing with her hands on her hips, wearing yellow gumboots, a violet polka dot apron and an orange bandana. I burst into tears.

'Now, now,' she says, striding toward me. 'No point crying over spilt milk.'

Mum is sitting at the dining room table, on one of the three chairs that aren't broken. With her head in her hands, she grunts; the sound is unnerving. 'Yeah . . . spilt milk.'

'Melinda,' Sasha says, stern now. 'Nothing is going to get better when you're being a sourpuss.'

'Mum . . .' Kate says. She is wearing rubber gloves, garbage bag in hand. 'Ease up, would you?'

Sasha takes two garbage bags, handing one to me. 'No time like the present, ay,' she laughs. The sound is as out of place in this depressing room as her vibrant outfit, and yet somehow it makes me relax.

We pick up bottles, broken glass, squashed cans and cigarette butts for over an hour before Dad emerges from the shed. Noticing Kate's car in the driveway he freezes mid-step on the lawn.

'Oh god,' Mum utters under her breath, her whole body tensing. She looks to Kate. *Has he seen me?*

Dad pivots and turns back toward the street.

Suddenly, Mum looks fierce. 'No fucking way,' she says, and rises from her chair, marching out into the yard. 'HEY! Come back here!'

Dad's face is white as he turns to face her.

'You're supposed to be my husband!' Mum screams and when he says nothing in return, just stands there in devastating silence, she rips off her wedding ring and throws it at him.

The ring bounces off Dad's shoulder. As Mum falls to her knees, Kate and Sasha rush to crouch beside her. I'm the only one who sees him pick it up before he takes off down the street.

Mum sobs into the trampled dirt. 'That's it, Ray. Walk away. Walk away from your family. Walk away from me . . .'

Kate rubs Mum's back.

'The only thing worse than loving someone who doesn't love you,' Mum says, her voice hoarse, 'is loving someone who *used* to love you.'

Sasha removes her headband and uses it to wipe tears from Mum's eyes. 'You know, honey, the first time your dad didn't recognise me, I walked straight out of the room. I got in my car and I drove and drove until I didn't know where I was.' She pauses to brush Mum's hair from her face. 'I pulled into a shopping mall car park and I just sat there. The nurses, the doctors, they all told me he'd forget sooner or later, but I hadn't really believed it. Your dad loved me, and I thought that was enough. Maybe that's why it was such a shock.' She takes a deep breath, as if trying to remember the next part of the story. 'So anyway, I just sat there, sat there in the car, for hours, trying to remember the last time he'd said *I love you*, and I couldn't figure out if it was when we'd lain in bed the night before, or if he'd said it that morning as I'd poured milk onto his cereal.'

I see tears welling in Sasha's eyes but she holds on to them.

'I wanted to remember so I could look back and know he still loved me in *that* moment.'

Kate gazes over Mum's shoulder to Sasha, 'Mum, why haven't you ever talked about this?'

'Don't interrupt,' Sasha says curtly, and Kate looks hurt.

Sasha takes Mum's hand and gives it a squeeze. 'You're right, Mel. Knowing they used to love you, it's the hardest thing in the world. But I still go in there and hold his hand. And I'll pour milk onto his cereal even though he's lost, because sometimes his heart wanders back.'

⌒

By midday, we're sweating in the summer sun, and as Mum goes inside to fetch some water, I follow. She fills a jug, adds ice cubes she cracks from the freezer tray and lemon sliced into quarters.

Pulling up a stool at the breakfast bench, I watch her move around the kitchen as if this is someone else's house, as if she's guessing what is in each cupboard.

'I'm sorry,' I say, too quiet for her to hear me. I try again, speaking louder now. 'Mum, I'm sorry.'

Turning to me, her face softens, and although she doesn't find the words to forgive me, I know she is trying.

Mum carries the jug out onto the verandah, calls out to Sasha and Kate in the yard, then takes a fresh garbage bag from the packet, closes her eyes and inhales air deep into her lungs. As she exhales, it is like the first breath of wind to touch the earth each morning, a new day. Opening her eyes, Mum walks back into the house, her confidence slowly building with each step down the hall.

I watch her make her way through the shadows. I watch her hand reach out, watch her fingers coil around the doorhandle.

I watch her enter Ben's room, and then, before my mind has time to register what's happening, my feet are carrying me down the hall. The thought of going in there horrifies me, but it's even more horrifying to think of her in there alone.

As I step through the door, I see my mum, her slight frame and bony shoulders, and I think of all the cakes, all the muffins, all the times she stayed back late at school. I think of how she turned this place into a museum. I think of all the nights she didn't even notice I was missing, how I'd thought of her as such a coward. Now she has dared to tread where I couldn't bear to.

In silence, we collect party debris and sweep up broken glass with a dustpan and brush. We strip his bedsheets, and as I carry them out to the laundry, Mum ties a knot in the rubbish bag and puts it out on the verandah.

Next she finds three flattened cardboard boxes. Taking them into Ben's room, she stands them up and I help her tape the bottom flaps together. Opening the cupboard door, I'm greeted by his musk. I close my eyes and it's as if Ben is stepping right out to embrace me. I've got a lump in my throat, but while it burns a little, it doesn't choke.

Mum and I pull jumpers and shirts off their hangers and empty his drawers, folding the clothes neatly, taping the flaps together when the first box is full. We then move to his desk, where we collect his alarm clock, pencils, notepads, lamp, magazines and schoolbooks. Mum saves a novel with a bookmark parting the pages close to halfway through and a framed picture of us on the beach after our first surf comp, setting them aside from the rest. All the while, we move to nothing but the sound of our breaths, and I think that's because there aren't any words that can fill this moment.

From under his bed, I pull out his shoes and skateboard and wonder if Ben was ever scared when he checked under my bed for monsters.

And then I empty Ben's bedside table drawer. I find a picture of Mia.

Her hair is loosely plaited like a forest fairy and she's wearing a pale green dress, off the shoulder, tight around the bust, loose and flowing over her hips. I look at the way the sunlight kisses her collarbones and recall how we'd all posed by the rock pool as Mum took pictures of us in our year ten formal dresses for the family album.

Sitting back now on his stripped mattress, I remember how Ben had bagged her that afternoon for not having a date, how she'd said there was no one worth taking and how he'd boasted of all the girls he'd had practically begging to go with him.

I pocket the photo.

Mum tapes a box shut and takes a moment to breathe. I follow her gaze through the shattered window to the yard where we see Sasha has found a bottle of tequila, half-full, at the edge of the flowerbed. Unscrewing the cap, she swirls the yellow liquid around a few times, sloshing it against glass walls, then sniffs, shrugs and takes a swig.

Mum looks at me and I look back at her, neither of us saying a word, then we burst out laughing. We laugh so hard that Mum collapses beside me on the bed. We laugh until we are limp, until our lungs ache, heaving for breath, until our cheeks are wet with tears. Finally, when we are both exhausted, Mum takes me in her arms and holds me to her chest, tucking my head into the nook between her collarbone and breast. As she cradles me in her arms,

I realise I have forgotten how this feels. I have forgotten how it feels to be loved, to be cared for.

Squeezing me tight, my mum whispers, 'Baby, I forgive you.' She takes a deep breath. 'I'm sorry too, so sorry. But I'm here now, and I'm not going anywhere.'

⌣

Though I'm the one who caused last night's ruckus, Mr Brown from across the road comes over to help us tape a sheet of cardboard over the shattered window, a makeshift fix until a professional can come tomorrow to replace the glass. I see his hands shake as he strains to pull the tape and ask, 'Is there anything I can do to help you or Mrs Brown at your place?'

A smile touches his lips. 'We're just glad you're okay.'

Sasha and Kate leave for the city just after two o'clock with the sun stretching into the afternoon. With them, they take several of the garbage bags to deposit at the tip just up the coast.

Inside, Mum unties her hair, tresses tumble down her back. 'You hungry?' she asks, opening the kitchen pantry. 'Whoa,' she laughs, eyeing off the remnants of caster sugar, two-minute noodles and potato chips. Opening the fridge, her laugh deepens. There's a single carrot, a slab of butter, wilted spinach, a stalk of celery turned brown, cheese, a half-eaten bar of chocolate and some eggs.

Checking the clock above the empty flower vase, I say, 'The markets are on till three.'

Reaching into the cupboard beneath the sink, she grabs a few of her tote bags, smiling. 'Best get a wriggle on then, ay?'

We take Monty for the trip and I think guiltily that this is the furthest he's been from the house in weeks. Despite his grey fur and achy joints, his tail still wags as we near the markets. A lot of the stock has already been sold when we arrive, but the upside is that whatever is left is heavily marked down. We fill every bag for half the price of a usual shop and have one of the boys working the fruit and veg tent carry a box bulging with fresh produce to the car for us. As we leave, I buy a strip of beef biltong and break it into pieces, feeding them to Monty on the drive home.

Filling the vase with the waratahs we purchased from the flower stall, I position them in a beam of sunlight and stand back to see them come alive. Monty lies on the kitchen floorboards between our feet as we stock the pantry and fridge until each is bursting with rich greenery and coloured fruits as vibrant as an Australian summer. On the shelves between, we stack grass-fed meats, fish fillets and organic butter. The last things Mum unloads are a bag of spelt flour, wild rice, spices and some macadamia nuts – ingredients I haven't seen in this kitchen since Ben died – and as the sun comes to rest on distant mountains, Mum rolls up her sleeves and *creates*.

We eat on the day bed outside with Monty beneath us and stars above. The night breathes like a sleeping baby as I take pleasure in the flavours of the cinnamon, nutmeg, vanilla and cloves in the raw carrot cake we've made for dessert.

Our meal nourishes our bodies like the sun nourishes the earth, and as I lie in bed, pulling a thin, clean sheet over my body, Mum leans down, brushing my hair off my face. 'Sweet dreams, honey,' she whispers softly and kisses my forehead.

⌒

The sweet scents of coconut oil and caramelised banana entice, gently drawing me from my slumber into the light of day.

The ocean gleams, a magnificent deep blue, as I change from my pyjama singlet into a T-shirt and pull my hair into a ponytail. Strolling out into the kitchen, I find Mum in front of the stove with a spatula in hand, standing in her paisley one-piece swimsuit. Her tresses are wet with the ocean and there are sandy, salty footprints on spotted gum floorboards.

'You went swimming?' I say, a smile rising like a wave out of the deep.

Mum nods. 'The water was beautiful.'

Thirty-Five

TIME

'They let me off for all charges,' Jake says, drawing back on a cigarette. 'Sympathy, probably.'

Sitting in the tray of his ute, facing the ocean by the beach at Tarobar, I tuck my knees up to my chest and wrap my arms around my knees. 'That's lucky.'

He laughs, and immediately starts coughing on the smoke still in his lungs. Spluttering, he finally catches his breath. 'Nothing about this is lucky.'

I look out at the water, cobalt waves breaking on grey rocks, gulls chatting by the cliff. 'Mia isn't talking to me,' I say at last.

He looks at me, his brow furrowed. 'And you care *why?*'

I shrug, thinking of the cold shoulder I've received from her at the shops and by the rock pool in the week since the party. Knowing that I deserve it doesn't make it any easier.

'She's a bitch,' Jake sneers. 'I thought we agreed on that point.'

'I found a picture of her in Ben's bedside table,' I say and Jake drops his cigarette into his lap.

'Fuck,' he stammers, flicking it away. There's a burn mark on his leg. I don't know if he's pissed off at me, or devastated by the weight of my words.

⌒

I rummage through a drawer in the laundry in search of candles. 'How long do you reckon the power will be out for?' I say, taking cautious steps back through the dark living room.

Mum finishes setting the table and hands me a lighter. 'Not long, I hope.'

As we eat, light flickers on her honey skin, bending around her cheekbone. Mum's lips are sunburnt and her eyelashes crisp with crystallised salt.

I wonder if Dad thinks of her.

'This is delicious,' I say. 'Especially the mushrooms.'

'Thanks, love.' Her smile stretches a little wider with each day that passes.

I swallow, wipe my mouth on my sleeve and listen to her complain about the stain it'll leave, the way she always has.

'Mum,' I say, 'she won't even look at me.'

'Mia?'

I nod, playing with the food on my plate. 'What should I do?'

'To be honest, I don't have an answer.'

My forehead creases. 'You're the adult. You're meant to know.'

'It doesn't matter how old you are. You'll never know *all* the answers.'

I fold my arms in my lap, watching wax drip down the side of the candle, pooling at the base, hardening.

'I think you have to figure this one out for yourself.'

I sigh, resigning myself to the fact that at least her last point is true.

⌢

Jackson answers the door and I step back as Oatley comes charging out, tail wagging, jumping up to my waist. Grabbing the dog's collar, Jackson pulls him back and apologises. I tell him I'm surprised to see him.

'Uni holidays,' he says. 'I'm down for the summer.'

Wiping my hands on my skirt, I glance around the yard. Mia's bike is on the grass, her shoes by the door.

'Do you want something?' Jackson asks in a tone I've never heard before.

I wipe my hands again, swallow and ask if Mia is home, but before Jackson has time to open his mouth, I hear her call out from down the hall, 'Tell her I'm at the shops!'

The afternoon heat is suddenly unbearable and I feel my body start to wilt.

Before all this, the longest a fight ever lasted between us was an afternoon. She had a tantrum when I mixed her playdough colours together and they turned brown. Her anger was amplified tenfold when Jake started eating the rest.

We were three, and if it weren't for Mia's dad continually retelling the story, I probably wouldn't even remember it.

As I make my way home, I take her photo out of my pocket. With tears running down my face, I apologise to him, promising I'll try again tomorrow.

Nearing the holiday season, stalls pop up at the markets with chocolates and candy canes, handmade gifts, cards and hampers, but it is hard to be excited about Christmas when half our family is missing. I point out a tray of fresh mangoes to deflect Mum's gaze and take her hand as she does her best to smile.

By the lemonade stand, I break a carrot in half and am feeding it to Monty as Nila Mathews strolls up to us.

Embracing us both, she asks how we are, saying she's so happy to see us. I leave Mum to do the talking. Nila's brilliant blue eyes are so much like her son's I find it hard to look at her.

'And what about you, Grace?' she says, roping me into the conversation. 'How are you? How did the exams go?'

I wonder if she asks Harley about me. I wonder if he'd even have answers.

'I'm good,' I shrug. 'Not too sure about the exams.'

'She sat them,' Mum says. 'That's the main thing.'

I should ask her about Harley, what he is doing now that school is finished, but I can't, so instead I change the subject.

'We really should thank you,' I say. 'For your gifts these past few months and the time you must have spent on them.'

Nila raises one eyebrow. 'Sorry, honey?'

'All the platters.'

Her brow furrows.

'You know . . .' I say. 'The food, all the dips and bread . . .'

'Oh!' She laughs. 'He's a modest boy.'

I cock my head to one side. 'I'm sorry?'

'I didn't make those,' Nila giggles. '*Harley* did.'

⌐

I catch a glimpse of strawberry blonde locks as we're loading the car with fresh fruit and vegetables. 'I'll be back in a sec, Mum,' I say, and dart across the field.

Standing against her dad's car, Mia sees me coming and immediately opens the passenger door, scrambling inside, slamming it shut behind her. As I come to a halt by the window, she locks the car from the inside, crossing her arms and turning away from me.

Oatley comes bounding up, pleased to see me.

'Hey,' Jackson says, strolling up behind him. He glances into the car and knocks with two knuckles on the window. When Mia doesn't respond, he turns to me with sunken eyes. 'Time, Grace, you got to give it time.'

Mum's Range Rover pulls up, loose dirt clouding the air as she winds down the window and calls for me to get in. I buckle my seatbelt, then let Monty climb onto my lap, clumsy and heavy, as we drive off the oval onto the street.

⌐

With our birthday and Christmas only six days apart, not only did we often receive one big present to loop the two celebrations together, we frequently received one big present to loop *us* together – a trampoline, our Nintendo, a cubbyhouse . . .

Kids at school always said we were unlucky, only getting one big present, but when the decorations were strung up in the Port Lawnam shopping centre each year, it always felt like they were for us, for my twin and me.

Turning off the juicer, Mum fills each of our glasses with juice – ginger, carrot, beetroot and lemon. 'Any idea what you want for your birthday?'

She knows she can't give me what I want. She can't just pop down to the shops, pick him off a shelf, swipe a credit card and bring him home.

'Ah well,' she shrugs. 'Still got two weeks to think about it.'

My phone buzzes. *Let's go to the Palms. I'll pick you up in fifteen?*

Caramelised onions make my mouth water as I climb onto the kitchen bench, sitting between vegetable scraps and the chopping board. My phone buzzes again. *Grace?*

Mum wipes her hands on a tea towel. 'Who's that?'

'Jake.'

I read his third and final message. *Okay then. Fuck you.*

Eating an early dinner of watermelon, mint and goat's fetta salad on the verandah, I look out to sea. The sky is pink with patches of grey cloud, lingering after this afternoon's rain. The sun pours through the gaps in the cloud, glittering on the surface of the water like finest fairy dust. As a rainbow stretches across the horizon, I think of Mia.

I think of her as I wash my plate, as I brush my hair, as I change into my pyjamas. As I climb into bed, I slide her picture beneath my pillow. Looking out my window into purple night, I tell him not to worry. *I have an idea.*

⌒

'We only have one banana left . . . and I went to the markets *yesterday*,' Mum says, dripping wet in her paisley swimsuit, with her arms crossed and one eyebrow raised.

Promising I'll explain later, I skip down the verandah steps, place the shoebox in the front basket of my bike, then ride out of the driveway and pedal through the morning light, kookaburras laughing and chatting in the gum trees that line our street.

Cicadas hum in bushes, neighbours water their plants and check their mail. As I sail down High Street, I smile at shopkeepers opening roller doors to their stores. Passing the bakery, I catch a glimpse of Margie, filling the shelves with fruit scones and finger buns, and remember the last Fat Friday we had before he was thrown through a windshield. I turn onto the Avenue, recalling how Mia had giggled, leaping onto Ben's lap, wriggling her bony bum; how he'd laughed, flipping her onto the floor, pinning her down, squishing his jam doughnut in her face. I remember him licking sugar and strawberry off her cheek and how her body relaxed when he smiled and kissed her.

I glance at the shoebox in my basket and pedal that little bit faster.

In her front yard, I tiptoe toward the side gate, carrying the shoebox under my arm. Her family are early risers, but I am cautious not to wake anyone, just in case. Mia is lying in bed, book in hand, when I peer though the glass doors that lead from her bedroom to the backyard. *This was a stupid idea*, I think, but as I turn to step away, I feel the crinkle of her picture in my pocket and I raise my knuckles to the glass. My first knock is barely audible, even to me. My second grabs her attention and her head spins.

'Can I come in?' I squeak.

'No,' she says, but before I really know what I'm doing, I have opened the door and pushed through.

'I've got something for you,' I say, offering the shoebox.

She just scowls at me, her eyes cold and hard.

'Mia,' I say, tears welling. '*Please.*'

Her lips wobble as she pulls her knees to her chest, tucking herself into a ball. 'I don't sleep, Grace. I can't,' she says, closing her eyes. 'I am hurting *too.*'

'I know,' I say, yet as the words slide off my tongue, I realise they are empty.

Shaking her head, Mia looks away, and I think of all the text messages I ignored, all the times I lied to her face, all the times I brushed her off.

She's so far from me because I pushed her there.

'You know,' she says, face to the wall, 'I sat in that courtroom and it was packed, like *fucking* packed . . . There were so many people you could hardly move, and yet I have never been more alone.' Mia turns and stares me right in the eye. 'I *hated* you for that.'

My tongue dissolves in my mouth and so I do the only thing I am physically capable of in this moment. I place the shoebox on the mattress beside her.

As Mia shifts toward me I catch a sudden whiff of Ben's musky scent and sway back against the wall. I catch sight of one of his jumpers wrapped around her pillow. Suddenly off balance, I slide down to the floor, my arse landing between a stack of books and some dirty washing, but she doesn't notice.

I rest my skull against the wall, smooth and cool on my neck, as I watch Mia, in silence, sit up and lift one of the fairy wands out of the shoebox. She bites into the skewered banana, and as rainbow hundreds and thousands pop and crunch between her teeth, the faintest smile blossoms on her lips.

I slip my fingers into my pocket, drawing out the picture.

'What's that?' she says, lowering the fairy wand into her lap.

I offer it to her with a slight tremor. 'I found it in his bedside table.'

As Mia takes it in her hand, she flushes a soft pink – the most colour I've seen in her face since she left Marlow with Ben to pick up the hampers for the raffle. And though the sun does not kiss her collarbones like it did in the picture, there is an inkling of magic in the freckles on her skin.

Thirty-Six

HOME

The night is black salt, clear skies, tiny stars and balmy air. I sleep beneath a thin sheet with my window wide open and an old, rusty fan on my bedside table. It clicks as it blows on damp skin.

Woken by a full, white moon, I lie, swathed in dreamy light, until a summer breeze drifts through the window and I think of Ben. I wonder if he's still out there, rising and falling with the warm, silver swell.

If I was insane, am I now sane enough for the delusions to have stopped . . . for him to have finally disappeared?

I rummage through my drawer to find a bikini, sneak out of the house, dart across the yard, then collect my board and make for our rickety gate. I fly down the hill, sprinting across sand, coming to a halt at the shoreline, suddenly unsure if I even want to know the answer.

Perhaps ignorance *is* bliss. Blindly believing he is out there may well be better than paddling out to find out he's not.

Yet I hold my rails and leap over white wash, stroking through currents as smooth as silk, propelled by the slight hope that he's out there, waiting for me.

~

'Hey, Gracie,' he says and I burst into tears.

Splashing water on my face, he laughs and tells me to stop being such a baby.

'Shut up . . .' I mumble and splash water back. 'I thought you were gone.'

'I told you,' he says, smiling now. 'I'm here for you.'

'And you love me?'

'Of course. Now quit being so corny,' he jokes. 'You're making me sick.'

I laugh as a wave climbs and I paddle over its lip, eyes closed, rising to my feet, swooping down the face, flying, free.

Returning to the line-up, I have a grin painted from cheek to cheek. Ben compliments my ride, and I sit up on my board, chuffed.

As we float with the swells in the brilliant moonlight, I try to savour every moment with him, afraid this magic may soon wear off. Ben looks me in the eye, his stare seeping through from the world of the dead into the world of the living, like the sky seeping into the sea after sunset, when the horizon disappears.

'Thank you,' he says.

My legs dangle. 'For what?'

'Mum swimming again.' Ben's gaze rests on the ocean as he adds quietly, 'And for reminding Mia the world is an enchanted place.' Ben makes small swirls in the water with his hands. 'She fell asleep tonight.' He smiles. 'She's sleeping.'

I surf in dark bliss, returning to Ben in the line-up at the end of each ride. We joke about the fart Monty did at dinner earlier tonight, my attempt to flip pancakes with Mum the other morning, and Sasha's swig of the tequila. 'Classic,' he laughs.

On shore, the first birds are waking and fluffing their wings. Their squawks are subdued, weary whispers. I tell Ben how Jake is pissed off at me for not going with him to the Palms and how I haven't heard from him since.

Ben's voice softens. 'Jake needs you. He won't admit it, but he does.'

'I know,' I say with a wobbly smile, and promise I'll find him.

A swell builds and I drop down its face, sailing down the line as stars fade in the sky above. When I return to the line-up, Ben's silhouette is purple.

Propping myself up on my surfboard, I draw a lungful of air. 'What really happens when you die?'

Ben rests his hands on the sea's silver skin. 'You go home,' he says.

The sky grows pale and his silhouette fades until I find myself alone in the absent moment between night and day.

I close my eyes, draw a deep breath, feel my lungs expand and when I open my eyes, I see her, a girl with soft cheekbones and smooth round shoulders.

'I love you and I'm here for you, Grace. I always have been . . . I'm a part of you.'

In an empty moment, stars burn out and I find myself sitting in still waters in the company of a girl I've known all along.

Staring into eyes as dark as the sea at midnight, I tell her *I love you too.*

⌒

Washing onto shore, I collect my board on wet sand and wander back across the beach, my shadow walking beside me, *with* me.

When we reach the rusty gate at the top of the grassy hill, I sit with her and watch night turn into day, and as the sun catches fire on the horizon, I look across the sea and I smile.

Thirty-Seven

SOUTHERLY CHANGE

Summer's first northerly rips down the coast. Whitecaps race across the sea like wild horses across azure plains, and as the wind whips the ocean, a fine salty mist rises above the earth. I can taste it, smell it, feel it – tiny salt crystals on my skin.

'Hey, honey, would you mind going to the fish shop? I need snapper for tonight but I'm giving Monty a bath.' Mum steers Monty out onto the verandah by his collar. 'There's some cash in my wallet.'

In the yard, I mount my bike and pedal down the street. Riding through the mist, flecks of sunlight fall through the trees like rain in a sunshower. On High Street, neighbours smile with warm eyes and wide lips, nodding as I sail past. With the wind combing through my hair, I smile back for the first time since he left.

The bell above the door rings as I enter the fish shop. The fishmonger, Rob, looks up and beams. 'Grace, how you doing?'

There's still a lump in my throat, but with every day, words seem to find their way around it with less strain. 'I'm good, thanks. I'd like some snapper please, if you have any. Mum's making yellow curry.'

He slips his hands into plastic gloves, reaches into the glass cabinet and draws a fillet of fish off ice. 'Ah, she's a great cook, your mum. Maybe she could drop in her recipe. Some other customers might like a crack at it,' he says, wrapping the fillet in paper then popping it up on the bench.

'I'll let her know, I'm sure she'd be happy to.'

'Here, complimentary,' he says with a wide grin. 'Some tiger prawns, fresh catch.' Rob winks. 'Will make for a great entree.'

I pay for the snapper, thank him and wander out to the street, popping the paper-wrapped package in my basket. Cycling back up Marlow's main road, I drop the fish off to Mum before pedalling back down the street, south to Tarobar Beach to check on the surf. Tucked behind the headland, I know it will be protected from the northerly.

Gentle, glassy waves peel around the rocks as I ride into the car park. I prop my bike against a signpost, stroll toward the grassy dune at the beach's edge, and then I see a familiar van is parked by the shower block. Gravel cuts into the soles of my feet. Turning to the line-up, I catch a glimpse of Harley rising to his feet, gliding down the face, as beautiful as ever. But then I think of flatbread, dips and daisies, all rotting at the bottom of a bin, and suddenly I am climbing onto the bull bar and up on the roof of Harley's van.

From the roof of his van, I watch him gliding, swooping, rising. He rides with his wetsuit top unzipped and hair loose. I feel my throat narrow, my breath becomes shallow.

When he glances back to shore after a wave he's caught right to the inside, Harley double-takes. Noticing me on the roof of his van, he paddles onto the next roll of foam, washing to the beach.

His steps across the sand are measured, coming to a stop a few metres short of the van.

'You all right up there?'

Ignoring him, I bite on my tongue as his brother wanders up behind him. Ryan glances up to me, then to his brother, and stutters, 'Uh . . . A few of the boys are over there, Harley. Um, I'm gonna go say hi.' He retreats to the opposite side of the car park, where a group of older guys, wetsuits peeled to their hips, are gathered around a Kombi.

'So, you just gonna stay up there?' Harley says, stripping off his wetsuit top, cocking his head to one side to get water out of his ear.

I shrug. 'Good view.'

'You'll probably fall off when I start driving.'

His words tug at my heart. 'Would you care?'

Harley drops his gaze, combs his fingers through wet hair.

The sun, creeping across the sky, burns the nape of my neck. All around, in the car park, people chat about the surf, about their last wave, about their plans for the weekend. Mundane conversation. Trivial.

Finally, he lifts his head. Harley's eyes rest on mine like a late afternoon sky on the sea. 'Yes, Grace, I would care.'

I remark, 'Find that hard to believe.'

'Look, can you get off the roof? It would be a whole lot easier to talk to you down here.'

When I don't budge, he wipes salt from his face with his hands. 'Fine,' Harley says, and dusts sand off his feet before climbing over the bull bar up onto the roof to sit beside me.

He sighs. 'I would care . . . A lot.'

I feel lightheaded. 'I know it wasn't your mum making the sympathy food,' I say, my voice breaking. 'Who are you trying to be? An anonymous benefactor?' I tuck my knees to my chest, squeezing my chin between my kneecaps. 'I'm not a charity case.'

Wave after wave laps the shore and he says nothing.

We sit shoulder to shoulder, the skin of Harley's upper arm, chilled by the ocean currents, cold against my flesh. Finally he cracks the sheet of silence. 'It wasn't my place.'

The sun bites my skin. 'I don't get it.'

'It wasn't my place. I couldn't just fix this for you.'

I lie back on the roof, black metal scorching.

'I couldn't just sweep in and make you feel better, Grace. You needed to do that on your own.'

I cover my eyes with my arms to conceal the tears, but then I start to sob, giving away the whole charade.

Harley lies back to rest beside me. 'I figured if you wandered back, I'd be here, waiting.' He pauses. Swallows. 'And I am here . . .'

A gentle sea breeze sways pine branches, brushes my cheek.

I take his hand, interlace my fingers with his and breathe.

'My mum's making fish curry tonight.'

'What kind of fish?' he says.

'Snapper.'

Harley's hand squeezes mine. 'I love fish curry.'

⌒

He wanders up our driveway for the fourth time in three days just after noon, when Mum and I are sharing a fruit salad on the verandah. Mum invites Harley to join us. Grinning, he sits down by my side and reaches for some grapes. As I lean against his shoulder, mango juice dribbles down over my skin, onto my chest, dampening my bikini top. He laughs, tells me I'm a messy eater. Mum agrees, says I always have been. I lick my lips, giggling.

'Want to go for a swim?' he says when Mum has gone inside with the empty fruit bowl.

I nod and he takes my sticky hand, leading me through the yard.

At the base of the grassy hill, we dart across the beach to the rocks, blistering sand scorching the soles of our feet. Beyond the rock shelf, turquoise tides sway. The sea is calm, as if it is dozing. Mere ripples kiss the shore.

As we step over rock pools filled with sea snails, periwinkles and limpets, a wave washes over them, and I marvel at the way they survive the flood of high tides and the drain of low tides.

'Watch out for oysters,' Harley says, helping me over a cluster of sharp shells to reach the edge of the rock platform, then counts, 'One . . . Two . . .'

'Three!' I squeal as we leap toward a sun-kissed sea.

Rising to the surface, Harley spits water in my face, a grin spreading his lips as I spit back.

Treading water, seagrass tickles my feet, and I laugh from the pit of my stomach.

⌒

We make dinner while Mum reclines on the day bed out on the verandah, Monty tucked under her arm, resting his head on her chest. I draw homemade flatbread from the oven, the heavenly scent of warm bread mixing with garlic and spices. Harley combines beef mince, garlic, fresh coriander and parsley, cinnamon and ground coriander in a bowl then rolls the mixture into balls and lays them to cook in a tomato and onion sauce, simmering in a skillet on the stove. As it bubbles away, Harley and I garnish a terracotta platter with fluffy couscous, roasted pistachios, marinated olives and sweet carrots.

Through the window, I catch a glimpse of Mum dozing with Monty and wonder if Harley's presence in the house is making Dad's absence pinch her heart that little bit tighter.

Walking back over to the stovetop, Harley takes the lid off the skillet and says, 'Now for my favourite part.' He takes three eggs and cracks them into depressions in the sauce. After a few minutes they have cooked to perfection and Harley beams. 'All done.'

I grab some paper plates and cutlery, pick up the terracotta plate and follow him as he carries the skillet by the handle out onto the verandah.

'Why don't we eat down on the grass?' I suggest.

Mum nods with a tired smile, and she and Monty walk with us through the gate to sit halfway down the grassy hill. As we eat, light is fading and soon dusk colours the sky with purple chalk.

'Mmm, this is delicious,' Mum says, flavours warming her skin. 'Well done, you two.'

I munch on a handful of pistachios, glowing with pleasure at the way her words have coupled Harley and me together.

The three of us eat here, on soft grass, until our bellies are full, and I feed Monty the leftovers. Mum licks her fingers and thanks us again before carrying the platter and skillet back up to the house, Monty in tow.

Lorikeets squawk in conversation in tall pine trees, silhouettes against a fading day. In silence, Harley and I watch the last of the swimmers wander back across the sand toward Marlow's beach park, where families pack up their picnic rugs and baskets. Harley checks the time on his phone. 'I should probably go home soon.'

I pause before responding, not wanting him to go. 'Jake and I found a box of old VCR movies a few weeks ago. They're in the shed.' I hesitate. 'They're classics . . . If you wanted to stay for a bit . . .'

'I'd like that.'

Hopping up, dusting grass from his shorts, he helps me to my feet. Then he crouches in front of me. 'Here,' he says, taking my hand, and looping my arm over his shoulder before piggybacking me all the way up the hill.

In the shed, he lays me down on the couch before taking a seat beside me.

'Impressive,' I grin and he laughs between laboured breaths.

'So do I get to pick the movie, then?' he asks.

I nod and he crawls to the cardboard box of movies.

Harley chooses *Aladdin* and puts the old tape in the VCR player. There's a blanket at the end of the couch but we leave it there. Inside the shed it's even warmer than outside. A droplet of sweat slides between my shoulderblades, another slides between my breasts.

'I can't believe how hot it is,' he says. 'Should I open the roller door?'

In the yard, cicadas buzz in the shadows. I turn the volume up on the TV to compete with them as Harley lifts the roller door, then lights a citronella coil to stop mosquitoes from swarming into the shed. Sweaty in the summer air, we watch the opening credits with only our hands touching. We're barely halfway through the movie when our eyelids start drooping, our bodies sedated by the heat, and in the moment before I fall asleep, I see Genie fly free from the lamp.

~~

In the early hours of the morning, the darkest before dawn, I am drifting in and out of sleep when there's a southerly change. Cool winds sweep across the ocean, blow over rock pools, lifting sand and rustling leaves. A chill runs down my spine, rousing me as goosebumps rise on my bare skin. I'm conscious of the drop in temperature, but have not woken fully enough to reach for a blanket.

I feel the movement of another body on the couch beside me and gravitate toward its warmth, my eyes closed.

His skin is smooth, his breath slow, steady, deep. Arms cloak my body and the brush of soft palms soothes, a relief in the shadows. Harley combs his fingers through my hair, kisses the hollow at the base of my throat, and with my eyes still closed, I feel him moving like currents in the night sea.

Harley's fingertips touch my cheek, my lips. His hold is deliberate, yet tender. As I relax my hand on his chest my heartbeat calms.

Harley's lips touch mine and it's not like I suddenly start to melt, or like everything becomes warm and fuzzy.

It's honest.

And as I sink with him into a serene, dreamless sleep, there's a softening of muscle around bones that have ached for hours.

~~

Mia, leaning against my doorframe, *knocks*.

A tender afternoon breeze cruises in through my open window.

I sit up in bed, wearing a singlet, undies, socks and a grin. 'Since when do you knock?'

She shrugs, the light catching her eyes. 'Thought you might have been asleep.'

'Nope, just dozing.' I reach across my bedside table and sip from my water bottle, quenching a parched throat.

'You're still the only person I know who sleeps with their mouth open.' She laughs. 'Wonder how many spiders you've eaten.'

My face twists with disgust and I whack her with my pillow.

'He kissed you, didn't he,' she says when the giggles subside.

'How can you tell?'

Mia takes hold of my hand, a gentle squeeze. 'You've never looked like this before.'

Another breath of sea air drifts through the window, lifting my hair ever so slightly. Mia's gaze drops and I notice her sparkly turquoise nails. 'I like that polish . . .' I say. 'Looks like mermaid scales.'

She looks up at me, tears like tiny birds in her sky blue eyes.

After a long, silent pause, Mia says, 'It's a good feeling, isn't it?'

'Kissing?'

'Falling in love.'

I stare, my mouth gaping.

'It's okay,' she says. 'For so long I've been fixated on that woman. What she took away from me, from us . . . everything she took away from Ben.' Mia wipes her eyes on the back of her hand. 'I didn't really stop to think about what he had given me.'

I offer her a sip from my water bottle.

She sloshes water around her mouth, swallows, and clears her throat. 'He loved me for all that I am and I'll never settle for anything less.'

Nodding, I bite my tongue, tears running freely over my cheeks.

'Ben gave me that feeling, and I know I gave it to him.' Mia pauses, shaking a little. 'She'll never take that . . . It's ours.'

I think about the times he shared with me, kept promises, played tricks, defended me. I think about the times he teased me, argued with me, waited for me, held me up, competed with me, scared me, protected me. I think about the times he cooked for me, the times he gave me the wave of the day – and all the nights he checked under my bed for monsters.

I think about the times he made me cry until I laughed. The times he made me laugh until I cried.

And then I think about the times he found me when no one else could.

Mia is right. No one will ever take that from us. It's ours.

Thirty-Eight

PINA COLADAS

This day is falling asleep when her mobile rings. Mum puts her spatula down on the bench, licks fingers, wipes her hands on her jeans and reaches for the handset. Her first breath escapes her. She doesn't take a second.

Sitting on my stool at the breakfast bar, this is the second time in my life that I have seen someone wear this face.

They've taken Dad to Port Lawnam and as we make our way down the highway, darkness saturates green paddocks.

Beneath a bruised moon, I wonder how someone can be so selfish . . . How when it all turns to shit, he can call the very woman he destroyed, asking for her help.

Mum pulls into the car lot, parking between two bays. 'Come on,' she says. 'Hurry up.'

I meander along behind her toward sliding glass doors. Mum ignores me when I suggest we take it slow . . . make him wait. Arriving at the nurses' station in the emergency wing, I cringe as a gurney is wheeled behind me. I catch a glimpse of an old man in the passing bed. He's so frail, a hospital gown on a coathanger.

'Please sit down,' the nurse says. 'A doctor will be out in just a minute.'

I notice Mum's legs shaking and steer her to a chair. In the waiting room, there are magazines from three years ago, a vending machine, people with wet cheeks and a kid with a scarlet rash from head to toe. I catch myself staring and he burrows his face into his mum's armpit.

'Do you have any coins?' I ask Mum.

She stares, her expression blank.

'For the vending machine – I want to buy a packet of chips.'

'*Seriously?*'

'I'm hungry. Can I please have two dollars?'

'Whatever,' she says, and leans back in her plastic chair, sliding her bag across the floor to me with her foot. I fish out gold coins and buy a bag of cheesy rings, wearing them on my fingers then biting them off one by one. The kid with the rash watches me eat, tugs on his mum's shirt. She shakes her head and he burrows his face back into her side.

A doctor approaches us with a clipboard. 'Mrs Walker?'

Mum nods, looking flushed and sweaty.

'We're running some extra tests, just to be sure, but at this stage all seems fine. He didn't go into cardiac arrest.' The doctor pauses. 'He had all the symptoms, but it looks like he's in the clear. Quite a scare, I'm sure. You can see him now.' Noticing the junk food in my hand she says, 'You can't bring that in with you. Sorry.'

'But I haven't finished them yet.'

Mum snatches the packet off me, throws it in the bin.

'Mr Walker,' the doctor says.

Grey skin. Grey stubble. Grey eyes. I'm not sure I even recognise this man.

He can't look at us, turning his face away.

Mum's hand grips the bedrail as the doctor says he'll be able to go home after a few hours of observation, but his drinking, his smoking . . . next time he might not be so lucky. Tears gather in his eyes.

Mum's knuckles are white as the doctor says he needs time off, he needs time to rest. 'I assume he's going home with you?'

'Yes,' Mum says, her voice cracking. She takes a seat in the chair beside his bed, her spine awkwardly straight against the plastic back.

'I'm going back to the waiting room,' I say, and walk out.

She catches me in the hall, grabbing my arm, yanking me to a standstill.

'He's still my husband,' Mum hisses.

Clasping my fingers around her wrist, I lift her hand, jerking it toward her face, waving her naked ring finger before her eyes. 'Is he?'

Mum slumps against the wall and starts to cry.

'I'm sorry, Mum.' I step forward, embracing her, and she buries her face in my shoulder. 'I didn't mean to . . . I love you,' I say.

Her words are muffled. 'We're all he has, Grace.'

I'm yawning in the car as we drive home in silence. Dad doesn't make a sound, just sitting there in the passenger seat, gazing out into the darkness, and I wonder for a moment if he's even breathing.

Gravel crunches, I've been dozing. Mum pulls the handbrake, unbuckles her seatbelt and walks around to open his door. Monty walks out onto the verandah and the sensor light turns on, flickering in the night. Tiny flying bugs buzz around it, hypnotised.

Mum helps Dad out of the car, but as they tread across the yard, Monty stands his ground at the top of the steps, chin up, and hairs raised. He guards his house, his family. He growls.

Suddenly, Dad loses it. His limbs fail him and he falls onto dirt and grass in a crumpled heap. A mess. Bursting into tears, he cries, 'I'm sorry! I'm sorry! I'm sorry!'

I call for Monty. He hobbles down the stairs, and I pat him, reassure him this is not a stranger. Monty sniffs Dad, circles him twice, before licking the nape of his neck. Finally, Monty wags his tail.

I help Mum lift Dad to his feet, supporting him as he staggers toward the house. Sitting him on the couch, Mum makes him a cup of tea while I bring blankets and a pillow out from the hall cupboard, laying them beside him.

'I'm *so* sorry,' he says again as Mum crosses the living room with the mug, passing it to him.

'It's late, save it for the morning,' she says and turns off the kitchen light.

*

I wake with the sun cracking on the horizon and an egg cracking in a pan.

I smell onion and garlic browning – nearly burning – as the kettle sings and sunshine dances on my windowsill.

Sitting up, I stretch my limbs and yawn as I notice the footsteps I hear are too heavy to be Mum's. I step into my uggs, pull a singlet over my head and tiptoe down the hall, unsure who I'm about to find.

Creeping into the living room unnoticed, I see Dad pull the kettle off the stove, pouring boiling water into the teapot Ben and I painted for Mum when we were in kindy. Sweet chamomile steam rises from the spout.

Piled beside the juicer are fruit scraps and three glasses filled to the brim with bright orange liquid. He's even rummaged through the drawers to find the twisty party straws and stuck a sliced strawberry to the rim of each glass. Two pans spit on the stove, bacon, eggs and hash browns in one and veggies in the other. The spinach is quickly shrinking, the mushrooms are near black and the halved tomatoes are saggy, but it's the closest he's ever come to serving a cooked breakfast. Dad stands shirtless in wet board shorts, water dripping from his hair and running down between his shoulderblades. He smells of the sea and I wonder how long he's been awake. When he turns, my presence takes him by surprise. 'Whoa!' he jokes. 'Do you want to give me a real heart attack?'

I shrug and refrain from saying *maybe*.

My silence wipes Dad's smirk from his face and he turns back to the stove. 'Oh shit!' He takes the bacon off the heat. I'm not sure whether you'd classify it as crisp or charred, but I have to admit he has done well with the hash browns, sizzling, crunchy and golden.

'You should probably turn the other one off too,' I suggest and he does, smiling at me from across the kitchen.

From the cupboard, Dad pulls out three plates, ceramic with blue and white swirl glazes. He lays them down on the bench and scrapes the contents of both pans onto the plates. Then, with his fingers, he arranges the food, trying to make it look at least semi-presentable.

Reaching over the bench, I pick a few petals off the flowers he's brought in from the yard and garnish each plate.

⌒

Morning tides glisten as I help him stand three camping chairs and the pop-up table under the fig tree. We spread a tablecloth and lay each plate down, placing the bunch of wildflowers in an old glass jar as the centrepiece.

As we wander into the house for the juices, Mum appears from the stairwell in her dressing robe with frizzy hair and pale cheeks. I assume she didn't get much rest last night, she looks exhausted. Rubbing sleep from her eyes, Mum notices the dirty pans stacked in the sink, the fruit and vegetable scraps scattered across the bench. She glances from Dad to me with a crease in her brow.

'You're not supposed to come down yet,' he says.

'*What?*'

'I'm not ready.' Stepping forward, he lays gentle hands on her shoulders and steers her back up the stairs. 'Five minutes!'

As Mum traipses back up to her room, I take the juices out to the table, grab Monty's bowl and fill it with dog biscuits from the pantry.

'One last touch.' Dad plugs our family iPod into the speakers.

The opening verse of *Pina Colada* plays through the living room.

He turns up the volume, as Mum reappears, her smile, though weak, is a beautiful curve on her lips.

She whispers along with the chorus.

⌒

The spinach is soggy, the tomatoes so overcooked they're watery mush, and the mushrooms and bacon barely edible, but the air is clean and the sky is blue. Rays of light streak between branches, specks of sunlight on our skin like tiny stars.

'Sorry, it's not great,' Dad says.

Mum smiles, shy, her eyes like ocean rock pools. 'It's not *all* bad.'

In the house, the song plays on repeat.

Dad reaches into the pocket of his board shorts. 'I have this,' he says and draws out a ring. 'I think it belongs to you . . .' He holds Mum's wedding ring tight between his thumb and index finger, smiling uncertainly. 'You know I'm not good with words, and I doubt I even deserve it, but if you can somehow forgive me . . . I would really like for you to take it back.'

The tide rises and water spills from the rock pools, tears running across her cheeks.

'You're my lovely lady, Mel.'

I think of Sasha when she crouched in her yellow gumboots.

Sometimes, they wander back.

Mum breathes in and holds out her hand. A warm breeze lifts her hair off her shoulders. Dad touches his lips to the back of her hand, warming honeycomb, and slides the ring back onto her finger.

Thirty-Nine

IN THE WATER

Answering my call, his voice is hoarse. I try to guess how old he is, and as he asks who's calling, I bite my tongue to avoid laughing at the absurdity of his contact name stored in my mobile – *GUY #5*.

'It's Grace,' I say. 'Grace Walker.'

'Grace! How are ya?'

'I'm looking for Jake. Have you seen him?'

Of all the people I have called this morning, GUY #5 is the first to give me a clue. 'He picked up off me last night – him and a few boys were going underground.'

I don't think to ask where or what *underground* is. 'Know where he is now?'

'Nope, sorry. You could try Henry,' he says, 'I'll message you his number.' Once GUY #5 hangs up, I wait for his message then key in the new number and see Henry is already saved in my phone as GUY #9.

'Hello?' he says. GUY #9's voice sounds young, compared to the others. Before I can even ask, I hear Jake in the background.

⌣

Pulling up to the kerb, my stomach knots, sensing this is the kind of street a local would know to bypass. Switching off the ignition, I wind up my window. 'You should probably stay here.'

Harley glances at the shabby fibro house with its front yard of yellow grass and patched dirt and then glances back at me, eyebrows raised. 'Seriously?'

I nod.

'I don't want you going in there alone.'

'Okay,' I resign. 'But when I find him, I need to talk to him alone or he won't listen to me.'

We're careful not to tread on glass as we walk down the driveway toward a house with a boarded window and a flyscreen front door left wide open. As we draw near, I hear chatting and the faint vibration of music behind the house, and we opt for the side path, squeezing between two rubbish bins overflowing with beer cans and pizza boxes.

I hear Jake laugh and tell Harley, 'Wait here, I'll be fine.'

The backyard is concrete, with a broken basketball hoop above the garage and a rusty Hills Hoist. Boys with clenched jaws lounge on tattered camping chairs. Jake raises his sunglasses and swears. 'What are you doing here?' he sneers.

I crouch beside him, almost certain that none of the other guys here have even noticed my arrival.

Jake takes a sip of his beer and burps. Skin is flaking from his lips and nose.

'You've got to stop, Jake.'

'Stop what?' he snaps. 'We can't just turn this off. We can't just press a button and bring him back . . .' He shoves me, knocking over his beer. 'I thought we were in this together.'

I shove him back, almost pushing him out of his chair. 'We are, Jake, and that's why I'm not gonna let you die in some gutter!'

⌒

Passing through fields along the highway back home to Marlow, two clouds part and I recall a story Dad used to tell. If there is enough blue sky to make a sailor a pair of trousers, the weather will turn out fine.

'My dad came back,' I say.

Jake is in the front passenger seat, Harley in the back. Jake winds down his window and dangles his feet out. 'Yeah? What's his story?'

'He was ashamed, I guess. Knew he'd fucked up and was too embarrassed to come home.' I glance across at him, but his eyes are fixed on the road ahead. 'He had some heart scare . . .'

'He all right?' Jake says. I hear the concern in his voice. He has started to thaw. He is here, where he should be, in the seat beside me.

'Well, he's off the booze. Mum's got him on some mad juice detox.'

Jake laughs. 'Bet he's loving that.'

'Doesn't really have a choice. The doctors said he can't work so he's at home all day every day . . . at Mum's mercy.'

'She's punishing him. I would.'

'I thought the same, but I'm realising no one is good, Jake. And no one is bad. Everyone is both.'

He says nothing.

'I guess Mum still sees the good,' I say.

Jake is silent a moment before looking over his shoulder at Harley in the back seat. 'And what's your story, *best looking*?'

'*Jake*,' I stress, warning him to play fair as I glance in the rear-view mirror.

'It's fine, Grace,' Harley says, and turns to Jake. 'You two were closest to him . . . I gave you space. I had to.'

Turning back to the dash, Jake shuffles in his seat and kicks his legs up once more, hanging his feet by the wing mirror. 'Well,' he says at last, eyes fixed on pea green hills in the distance, 'don't fuck Grace over.'

⌒

Mum insists on writing birthday invitations and riding to each of my friends' houses to pop them in their letterboxes. 'You only turn eighteen once,' she says.

'We're having a *barbecue* . . .' I remind her. 'At the *beach*. It's hardly a party.'

Ignoring me, Mum licks the final envelope seal, runs her fingers across its edge and pops it in her bicycle basket with the others. 'Come on,' she says, motioning toward my bike, balanced against the shed. 'You might not think it's anything special, but you'll look back one day and see, for more reasons than one, it was worth the celebration.'

Together, we sail down High Street, and as golden light bounces off her naked shoulders, I realise I'd forgotten how beautiful my mum is.

When we've delivered the last invitation to Toby's house, we pedal back up High Street, stopping every few shops for Mum to greet someone. I don't mind. She buys me lemonade and I cruise along by her side, listening to the way she inspires laughter, crafting something out of nothing.

Back home, Mum lathers homemade choc-hazelnut spread on slices of spelt toast and lays them on a plate between us. When Dad pulls up a chair beside me at the kitchen bench, Mum hands him a glass. Ice cubes bob in a sea of juice. 'Carrot, ginger, cucumber and apple.'

As Dad sits down, he takes a gulp and, for the first time since the detox started, swallows without scowling. Instead, he thanks Mum. Something passes between them on a breath of sea air. Respect.

A wad of creamy chocolate softens in my mouth as Mum places her hand on mine. I love the way her rose gold wedding ring wraps her finger. Brushing my knuckles, tiny bone hills, she says, 'We have something to tell you.'

Dad rests his elbows on the bench, rocking his weight forward.

'Ben's savings . . .' he says. 'We've transferred the account into your name.'

I don't know what to say.

Dad's laugh rouses Monty from his nap beneath my feet. 'Hon, you all right?'

Nodding, I recall I never actually asked Ben how much was in his account. Dad pats me on my back, jiggles my shoulder. I try to figure out how much it might be, all his endorsements, all his sponsorship deals, and all his prize money . . . I lose track before I even consider the first major contract he signed at fifteen.

'We trust you'll be responsible,' Mum says. 'And if you want to put some away in a locked account, you know, or invest in something, Uncle Mark can help.'

'But at the end of the day, it's yours,' Dad says.

'Thank you,' I say at last. I bite down on my toast, crumbs bouncing off my plate.

Dad rubs my back. 'Don't thank us.'

⌒

I remember the knot I had in my stomach when they told us the exam results were going to be released on our birthday, Ben's and mine. I'd been so sure one letter in the mail would make our eighteenth either the best or worst birthday I'd ever had. Ben was completely unfazed. At recess, he'd reclined against the pine's great trunk, munching on his muesli bar, joking with Jake, his voice as calm and as light as late summer dusk. An exam mark wasn't going to define him. Nothing anyone could say or do ever would.

He'd already done that all on his own. He was the sun, catching fire on the horizon.

⌒

Mum rouses me from my sleep. A peach sunrise stains my bedroom walls. 'Here,' she says, as I rub my eyes, and holds three envelopes out in front of me. Dad strolls in behind her and plops himself down at the end of my mattress.

Opening the first envelope, pink with my name scribbled on it, I draw out a birthday card. Opening it, glitter falls out, rainbow flecks in morning light, and as it starts to play a sassy musical number, I realise that I've left him behind at seventeen.

Under the message – which I'm almost certain Sasha wrote with a glass of whisky in hand – is her signature and, in the same handwriting, Pa's signature.

The second envelope is sky blue and contains a card from Mum, Dad and Monty with a picture of a mermaid. The third is white with my name and address printed on a sticker on the front.

I open it and unfold the piece of paper inside. Mum rests her hand on my leg as I read my score once in my head, once aloud. Reaching forward, she wraps her arms around me, her tears warm on my naked shoulder. 'I'm *so* proud of you,' she whispers, and it doesn't matter that my score is barely a pass. A number cannot define me.

⌒

Just after three, the clouds part and liquid gold pours through the opening. 'See,' Dad says. 'It's clearing.'

Mum, in the yard with a picnic basket in one hand and a beach towel slung over her shoulder, points to the sky. 'Told you . . . There's no way he'd let it rain on your birthday.'

Under a pine where the park meets the sand, we unroll picnic rugs, set up the barbecue and arrange camping chairs. Dad runs across the road to grab a bag of ice and fills the esky. When Mia arrives with her family, Jackson carries a plate of fairy bread, her dad a sixpack and her mum a fresh fruit salad that she places beside my mum's pavlova. The vibrant jumble of watermelon cubes, sliced strawberries and juicy mango cheeks makes my mouth water as Mia hands me a present. Putting it down at my feet, I hug my best friend. Her skin is as hot as a roaring westerly and I tighten my hold, suddenly appreciating how difficult it must have been to wrap one present instead of two.

With little encouragement, I open the envelope and laugh at the flying unicorn on the card's rainbow cover. Inside, it reads

Happy 5th Birthday, only she's crossed out the 5 and written 18. Mia shrugs with a guilty grin. 'All the birthday cards our age were boring.'

I unwrap a box and find, inside, a necklace. Hanging on a thin silver chain is a tiny stone pendant. I glance up to see Mia reach inside her shirt and lift out the same stone pendant dangling from an identical delicate chain around her neck. She rubs her finger over the stone on her necklace, and then touches the stone on mine. 'Larimar,' she says, her ears shining pink in the late afternoon sun. 'It's the stone for the sky and the sea. The Atlantis stone.'

As we embrace, her shoulderblades dig into my forearms; she's lost weight over the winter.

'I got offered a scholarship to study a combined degree,' Mia says. 'It's a bachelor of law and bachelor of international studies. Quite a mouthful to say, ay?'

I feel the weight of this news, but it's not painful.

'I'm moving to the city, Grace. I'm going to live with Jackson while he does his honours year.' Mia takes both my hands, I feel her heartbeat in her fingertips, quick and jumpy. Is she afraid? Is she afraid I'll hate her for leaving me, like I'd hated him?

I wonder then if Mia had hated him too. Has she forgiven him?

'Are you okay?' she says. My cheeks are wet. Tears drip from my chin, full and heavy like droplets from leaves in the silence after a rainstorm.

I nod. 'I don't hate you,' I say.

She's crying now too.

'Mia, I'm really proud of you.'

⌣

Dad lights the barbecue as Jake skates through the car park, clutching a wrapped gift. Toby, his parents, and his younger sisters arrive soon after with a present, a bowl of coleslaw and a handful of balloons, which Toby's mum ties to the branches of a nearby pine. Their puppy, bouncing with a bandana tied to its collar, runs rings around Monty as he waddles behind Mum. I sit on the picnic rug and Jake insists I open his gift first.

I give him a cheeky smile. 'But Mum always said *read the card first*, and you haven't given me one.'

'I'm shit with words – just open it!'

I cross my arms.

'Fine! I love you, I love you, happy birthday, you're a bloody ripper, blah, blah, et cetera, et cetera!' he says and starts tearing at the wrapping paper as I laugh and squeal. It's a pack of twenty-four cinnamon doughnuts, and he's the first to take one.

Toby's family have all signed his card, including his youngest sister, who has spelt her name wrong. Before I unwrap his gift, I ask him how his exams went.

He gives me a grin I've never seen before. 'I've been offered an early placement for a bachelor of advanced science.'

Mia wraps one arm around his shoulder, holding him in a headlock, ruffling his hair, jiggling his lanky arms. 'He's going to move in with us!' She plants a slobbery kiss on his forehead and he squirms. 'Roomies!'

Toby wriggles out of the headlock and I congratulate him before unwrapping his gift. Holding up my new wetsuit top and bikini bottoms, I thank his family over and over, feeling very chuffed.

'Nila!' I hear my mum say and glance up to see the Mathews walking through the park. Nila kisses Mum on the cheek and hands

her a bowl of couscous. Behind her, Ryan pushes his dad down a
paved path, the wheels of his chair digging in as they cross the grass.

Harley says hi to my mum, kneels at my side, kisses my cheek
and hands me a bunch of flowers. Daisies tied together with a fine
blue ribbon.

～

Dad turns sausages, flips patties and browns onions with a ginger
beer in one hand and tongs in the other, laughing and chatting with
the other dads. He's wiry and a shoelace belt holds up his shorts,
but there is colour in his lips, his skin, his hair.

I load my plastic plate with salad and couscous to please Mum
before smothering my sausage sandwich with tomato sauce and oily
onions. When I take my first bite, juices spill down my chin and I
lick my lips and my fingers. My hair is matted at the nape of my
neck, wet after our swim, and I glance down repeatedly to admire
my new bikini bottoms. In the pine trees above, cockatoos gather,
flapping and yapping. I imagine they are laughing and carrying
on about all the things they've seen today.

Beside me, Jake chews with his mouth open, crumbs flying.

'You smell different,' I say, taking another sniff and learn it's not
so much a new smell but rather the absence of one. It's an absence of
dirt, an absence of sweat, an absence of tobacco. 'You quit smoking?'

He smiles, his lips glazed with barbecue sauce. 'Five days now.'
We high-five. 'Piece of cake, really.'

'Speaking of cake,' I hear Mum say. She takes a mud cake out
of its container and pokes it with candles.

Ever since I can remember, we've always put twice the number of
candles in our cake, saying that twins live two lives in one. I want

to thank her for making this year no exception, but the words don't
find their way out. Mum pulls a box of matches from the picnic
basket but I stop her before she sparks the first light, announcing
that I'm going to make a speech. Everyone gathers round as I reach
into the basket and pull out three envelopes.

Starting off, I thank everyone for coming, and for the delicious
food. One of Toby's little sisters burps and turns bright red when
we all laugh.

'My birthday has never been *mine*,' I say. 'But because Ben's
not here to share it with me now, I figure he'd want me to share it
with you instead.' I tell my guests that I've been given Ben's savings
account and hold up the three envelopes. I pass one to Mia and
one to Toby, congratulating them on their results.

As everyone applauds them, Jake pinches Mia on the arm with
the tongs. 'Well done, fairy.' Mia yelps, giggles and pounces on him.

As he breaks from her grip, I hand him the third envelope. 'Jake
has started working again for Dad at the factory,' I announce.

'Don't embarrass me,' he says but he's already blushing.

'And I have a proposition,' Dad says, stepping forward. 'Next
year I'm pulling back. I'll only be working one or two days a week.'
He pauses, wraps an arm around Jake's shoulder. 'I want you to
come on full time. I want you to take over when I retire.'

Jake swallows. He nods, hesitant at first, then deliberate. 'Does
that mean I can change the name? *Jake LEGEND Surfboards* has
a nice ring to it.'

Dad laughs.

'That wasn't a no,' Jake says.

'It wasn't a yes either,' Dad chuckles.

Mia opens her envelope. 'A thousand dollars! Are you serious?'

'Yep,' I say as Toby and Jake rip open their envelopes to find cheques of equal sums. I tell them they can use the money to set themselves up next year and all three come bounding up, tackling me to the ground. Toby's two youngest sisters cannot resist the activity and throw themselves on the pile.

When everyone is back on their feet and dusting grass from their skin, Mum lights the candles and I watch flames flicker as they all sing happy birthday to me, their voices out of tune. I find myself singing with them, like I always have, singing happy birthday to Ben.

I blow out the candles, make a wish and slice the cake, pulling out the knife. 'It's dirty!' Mia squeals. 'Kiss the closest boy!'

As I glance over my shoulder, Jake, the closest boy, steps back with his hands raised, as if to say, *Don't shoot!* He laughs and points to Harley, who is standing with a shy grin across the circle from me. '*He's* the closest boy,' Jake says, and as if no one else is here, I stride toward him, take his face between my hands and kiss him like there's no tomorrow.

When everyone is laughing and yahooing, I step back, unsure if it's Harley or me who is more surprised.

Mum slices the cake and serves giant portions on paper plates, topping each serving with fruit from Mia's salad. I sit beside Harley and he laughs at the sand on my olive skin. 'You look like a lamington.'

I giggle, inhaling a mouthful of cake.

'I have a question,' he says. 'Ryan is leaving in a few weeks for his trip. He was the main person driving the van, so my parents are gonna sell it.'

I fork a piece of chocolate icing.

'I asked if I can take it on a road trip . . . a last hoorah.'

My pulse is as thick as the rich dollop of chocolate.

'My parents said I can go for a few days. And, uh . . .' He stutters, then spits it out in a single breath. 'Do you want to come with me?'

All I manage at first is a nod, as chocolate icing coats the walls of my mouth, my throat. 'Are you asking me on a date?' I joke.

Harley laughs. 'I guess so.'

'I've never been asked out on a date,' I say.

'I've never asked anyone out on a date.'

'You asked Maddie to the formal.'

'She invited herself. She wanted to make George Collins jealous.'

'Well,' I say, blushing a little. 'Should we go north or south on this road trip?'

⌒

As we pack up the picnic rugs and Dad folds up his portable barbecue, Jake remains sprawled in his camping chair with his feet kicked up on an esky. With a mouthful of food, he says, 'Do you ever wonder where he is? Like if there really is a heaven?'

I turn and gaze across the beach. Soft pink clouds float on the sea.

There's a warming in my chest. 'I know where Ben is,' I smile. 'He's in the water.'

Forty

HORIZONS

I'm about to shut the van's back door when I notice Monty hiding between Harley's longboard and a tarp. He whimpers as I coax him out. 'Sorry, buddy,' I apologise, taking a carrot from the esky and snapping it in half for him to eat. Going over the contents of the van, I tick items off the checklist in my head, yet even as I pull down the door, I'm almost certain we've forgotten something. I can't remember a trip where I haven't. Whether it's gas for the stove, a sleeping mat or a wetsuit, something is always left behind, but no matter what it is, I've always marvelled at the way we carry on without it, the way we adapt.

Dad encourages us to be safe, as all dads are meant to, while Mum kisses my forehead and both my cheeks and my forehead again. I wave goodbye as we pull out of the driveway with a box of special road trip snacks on my lap. Opening it when we turn onto the highway, I discover an assortment of Mum's homemade treats — spelt biscuits with chocolate chips, puffy apple and cinnamon muffins and chewy honey oat muesli bars.

'Reach into the glove box, there's a CD folder. You can pick whatever you want,' Harley says. I pass him a biscuit and flick through the folder. In a van with a sound system as outdated as this one, I am hoping we're not going to end up stranded somewhere with a steaming engine. I chuck on a Fleetwood Mac CD because Ben loved it and used to know all the words, and I'm hopeless with music and don't recognise any of the other band names.

'I've never been on a real road trip,' I admit.

'What do you mean?' Harley says, shifting into fifth gear. 'You travelled all the time for surf comps, didn't you?'

'Yeah, but we were always going somewhere. This is different. I don't really know where we're going.'

His smile is wide as he reaches one hand across the gearstick to rest it on my thigh. Warmth radiates through my leg, through bone. 'That's the best part about travelling,' he says. 'The not knowing.'

I can feel myself blushing and let a lock of hair slide over my cheeks, hiding my rosy skin. 'The scary part.'

He squeezes my thigh. I turn up the speakers, winding down my window and letting the wind beat my face.

An hour passes, his hand leaving my thigh only to change gears, returning to rest on my skin every time. Out the window, Australian bush flies past in strokes of ochre and sap green, and then I notice strokes of red, strokes of black beneath a striking blue sky.

The road bends and opens onto a stretch of burnt forest. 'Oh look!' Harley says, pointing up ahead to a stall at the front gate of someone's farm. 'Should we get some peaches?'

Pulling over, hot gravel crunches, kicking up clouds of orange earth. The farmer we bought fruit from all those months ago, dressed now in faded jeans and a white T-shirt, with old stains that haven't fully washed out, hoists a tray of fruit off his wagon. While he chats to Harley, I step back and find myself in awe of the forest. Tiny green buds sprout from charcoal trunks.

Bush always grows back . . . he had said, *I'll stand by it until it does.*

⌐

'Let's play a game,' Harley suggests. 'Have you ever been down that road before?' He points ahead to a big brown sign with an arrow that says *Scenic route*. I shake my head and he flicks on the indicator.

The road weaves through national park. He slows down, the wind softens on my cheek and I hear birds chatting, bushes rustling, a stream bubbling as we cross a bridge. 'Grab my wallet, Grace. Should have some coins,' he says. 'Pick one.'

I unzip the pocket and pull out fifty cents. As we near a fork in the road he leans across. 'Left is heads, right is tails. Flip!'

Tossing the coin into the air, I catch it in my hand and I turn it over onto the back of my other hand. 'Tails!' I laugh and he veers off to the right.

We flip at every crossroad until we turn onto a fire trail that leads us to a beach. Parking the van on cracked earth, we wander over sand dunes, hand in hand. Tiny crabs and insects have left trails and dug holes in the sand and I wonder how long it's been since someone last trod here.

Clouds have gathered in puffy clumps, and as we make our way down to the wet sand, my chest expands, air cutting into my lungs. The coastline – ragged cliffs, lone seabirds, shores stripped raw – is here before me in all its mighty grace, and I revel in its glory.

'You up for a swim?'

'Our swimmers are in the van,' I say, but Harley has already taken off his top. I feel my cheeks stretching with a smile as he steps forward, hands sliding beneath my shirt, around my waist. I raise my arms like they do in the movies, but as he lifts my shirt, his elbow knocks me in the side of the head and my sleeve gets caught on my watch. I don't mind, though, because he's blushing too.

As I kick my pants from my ankles, and step into the sea with him, this moment is foreign, yet it has never felt so natural to be naked.

I dive beneath the water and my bones chill. Rising through the back of a foam wave, my skin is fresh, my limbs slippery. Kicking, my feet touch the sandbank, and I stand with the water lapping around my hips. Looking across to Harley, I marvel at the wild blue flare of his eyes, set against a wash of grey surf. A smile curls the edge of his lips, faint but ever present, as he wades toward me through this frothy soup, and as the ocean roars, I discover love as deep as the sea.

⌒

Woken by birds at dawn, we jump back into the front seats, drive out of the national park and north for half an hour before turning off the highway and passing through a coastal town. The houses are old and still asleep. Harley pulls up in the car park beside the local surf club and suggests we go for a swim.

We flounder, dive and float in warm currents. Harley lifts me onto his shoulders and throws me over a white wash. I emerge, laughing and spluttering, leaping onto him. We fall back and splash beneath the surface.

When my tummy rumbles, we swim to shore and wander back across the sand. On the grass, with not a single person in sight, we shower naked, in broad daylight, beneath a public shower. The sky is low hanging, the air quiet and still.

'You're mad!' I say.

'You're beautiful.'

⌒

On the road again, we pass a dusty paddock. The sky is pale and sleepy.

Alone on a hill stands a huge, dry tree trunk with branches twisting high above the earth. Time has drawn flesh from its bones. It is without foliage, and I find myself fascinated by its unruly shape.

Gazing at the splinters of a life once lived, I finally come to see life for all that it is. We breathe, for a while, and then we come to rest. We become the earth, the clouds and the deep-sea currents – the summer swells and the winter tides.

⌒

We weave through another national park, further north, as the day winds down behind a mountain. Harley points to an opening between spotted gums. 'Do you think we'll make it down there?'

The trail is overgrown with wild grass sprouting through tyre marks, cracks in yellow earth. 'I don't know . . .' I say, and smile. 'Let's find out.'

'Adventure!' His grin explodes. 'Now you're getting it!'

The van bounces and jumps like it has hiccups. We struggle over rocks, fallen branches and mounds of soil until we reach a clearing where dirt and grass turn into sand. 'Sweet,' Harley says, eyeing off a majestic blue sea. 'How good's this!'

We park at the edge of the grass and unload our esky, lay out a picnic rug and set up our camping table and chairs. Harley gets out the gas stove and boils water to make chai, which we drink while nibbling on Mum's cinnamon and apple muffins.

'I've been thinking,' I say, and he puts his mug down on the table. Curls of steam swirl like tiny dancers. 'I'm going to put the bulk of Ben's money in one of those accounts where I can't touch it. You know, to save for later. For uni, or a deposit or something.'

Harley nods, approving, waiting for me to continue.

'With the other bit, I'm going to go travelling.' I pause, feeling my skin glow, proud these words have made it off my tongue, proud of my conviction. 'Maybe Europe, Asia, I don't really know.' I grin. 'But not knowing, that's the best part, ay?'

Harley touches his thumb to my cheek, wiping away a tear I didn't even know was there.

'I think that will be really good for you,' he says. 'I haven't told you, but I'm taking the year off. The bloke Ryan is labouring for said I could take his place when he flies out. I was thinking I'd work for a few months, save up, go travelling as well.' He draws a deep breath. 'Maybe I could come meet you?'

My skin tingles beneath the warmth of his palm. 'I'd really like that.'

We dive in the ocean after our chai and when we return to the van, our bodies are dripping wet, salt crystals on our eyelashes, our eyebrows and our lips. Naked, we dry ourselves, then hang our towels on a nearby tree. I wrap a sarong around my waist and sit down beside Harley at the table. He makes me another cup of tea and asks, 'What should we have for dinner?'

'Bacon and egg rolls.'

His laugh is short, then he's silent, waiting for me to tell him I'm joking.

'Breakfast . . .' I wink. 'The most important meal of the day.'

He tells me he likes the way I think and lays two strips of bacon in the pan. As the strips sizzle and spit, Harley cracks two eggs while I cut apart the bread rolls. When they're ready, we squirt barbecue sauce on top of each egg and carry our chairs away from the table to the edge of the deserted beach, our feet resting on sand.

Above, the sky is pastel pink and blue, as soft as petals. The sun has not yet set, but the moon is already rising on the horizon, a delicate white orb.

'When there's still daylight . . .' Harley says, 'that's my favourite time to see the moon.'

ACKNOWLEDGEMENTS

This book is for my sister, Georgia Grace. Thank you for the bouts of uncontrollable laughter. I love you unconditionally.

This book is also for Gemma, my second sister. You've been at my side since the day I was born and I cannot think of a better way to describe you. Thank you for making friends with my characters when we were thirteen and talking about Ben and Grace while riding our skateboards in your street.

Thank you also to my parents, Lindy and Will, for giving me this life. Thank you Nanna Bunny and Nanny Margaret for your eternal love. And thank you Pa for sharing your wisdom. Thank you for challenging me. I know how much you would have loved to have seen this book on the shelves.

I would like to thank Chloé Rymer, Alexa Kaufer and Isabella Dobrijevich for reading this book when we were fourteen and it was still called *Horizons* and handwritten on loose sheets of paper. Thank you Gwen Flynn-Pye for your encouragement and constructive criticism. Thank you Geoff Bentley for reading the *Breathing Under Water* manuscript the day I finished writing it. Thank you for believing in my characters.

I'd like to acknowledge and thank my agent Selwa Anthony and her beautiful daughter Linda Anthony for going above and beyond for me. Thank you to Sha'an d'Anthes for bringing Grace to life on the cover, and to Chris Loutfy for helping me connect with Sha'an. Thanks also to everyone at Hachette Australia and Hachette New Zealand. Thank you Vanessa Radnidge. You amaze, inspire and support me every day. And thank you to my editors Kate Stevens and Elizabeth Cowell, your work is beyond incredible and I can't thank you enough. Thank you Ashleigh Barton and Jackie Money for the giggles and for taking such good care of me. Thank you also to Louise Sherwin-Stark, Justin Ractliffe, Fiona Hazard, everyone else who worked tirelessly on this book in the office and all the sales staff around the country who championed it. Thank you for helping me connect Grace and Ben's story with readers.

Last, but certainly not least, I would like to thank my greatest supporter, the boy with the icy blue eyes. You balance me in a way no one else can and, for that, I am eternally grateful.

Sophie Hardcastle is an author and artist currently studying a Bachelor of Fine Arts at Sydney College of the Arts, majoring in painting. Sophie's memoir, *Running like China*, is published by Hachette and was released in September 2015. *Breathing Under Water* is her debut novel.

In addition to her books, Sophie has written for various magazines, including *ELLE*, *Harper's Bazaar* and *Surfing World*, and has also written for theatre. Sophie is now a mental health spokesperson for Batyr. She shares her experiences with bipolar 1 disorder by speaking in schools around New South Wales.

If you would like to find out more about Sophie you can visit her website or follow her on Twitter or Instagram:

sophiehardcastle.com
twitter.com/Soph_Hardcastle
instagram.com/sophie_hardcastle

hachette
AUSTRALIA

If you would like to find out more about Hachette Australia,
our authors, upcoming events and new releases you can visit
our website, Facebook or follow us on Twitter:

hachette.com.au
facebook.com/HachetteAustralia
twitter.com/HachetteAus